INCIPIENCE

Incipience

Book One in the 'Incipience' Series

L. Gourley

ISBN 978-1-9196027-0-7 (eBook)

ISBN 978-1-9196027-1-4 (pbk)

This book is dedicated to the people that got me this far, and to everyone fighting battles that nobody else can see.

This book contains themes of fantasy violence, injury detail/gore, trauma, bereavement, and death, which may be unsuitable for some readers.

For a full list of advisory content warnings, visit
https://incipiencenovel.wordpress.com/incipience-content-warning/

Someday I will breathe again
The tide will set me free
And on the shore, I'll feel the rain
A farewell to the sea

Someday the dark won't pull within
The dark won't weigh me down
And as I let the light in
I'll fight the urge to drown

Someday the storm will end
The waves will break and calm
Slowly I will start to mend
To re-learn who I am

Someday the colour
Will come back into my world
No vibrant scenes left duller
Iridescent scenes unfurled

Someday is not today
Someday looms just out of sight
But I will not fade away
For Someday, I will fight.

Prologue

It had been a long time coming, Kali knew. This point. This precipice. This pain. Forever, even before she got here, there had been a sickness inside her. A darkness that permeated every fibre of her, threatening to consume her. A lifetime of battles, before she even knew what she was fighting.

She learned early in life not to talk about it to anyone; the slightest mention of it was enough to earn stricken glances between her brothers and her father. Glances that brought with them an ominous secrecy to which Kali always sensed a burden she was not ready to know.

As she grew older, she channelled the rage she felt into her training – combat, tactics, strategy. The dizzying darkness that threatened to drown her kept forcefully at bay by militant discipline. On the surface, she was all that someone of her family name should be, on the inside, a war raged.

Life hadn't always been so onerous, though; true to her species, Kali experienced joy in a way that no other being was capable of. She saw the world with a purity that only seraphs could and lived with her kind in relative comfort as the daughter of a respected general.

Her mother had died in the war that earned him his title, and she learned at a young age never to ask questions about her. She had never known her, but for her brothers and her father the grief was still tangible. Even family friends dared not utter her name in their presence, and Kali grew up knowing little about her.

For the most part, her early childhood was a happy one full of education, travel, and other privileges. Her power manifested itself at an early age in an affinity for animals, and nothing delighted her family more than watching her toddle after the wildlife that was drawn to her, that protected her, and that seemed willing to obey her every wish.

At her Revelare Ceremony, the Elders declared this to be a sign of pure spirit and kindness, and her father had beamed with pride, and barely concealed relief. When other powers started to surface, it wasn't immediately a cause for concern; rare, yes, but not unheard of for the children of prominent bloodlines to develop two or in extreme cases, three defined powers.

So, when during an argument with her eldest brother, Mattias, the plant life around her began to sicken and die, it did not raise suspicion in Kali. New flowers were planted, and when they refused to grow in the blackened earth, Kali's father had the spot paved over without a word.

Throughout her life, her father and her brothers were protective of her and pushed all manner of fighting styles and combat lessons on her. No sooner had she mastered a weapon, she was moved onto another, always practising, always honing.

With many seraphs being trained as warriors and her family's history, this made sense to Kali. What didn't make sense to her was her family's obvious and increasing sense of desperation each time a new power surfaced.

Thrilled initially that she was living up to her family name, she was left disappointed when rather than show pride at her ability to repel her father's sword with a burst of energy from her hand, he grew pale and abruptly ended the day's lesson. When she awoke the next day, she found her training schedule had been made even more intense.

Finally, after several similar occurrences, Kali's father announced they were to leave.

He claimed he wanted to travel, to "see the world as the humans do." It would be educational. Fun. Kali wasn't sure who he was trying to convince. Despite his broad smiles and words of excitement, she sensed the uneasy tension bubbling just below the surface.

At first, despite her early misgivings, Kali enjoyed their nomadic life, full of adventures. Spending their days hiking through new terrain, seeing forests, seas, mountains, and astounding views that she had only ever seen in books. Seeing the humans up close, their eerie similarity to the seraphs, just slightly less beautiful and a little more fragile was incredible to Kali. She loved spending the days exploring with her brothers and recounting their days to their father at dinner.

As time wore on, however, she began to realise that her father was hiding them, hiding her, and that rather than experiencing the world, they were running from it.

Amongst the humans, they blended in well enough, but Kali was forbidden from ever being alone with them, from making any true friends. If they encountered any of their own kind, out on scouting missions or similar "educational" experiences, her father would show all the courtesies expected, nights of dinner, drinks, and laughter, and then they would leave the next day, never to return.

Their last stop before her father, paled and anxious, finally told her the truth was a secluded cabin in a dense forest; a spot chosen by her father supposedly for the benefit of improving their navigation and general survival skills.

The location seemed only to underpin Kali's sense of isolation and growing increasingly frustrated, Kali was unable to keep up the pretence any longer. Her tension boiled over, and she demanded to know what her father and her brothers were keeping from her.

Taken-aback, her father recovered quickly, telling her she was imagining things, and when that didn't work, begging her to leave it alone and to trust him. Growing steadily more angry, desperate, (and although she would never admit it, scared) she was barely aware of the acrid smell filling the air around her, or the heat, until flames had surrounded her entirely. They formed a wall around her and crept up the walls, consuming the building from the inside out. Every attempt to reach her caused the flames to intensify, and eventually her family – including her brother William, whose power usually allowed him to control fire – were pushed back by the heat, forced to flee and watch as the cabin, with her inside, burned.

The fire burned well into the night, and in the morning, when she woke to her father picking her up, unhurt, from the rubble of the house, it was the only time she had ever seen him cry.

When she saw the smoking ruins of the house, she apologised profusely and assured them that she had not been in control of what had happened. With a stomach full of lead, she promised herself that she would never tell anyone about the cold sense of rage and power that had rooted itself and spread through her as the flames burned higher; never acknowledging that in fact, she had never felt more in control.

Resigning himself to the fact this could not continue any longer, her father sat her down, looking haunted, and told her everything.

Chapter One

When God created angels, He was convinced His work was perfection.

He doted upon the angels, and they loved Him with the kind of fiercely burning loyalty He always intended for them. He gave them everything they could ever want, and in turn, they loved Him, protecting Him from the mysterious darkness that lurked beneath the surface of the Earth.

After a time, however, God yearned for something deeper and more meaningful. His angels loved Him and were loyal to a fault, but He wanted creatures that could rebel, that chose to love Him freely – not because they were designed to, but because they chose to. Although He loved His soldiers dearly, God decided that the angels needed a higher purpose, something other than Himself to watch over.

He created humans, and although initially pleased, to His dismay He watched as they formed factions that tortured, killed, and inflicted terrible pain on each other. Although goodness and love existed within them as He had envisioned, the humans could be petulant and spiteful, and willing to inflict pain for trivial reasons. Disheartened, He turned to one of His favourite sons, Lucifer, for guidance and counsel.

Although some say that it was the humans that drove Lucifer to rebel against God, out of jealousy and pride, that he began a revolt against Heaven to protest their creation, the truth was that Lucifer was rather fond of the humans. He saw in them the beauty his Father had created, the wildfires in them that burned brighter than anything else in existence, but which were quickly extinguished by their mortality.

He told God that He had created two beings, perfect in their own way and that He should be proud. He pleaded with his Father to turn His attention once again to His children in Heaven, who were growing increasingly restless.

Yet still, God remained unsatisfied.

Deciding that He would make one last attempt, God sought to create a being that combined the parts He loved most of each the angels and the humans. It was not the humans, but this – God's third and final creation – that caused Lucifer to lead a war against Heaven.

When God created the seraphs, combining the power of the angels with the free will and mortality of the humans, Lucifer saw this as an affront to both species. He grew jealous of God's affection for them, and of their power and freedom.

Perhaps thinking he could prove to God that angels were capable of the free-spirited disobedience He craved, perhaps driven purely by envy and spite, Lucifer gathered an army of loyal followers – other angels offended by the creation of the seraphs – and delivered God an ultimatum: destroy the seraphs or face a civil war within the gates of Heaven. Incapable of the genocide that Lucifer demanded, and unwilling to bow down to His creations, God refused, waging war and ultimately killing Lucifer's followers and banishing His once treasured son from Heaven.

The peace that followed was tenuous and mournful. Loyalties, once unquestioned, were strained and fraught. A turbulence hummed just beneath the newfound calm, and God, concerned for the safety of the seraphs, decreed that they should leave Heaven, too.

Sent to an Earthly realm the humans could not reach, their relocation felt like banishment, but the seraphs did not protest. They knew it was the easiest way to prevent the provocation of similar resentment and rebellion from the other angels, and so they obeyed. Believing all His creations to be safe, Heaven was quiet at last.

Unbeknownst to anyone, however, Lucifer had fallen to Earth as the Morning Star. His fury was an inferno, and the force of his impact so great that it ruptured the ancient barrier created to seal away the very darkness the angels were designed to protect against.

Hurt and full of vengeance, Lucifer fashioned a sickness out of this darkness, designed to enter souls and corrupt the victim utterly and unrecognisably. He entered the homeland of the seraphs, and unleashed the disease, watching from a distance as it infected them one by one. Out of it, creatures that lusted for blood, murder, power, and suffering were borne, still wearing the faces of those they were before. Beings without conscience that thrived in pain and anarchy, that existed in a state of perpetual murderous rage ran forth into the night.

Demons ran forth into the night.

The seraphs looked to Heaven for help, but now impure, the angels barred their doors to them. Unwilling to risk the sickness reaching Heaven and corrupting the angels, or even God himself, they ignored the seraphs' plight. Left with no choice but to fight or die, a bitter, bloody war broke out amongst the seraphs, with parents killing children and siblings turned against each other in an effort to destroy the disease.

Their souls now severed from Heaven's energy, most of the infected lost their angelic powers or found them diminished, but they all developed a new and fierce strength that, combined with their thirst for blood, made them formidable foes. The fight soon spread beyond the seraph homeland and the demons, intent on nothing but bringing chaos and agony, sought other souls to infect. The disease spread to the human world and the seraph warriors, though battle-weary, grew confident that Heaven would now intervene to assist their thinning resources; their calls for aid, however, remained unanswered.

The humans reacted to the sickness differently, but retained their thirst for blood and suffering, causing tales of undead creatures that hunted at night and of monstrous beasts to sweep through the human communities. The seraphs resigned themselves to fighting alone, infiltrated the human world to destroy any infected creatures that lurked in the shadows, and eventually, the demons were pushed back.

Those not fighting in the battles worked tirelessly to find a way to stop the disease from burning through the world, experimenting with wards, elemental purification, and poultices, until it seemed, finally, the sickness' virulence was sufficiently tamed. Bored, unable to infect any more victims and deprived of the blood they craved, the remaining demons retreated and sought refuge from their creator, Lucifer. For a time, there was peace.

With a significantly diminished population, the seraphs began to rebuild, electing a Council of Elders out of their most valiant warriors to lead them.

One such Elder, Kasandra, had a gift for predicting the events of the future, which allowed the seraphs to foresee attacks and drive the demons back in the war. It was widely regarded that in the absence of angelic warriors, her visions were a turning point in the war, leading the seraphs to victory. As a beloved war hero, she was amongst the most trusted and respected members of the Council.

When she sickened in her old age, crowds gathered to say their goodbyes. It was then, moments from her death, that she predicted another war, one more terrible than the first. The triumphant side in this war – seraph or demon, the light or the darkness – would be determined by a child. She prophesied that the child would have more power than any seraph or demon that had come before because it would share the blood of both creatures yet was borne from love. Astounded, those around her asked her to explain, to clarify, but with a troubled smile, she drew her last breath and died, leaving her visitors, now mourners, in stunned silence.

With Kasandra's death came terrible uncertainty; Kasandra was never wrong, but the seraphs knew that of which she spoke was not possible. It was well known demons were not capable of love and that they preferred to destroy life rather than create it.

Divided, and unsure of what to do next, the seraph Elders soon discovered that demons had learned of the prophecy and a small faction had become emboldened, trying to fulfil it. In the dead of night a few days after the death of Kasandra, these demons attacked and, although the battle was short-lived, many warriors were wounded.

Most troubling, their most celebrated Healer, Persephone, was captured by the leader of the demon faction and taken to the demon homelands with them. She was never to be rescued.

An uneasy doubt crept across the seraphs, and they decreed that all children would be monitored for any sign of demonic or destructive power. This formed the basis of what would become a core part of seraphic tradition – the Revelare, in which a child's power was announced to the community and sorted into four distinct categories.

Children classified as Empaths (powers regarding any affinity for nature, animals, healing, or the emotions of others) were considered minimal risk, with most becoming healers and peace-makers. Those with Prophetic powers were regarded as moderate risk, due to the potential for influencing events with their knowledge, as were Warrior children (those with abilities such as telekinesis, strength, and the ability to control elements).

The only category truly deemed a risk to the existence of the seraphs were those with Dark powers (an ability to cause sickness, death, or destruction), a rare occurrence that often resulted in the child being taken away and raised under the close supervision of the military. Due to the reputation of those with Dark powers, families often attempted to conceal children with Dark powers, or simply abandoned them.

Such was the fear amongst the seraph Elders, it became compulsory to submit all seraph children before the Council when their powers manifested to be categorised, with failure to do so punishable by death. With compliance mandatory, all children were brought before the Council to be assessed. Under public scrutiny, a pattern of mysterious disappearances befell Dark children; the quiet unease that accompanied the missing children was insufficient to stir the seraphs into action, who were largely reluctant to ask if the source was familial, vigilante or Council. Even the most concerned were unsure if they wanted to know the answer.

By the time Kali's father, Malakai, met his wife thousands of years later, the old fears were regarded as meaningless superstition. The Revelare was no longer a legal requirement, but instead an important part of seraph tradition, and although a stigma surrounded any child with Dark abilities it was not believed that the ancient prophecy held any truth. Such children were not subject to the same sinister fate as their unfortunate predecessors, and the sickness that caused the First War was believed to have been vanquished.

When Malakai met Liliana on his first day on patrol with the Guard, he was immediately taken with her. She seemed so fearless and, struck by her beauty, he found himself desperate to impress her. So desperate, that he volunteered to do extra patrols out beyond the seraphic lands, where the protective wards were weak and demon attacks were frequent. When he returned, having inevitably found himself overwhelmed and injured, she had regarded him coolly, before offering her services as a trained Healer to assist him. Within the year, they were married.

As they rose through the ranks in the Guard, Malakai was initially reluctant to start a family, but he saw how Liliana longed for children and was thrilled when their eldest son, Mattias was born. When Mattias was declared a Warrior at his Revelare ceremony, Liliana was heavy with child again, and a short time later gave birth to their second son, William.

Several years after William's birth an unexpected uprising of demons near a human city caused the seraphs to go to war for a second time. Malakai and Liliana were relocated to a far corner of the world to fight and push the evil back, with Malakai leading the army to win an important battle that turned the war in their favour.

It was during a lull in the fighting, at which point they were allowed briefly to return home, that they realised Liliana was pregnant with a third child. After requesting that she be put on scouting patrols, rather than frontline battle, Liliana was charged with leading a squadron of newly qualified seraph soldiers. Thinking of Malakai, she was amused but wary of the eager arrogance that often accompanied new warriors, keen to prove themselves, and resolved she would never allow her team to become complacent to the dangers they faced. Even so, one night the squadron found themselves ambushed and outnumbered by demons. They managed, barely, to slay the demons, but they suffered heavy casualties and Liliana was injured.

After meeting a frantic Malakai at the medic station, she assured him that both she and the baby were in good health. As the days passed, however, she noticed one of her wounds turning a sickening green colour, with black, spidering veins spreading out from its centre. Perhaps she would have asked for help, reached out to Malakai in fear if not for herself than for their child, but she had begun to feel a depthless emptiness inside her, a hollowing cavern that nothing seemed to fill. After the emptiness came the rage, the nauseating hatred so all-consuming it was as though her innards had been replaced with boiling, acidic poison.

When, unable to hide the changes any longer, Liliana made Malakai aware of the situation, his denial afforded her the time and protection she needed to complete her transformation. By the time she gave birth to their daughter, the sickness had already taken her, and it was clear that nothing remained of the woman Malakai married. She left in the night without the child, without a word, and without a trace.

Fearing for his daughter's safety and unsure of how the sickness may have affected her or how the Elders would react to her, Malakai realised that although he was duty-bound to report a case of demonic infection, he needed to leave his new-born daughter out of the story. He staged an attack overnight, lying – only partially – that a demon had taken his wife from him shortly after the birth of their child, and that she had transformed before his eyes before fleeing.

Regarded as a war hero, Malakai returned home to his two young sons, now without a mother, with an infant daughter he knew may be infected. For nights on end he would watch her sleep, watching her tiny chest rise and fall, willing her to stay seraphic. When he did sleep, his dreams were filled with horrific scenes of his wife, terrible in both her similarities and her differences to the woman he knew, slaying his family as he watched, and babies with emotionless, dead eyes.

As he watched his daughter grow, cry for him, giggling at her older brothers, he knew, he *knew* she wasn't evil. He could finally breathe again.

The prophecy, now just a fairy-tale, didn't even cross Malakai's mind until Kali was two years old, and the family attended a memorial service for lost warriors. Afterwards, the Council talked of the First War, and how the great Kasandra had foretold of the war they fought and won just two years previously. They rejoiced that the prophecy remained unfulfilled, that no such child ever came forth, and that the seraphs had emerged victorious.

Not truly believing, Malakai assured himself that he would keep a watchful eye on his daughter, observing for any sign that she was capable of being the child the prophecy spoke of. When she was declared an Empath at her Revelare, he almost wept with relief and scolded himself for allowing himself to become burdened with ancient superstition.

The day that Kali's second power manifested, and he saw the plants around her wilting and dying, it was like seeing Liliana before him again, changed. It felt like the air had been knocked from his lungs. Although he tried to remain stoic, his oldest son noticed his panic, and it was then that he confided in Mattias, the only other person he had ever told. Perhaps, he ruminated later, it was unfair to place that burden on a child's shoulders, but seraphs were warriors older than their years, he rationalised. Deep down, he knew he was just tired of being alone, with nobody to trust.

He wasn't aware of Mattias telling his second son everything, but one day he noticed William watching his sister closely, protectively. Before he realised it, the three of them were bonded by this secret, this mission to protect Kali and keep her true nature a secret.

With every new power, his panic intensified. He knew his daughter, knew she wasn't capable of leading demons to victory, but would the Council see that? As a general, he knew the two strategies that lay before the Council if the prophecy rang true: weaponise his daughter, the child that still giggled with delight whenever she coaxed the birds down from the trees around her, or kill her to neutralise the threat. That was the seraphs, he couldn't even think about what the demons might do to her if they found out she might eradicate them.

So, he did the only thing he felt he could – he packed their things, and he left with his children. Knowing he was on borrowed time and that he couldn't lie to his daughter forever, especially as she grew older, he prayed for just a little bit longer. He prayed he was wrong; he prayed that his daughter was safe.

The night Kali burned down the cabin in the woods confirmed everything he had been denying for almost twenty years. Although his daughter promised she had no control, he had faced enough demons on the battlefield to recognise the shadow that passed over her face as the fire raged around her. He knew, at that moment, that his daughter would never be safe.

Chapter Two

After her father finished speaking, his voice hollow, recounting the truth about her mother, the prophecy, her abilities, Kali felt like she had been dropped into a nightmare. With bile rising in her throat, she barely suppressed the urge to vomit.

Her blood pounded in her ears, hot like lava, her stomach churned; she could *feel* it, the darkness creeping through her veins, choking her, and bubbling in her gut. It didn't even occur to Kali to disbelieve her father, to argue that somehow, he was mistaken because she knew, as she had always known, that something existed within her she didn't understand. A nameless threat that pulled beneath the surface, always present like an ominous shadow.

As her breathing grew steadily harsher and more frantic, everything around her became distant and distorted. She could see her father talking to her but couldn't hear the words. It was like being submerged underwater, in a world where nothing was quite real, spinning in a limbo that somehow managed to be deafening in its oppressive silence. Dropping to her knees, every breath began to feel like a knife's edge.

William's face appeared in front of her. How peculiar, she thought, that he too seemed to be silently shouting. He grabbed her by the shoulders and began gently shaking her, his voice slowly beginning to reach her through the bubble.

"Kali, Kali, it's okay. It's *okay*!" William looked at his father, desperate, but he too seemed lost. Mattias was watching warily, reluctant to get too close to his sister, looking at her like a bomb about to detonate.

"Kali, look at me. Tell me what you see. Where are we? What do you see?"

Kali looked at her brother, confused. "Trees?" she replied questioningly, wondering if her brother was also going mad. She was a *demon,* who cared about *trees?*

"That's good! What else? What can you hear? What can you smell?"

Bewildered by William's questions, Kali focused on the world around her. She could smell moss, and the earthy dampness of the forest floor; the sweetness of the flowers in bloom, covered with the smell of natural decay. She could hear the birds chirping inquisitively, as they returned to the trees above – she supposed she had been the cause of them leaving – along with the rustling of small animals in the undergrowth. She sensed the calmness of the forest around her, and the silence became less dense, less menacing the more she let it in.

She looked at her brother, and inhaled shakily, feeling the air fill her lungs in what felt like the first time in an eternity. He smiled encouragingly as she took another breath.

"Good! It's okay, Kali, it's okay. You're okay."

"How did you do that?" she felt her breathing return to normal, considerably impressed by her brother.

With a tiny jolt of hope, she wondered if he too had more than one power, something that connected them, that would lessen the differences that set her apart from everyone she loved. William, who always seemed to know what she was thinking, looked at her with a sad smile.

"It's not magic, Kal, just something I picked up along the way, to help you stay grounded. I'm glad it worked, I've never tried it out before."

"Glad to be your guinea pig then," she said with a hint of sarcasm, swallowing her disappointment.

Slowly, she began to stand. As she did, she noticed that the ground below her was charred black, with fissures running through the centre of where she stood. Stricken, she looked at her brother in shock.

"Kali, don't—it's fine."

Before she could reply, he grabbed her arm and dragged her past where her father and oldest brother stood, still motionless, into the cover of the trees.

"Will, where are we going?" She struggled against him, but his grip didn't loosen. "Will? *Will!*"

William stopped walking and turned to face her.

"We're going for a walk and we're talking about this. We've buried these secrets for too long and I've been telling Dad and Matt to come clean for months now. I *told* them that at this point it wasn't protecting you, just setting you up for a spiral and I was right. So, you're not shutting me out of this, and I'm not lying to you. About anything. We'll stay out here as long as we need to until you stop feeling like you're going to lose your shit."

She considered her brother for a moment. Being the middle brother, William always seemed to let Mattias take the lead, being more of a soldier than a leader, and more of a brother than a protector. The one who stayed up at night to read her stories, and to give her that look when Mattias came in and lectured him about keeping her up too late. Now she saw him, his strength, and in spite of everything, she smiled.

"You know you're in danger of being my favourite, right?" she grinned at him.

"God forbid," he smiled back.

For a moment, a tense silence settled over the two.

"How could you keep this from me, Will?" she asked in a low voice.

He sighed.

"I was a child when Mattias told me, it's been normal to me my whole life. Well, not exactly *normal,* but..." he trailed off. "Look, we should have told you before now like I said, I've been telling them for months, it should never have got to last night."

Shame burned through her, looking at his clothes, still stained here and there with soot and ash, and she turned away from him.

"Kal, I'm not blaming you. I mean, if we had told you sooner, you'd probably be able to control it by now. But you have to understand, Dad was terrified that the Council would find out and hurt you, or that demons would find out and hurt you. All he wanted was time. Time to figure out what to do, to teach you how to defend yourself, to—"

"Figure out if I was a threat?" Kali turned back to face her brother. She expected him to avoid her gaze, but he met her eye, steady.

"Yes."

This didn't come as a blow to her. Of course that's what her father would have done, he had already told her as much. In truth, it's what she would have done in his position; she just wanted her brother to acknowledge it. She wanted confirmation that amongst his tales about protecting her, a small child, and a victim of circumstance, that he recognised she was, at least partially, a threat too.

"So, our mother is still…?"

He flinched at the word "mother" but didn't deflect the question.

"Out there? As far as I know, yes. Dad barely talks about her, and people rarely mention her in his presence. Over the years I've heard this and that; it seems she kept her talent for leading because the last I heard she was some sort of general for a faction out near the borderlands."

Despite the cool detachment of his tone, there was pain in his eyes as he spoke.

"What was she like?" Kali asked quietly.

He looked down at his hands as if they held the secret of the words that would upset her the least.

"Honestly, Kali, I don't remember her very well. I remember she was kind. I remember she would sing to us before we went to sleep, and when she woke us in the morning. I remember her laughing when Matt and I would chase Dad with our toy swords, and how she stroked our hair and told us we'd be fierce warriors. I remember how excited she was when she told us we were going to have another brother or sister—"

When he saw that tears were streaking his sister's face, he stopped and was surprised to find his own face was wet.

"I took all that from you," she whispered, horrified. "You had this happy childhood and then I was born..."

"No, Kal, how can you even think that? *Demons* did this. They took her, they changed her, you didn't do anything!"

"But I'm *one of them!* And your whole life, keeping this from me, living in secret, always running, because of *me.*"

"Listen to me, we never saw it like that. We love you, we always have, and we've always wanted to protect you. You have never been, nor are you now, a burden to us. Understand that. And you're *not* a demon, so stop saying that."

For a moment, she was overwhelmed by the weight of everything – the truth about her, the strain it had put on her family, the fact that she had been robbed of ever knowing her mother, this kind, fierce warrior that doted on her children. She felt rage. Rage at the demons who had taken so much from her before she even lived, and grief for the life she never had, the life her brothers had lost, and the life she knew she could never have.

They talked for a few hours, not realising that time was passing by. Gradually, the training, the protectiveness, private education, everything, began to make sense. Hearing her brother detail everything they had done, every sacrifice they had made for her, filled her with an equal mix of sadness and gratitude.

As they walked back to where the ruins of the cabin lay, their now makeshift campsite for the night, Kali stopped one last time to ask the question that had been playing on her mind all day.

"Do you think....do you believe Kasandra's prophecy is true?"

William regarded her for a moment.

"As in, do I think you're some Messiah for the seraphs or the demons?"

She nodded. He sighed.

"Honestly, I don't know what I believe anymore. It seems impossible, but most people would say that *you're* impossible, and yet here you stand, and here we are having this conversation. What I *know* is that you're a good person, Kali. A regular pain in the ass, sure, but a good person. And I've always got your back."

Unable to find the words that would express just how much that meant to her, or how he always knew what she needed to hear before even she did, she hugged him tightly, refusing to let herself cry again.

"Come on, I'm starving. Plus, we can't deprive Mattias of the chance to lecture us to death about running off into the woods in a time of crisis. I bet he's been practising all day," William laughed.

"Oh, do you think he'll tell us how disappointed he is in us?"

"Maybe if we're really lucky."

Laughing, they continued their walk in good spirits, with Kali feeling lighter than she had in months. The threat that seemed to permanently loom over her now had a name, a face. It was something she could fight now that she knew what it was, and despite the initial shock of the truth, Kali knew it was far better to know than to live in the uneasy ignorance she'd known for so long.

As they drew closer to the campsite, Kali felt William tense beside her.

She turned to ask him a question, but he raised a hand to silence her. Suddenly, she heard it too.

Clanging metal, shrieks of pain, and their father's voice shouting above the noise of monstrous screams of something inhuman.

"*Demons!*" growled William.

Without a word, they both sprinted towards the campsite.

Chapter Three

As soon as they started running, everything else fell away; the emotions of the day gave way to training and instinct, and both of their weapons were already drawn when they reached the camp.

The sight before them was something that Kali's father had always tried to prepare his children for, but he could never convey the horror of demons in stories – the cruelty and hatred in their black eyes, their twisted, almost-human features, and the relentless ferociousness with which they attacked. Living weapons, from their unnatural strength and their razor teeth to their clawed hands, they were unburdened by fear, undeterred by pain, and they fought like it.

Kali leapt over the corpse of a demon as she entered the clearing with William beside her and assessed her surroundings. To her left, Mattias fought four demons, and they were beginning to push him back into the forest. To her right, her father was encircled by ten of the beasts, blood trickling down his face. Without breaking pace, Kali ran left to help Mattias whilst Will joined the fight with his father, hacking a path to him through the demons.

As Kali approached where Mattias was fighting, she vaulted over a fallen tree and sprung onto the back of one of the demons, plunging her sword into its back. Black blood spurted from its mouth as it fell to a heap on the ground, snarling and gurgling, still trying to stand and fight. She twisted the sword free and brought it down on its head, just as another demon loomed behind her.

Turning, she caught her would-be attacker in the face with a slash from her sword, causing it to momentarily lose balance but then carry on towards her, enraged. It lunged at her with alarming ferocity, slashing at her with wicked-looking daggers which curved to a point and were punctuated with deep serrations. With every advance, the demon grew more impatient and she noticed that in its frenzy, it was throwing too much of its weight forward, becoming susceptible to losing balance.

She danced closer to the demon, parrying its blows and drawing it nearer to her; as it lunged again, she spun to her right, kicking out at it as hard as she could. It stumbled and she took her opportunity, driving her sword through its spine and beheading it before it hit the ground.

She turned to see Mattias finishing off the last of the remaining demons and, knowing he no longer needed her help, ran to their father and William. They were fighting five remaining demons, but these were different from the ones Kali and Mattias fought. They were much bigger in stature, appearing more controlled than those Kali had killed, which was making the fight more difficult. She paused briefly to find the best opening and was about to start forward when Mattias sprinted past her. She was about to call out to him, to strategise, when a spear hurtled through the air and caught him in the stomach. She froze, aghast; trapped in a horror so strong it seemed to momentarily stop her heart, her blood turning to lead in her veins.

Mattias stood for a moment – startled by the unexpected opposing force – and then fell backwards to the ground. To Kali, watching him seemed to take an eternity.

"NO!"

Her shout broke the focus of her father and William, who took in the scene before them and temporarily faltered. Her father recovered quickest, slaying the demon directly in front of him then dragging

William from the centre of the battle to where his eldest son lay.

It was Kali who reached Mattias first; blood bubbled at the corner of his mouth as he tried in vain to sit up and already, he looked pale. Kali had never manifested a power to heal but if ever there was a need to then surely this was it, she silently willed herself. She held her brother's hand, aware that this position made them vulnerable but unable to bring herself to move. It was her father's voice that roused her.

"Kali, you and William need to cover us!"

She met his gaze and nodded, springing to action as her father knelt beside his son, gauging the damage and prognosis. Malakai lifted the shirt of his son and saw not only the spear protruding from his abdomen, but the toxic ooze spreading from the wound – *poison.*

* * * *

Kali and William had always made a great team – even in their youth at sparring competitions with the other children they always placed first – and they carried that momentum with them now. They fought almost as one unit, always aware of the others positioning, vulnerabilities and opportunities. When Kali saw a dagger heading for William's head, she cut it down mid-flight with her sword and sent it hurtling back at the demon responsible with a burst of telekinetic energy, where it lodged itself firmly in its forehead. They cut their way through the remaining demons, never pausing to look at their father and brother, focusing only on keeping them from harm and staying alive.

The last demon was without a weapon and this struck Kali as odd – the other demons had been equipped with terrifyingly brilliant weaponry. She scanned it, looking for weak points in its armour or for hidden weapons, becoming increasingly perplexed when she saw that it was unarmed. It stood unafraid, grinning maliciously at them before turning its gaze to their older brother, whose breathing was becoming heavier and shallow.

The demon strode towards them, looking at their brother like a hunter claiming its prey, and they seemed to realise simultaneously that this was the demon responsible for wounding Mattias, William letting out a low snarl as Kali formed the thought. She watched the demon advancing, and a venomous rage poured out of her.

She directed all her hatred and her fury towards the monster in front of her, as William raised his sword. The demon was mid-stride when it stopped, clawing desperately at its throat like it was drowning. Kali didn't know how she was controlling this power, but she knew it came from rage; she threw all her power behind her attack, enjoying how good it felt to watch the demon choke, blood streaming from its eyes and mouth as it fell to its knees.

A thrill of power ran through her as the demon took one last gasp, shuddered, and collapsed face-first into the grass. She could sense William, who still looked poised to meet the demon head-on in combat, watching her from the side of his eye. There was half a second of silence before they heard their brother cough, and they returned their attention to their father and Mattias.

Kali's heart sank as she took in the scene before her. Her father's expression was grim as he tended to his son's wound, sweat lining his forehead as he tried in vain to clean it with his limited supplies. It was plain on his face that Mattias' prognosis was not good.

"We need to get back to the city, now. I

have antidotes there that can help," her father finished covering Mattias' wound and glanced up at them as they approached.

Kali nodded and began to reach out to him when an odd look crossed his face. He looked across the clearing like a man seeing both a miracle and a tragedy, pain and confusion etched in the lines of his face. She followed his gaze and saw a woman, beautiful and terrible, almost gliding towards them. Thirty or so demons followed her, not daring to break rank or cross her path, watching her intently as though waiting for her signal.

William made a noise of surprise in his throat, as their father stood, slowly and protectively over Mattias and in front of his other children.

"Malakai, darling, what have you been doing to my beautiful children?"

Shock kicked Kali in the gut, hard. Beside her, William took a step backwards.

She regarded the woman before her, the woman that should have been her mother, and her heart did somersaults every time she noticed something familiar in the otherwise strange face – William's jawline, Mattias' nose, her own facial structure. But the woman's eyes were pure black, giving no hints toward the woman she was before, or the mother she might have been to Kali, and the cruel smile the woman wore bore no resemblance to any of her other family.

"What are you doing here, Liliana?" her father sounded far more composed than she could ever have expected, his hand resting on the dagger strapped to his lower back.

"I heard the call of our daughter, and I came to welcome her home!"

She saw her father flinch, almost imperceptibly. Dread weighed Kali down as she tried not to look at her brothers – Mattias breathing heavily on the ground and William standing rigidly beside her. She had brought this upon them; she had no idea how, perhaps it was when she lost control, perhaps the fire called to her somehow, and now one of them lay dying in the grass.

"You are not wanted here. Leave this place and take your horde with you."

The woman that was once Kali's mother flashed her father a dangerous look.

"Do you propose to stop me, Malakai? You and your green children who have never seen war? It seems like one of them is fading from this life as we speak, perhaps you would be best placed turning your attention to him…or have you finally recognised a lost cause when you see one? Pity, that a child of mine could be so weak."

A snarl left Kali before she registered the woman had finished speaking. Blood pounded in her chest, her throat, her head; all she knew was adrenaline and anger and shame. Teeth bared, she felt poised to tear the woman's throat out, this pretender that wore their mother's face and mocked her dying brother. Without thinking, Kali lunged towards her mother, disappearing and re-materialising in front of her, using a pair of daggers like scissors to slice the woman's throat.

Shock, then glee, lit up the woman's features as blood burst from the wounds on her throat. Her mangled laugh gurgled in the stunned silence around them. The demons became restless as Kali's chest rose and fell. She moved past her mother and prepared to battle the next onslaught of demons, hearing her father shouting unintelligible words behind her as she did so.

As she re-sheathed her daggers and drew her sword, she felt a cold hand on her shoulder. She turned and saw with a jolt that the wounds on her mother's throat had already faded to angry, red scarring and she seemed relatively unharmed by her assault. In fact, she seemed delighted by it.

"Well, *here* is an offspring to be proud of, Malakai! I like this one's spirit. She will make a fine soldier," she turned her attention to Kali. "Come along, now," she chirped, as though nothing had happened.

Kali's father always taught her that the key to success in battle was to never be shocked by anything, to react without hesitation, but something seemed to have rooted her to the spot as she tried to figure out her next move. She looked to her brother and father and saw that they seemed to be trapped behind some sort of barrier or forcefield. Unable to reach her, they threw themselves against the invisible wall repeatedly, trying to break through.

Behind them, Mattias lay still – too still – and Kali knew, above all else, she needed to get him out of here. She tried to teleport back to her family, only to be stopped by the same invisible barrier holding them back. She bounced off it painfully and rolled back onto the grass.

"Get Mattias out of here!" Kali stood and tore her gaze away from her family, wide-eyed and frantic, as she prepared to fight alone, adrenaline drowning out any of her mounting fear.

Attempting to kill her mother had been fruitless, and she sensed her mother's power far surpassed that of the average demon – to waste energy on a second attempt seemed futile, but she would not be taken prisoner. She would not be taken alive for this woman to make her into a weapon, or to be broken down into a slave. Yet escape now seemed impossible, the barrier between her and her family entirely within her mother's control.

Kali decided that if death was her only way out, she would at least take as many demons with her on the way as she could manage. Maybe, she thought, it would give her family a better chance of survival. Without warning, she materialised herself into the crowd of demons, hacking and slicing at everything around her, expecting to be ripped apart at any moment. But although they howled, they hissed, and they snarled, the demons did nothing as she tore her way through them. Her mother watched on as though fascinated, refusing to give the demons the order to kill.

Only when Kali had killed around half of them did her mother finally react, barking something in a harsh language, and the demons began to move around her. She braced herself, yet even still they did not swarm her as she expected them to, instead choosing to fight in groups of two or three at a time. It seemed that her mother did not want her dead – at least not yet. When the last demon fell, Kali was breathing heavily and covered in blood – she wasn't sure how much was her own – the hot weight of it sinking into her clothes.

She faced her mother, defiant. Her plan to die had failed – her mother had made sure of that – and she was running out of options. Looking into those soulless, black eyes and imagining the woman that sang her brothers to sleep seemed to hollow her out, but she held her gaze.

"That was quite the show. Let's hurry along, now!" Liliana looked at her almost impatiently, appearing supremely unbothered by the demons that lay slain all around her.

Kali looked at her, incredulous. "You think that I would go anywhere with you, *demon?*" she spat with as much rancour as she could muster.

Her mother narrowed her eyes.

"You say 'demon' like it is an insult, my child; but it is what makes you special! It's what fuels that fire inside you and stokes your power – without it, you'd be nothing more than average. It was I that made you, demon blood that made you. Soon you'll learn to accept that it is a part of you and that those seraph *scum* will never accept you as you are. Only I will see you for all that you are! They will reject you, denounce you, seek to destroy you, but I will give you the world."

Her mother spoke fanatically, and everything about her presence screamed danger. Kali knew her options were limited. She looked one last time at her family; Mattias lay motionless, whilst her father and William still fought to find a way through the invisible barrier separating them. She was alone.

She looked at her mother coldly and dropped her sword as if to accept defeat. Triumph blazed across her mother's face, with a cold smile that sharpened her features. Kali could hear the desperate shouts of her family as she withdrew one of her daggers. Upon seeing the dagger in her hand, a look of amusement passed her mother's face…until she brought the blade sharply to her own throat.

She waited for the pain to come, anticipating the choking feeling she had witnessed others act out as their life drained out of them. She waited to watch the world turn dark.

But nothing happened.

Instead of feeling blood stream down her throat, she felt only sweat, and when she looked, the dagger was no longer in her hand. Perplexed, she looked to her mother, who inexplicably held the dagger in her hand and was wearing a look of cold fury. Before Kali could ask how her mother had stopped her, or draw her remaining dagger, her mother gave a cry of rage.

"If you aren't ready to join me, child, then so be it! Let's see if your mind changes when your world turns to ash. I promise you this, one day you will beg to join me," she snarled, before expertly launching the dagger across the clearing, where it found its target in Malakai's heart.

Chapter Four

Kali let out a cry, scarcely aware of Liliana turning and leaving as she stared transfixed in horror at the knife embedded in her father's chest.

He fell to his knees as she ran to him. The invisible barrier that held them back was now gone, but William had abandoned all attempts to reach her and was instead frantically trying to keep their father awake. Kali sank to their side, glancing over at Mattias – who was now clearly dead – and forced down the panic and bile rising in her throat.

Killing a seraph was difficult – far more so than killing a regular mortal – but the metal that forged Kali's dagger and the sigils engraved within it were designed to kill all mortal and non-mortal creatures. Whilst demons often carried runed weapons of their own, as well as the rare but fatal poison used to kill Mattias, seraphic-made blades were made with more skill and precision. They seldom failed. Met with the precision of Liliana's throw, it was a lethal combination.

As she watched the blade rise and fall with the fading breaths of her father, Kali knew there was little they would be able to do, out here alone in the woods. Even if they could make it back home to the seraphs, she doubted there was anything anyone could do with a mortal wound like this. It was eerily silent around them, with the corpses of the slain demons intruding on their grief. She took her father's hand, as she had done with Mattias – her last and impotent goodbye to her oldest brother – and met her father's eye.

"I'm so sorry," she said, tears blurring her vision.

"No...I'm sorry," he choked, looking at both her and William. It was clear that he wanted to say more, but his breathing was already becoming laboured and his lips were stained with blood. Kali gave her brother a pleading look but saw only her own pain and helplessness reflected on his face.

"I love...you...both." Their father gave them one last look full of love and grief and then looked at his oldest son, stretched his hand towards him and lay still.

"I hope he's waiting for me," he exhaled a long, shuddering breath, then breathed no more.

Looking at the empty shells of her brother and her father, it was like something had broken inside of Kali. She didn't feel rage or anguish, she didn't feel a rush of terrible power, she felt nothing. It was like a part of her had died with them. Mattias, who died alone on the ground as her family tried to save her. Her father killed by the blade she couldn't end her own life with.

They were both dead because of her.

She lay in the grass beside her father, hardly feeling the grass tickling her face, or the ache in her bones from the battle, or the burn of the wounds she sustained. She didn't feel the ache in her heart, it was as if she was observing all these things through someone else. William was crying silently, his hands in his hair, and Kali supposed that at some point soon the guilt would crush her, but at that moment, there was nothing.

Kali didn't know how long she lay there for, awake but not aware. William began the laborious task of conducting an inventory of the demons and using his ability to conjure fire to burn their corpses – anything to avoid looking at the broken remnants of his family, she guessed – but she still hadn't moved by the time he had finished. She didn't think she would ever move from this spot again. It should be her lying dead, not them, she thought as the tears finally came. *It was supposed to be me.*

"Kali, we have to go, we can't stay here." William finally broke the suffocating silence.

Didn't he understand there was nowhere to go? There was nothing. Only nothing.

"Kali?"

It hurt to breathe. There was nothing left.

"Kali!"

She was drowning. She could *feel* her lungs burning.

William kneeled beside her and turned her around so she was forced to look at him, instead of her father. She stared blankly ahead at him. Nothing made sense anymore. Nothing mattered.

"Kali, you're bleeding! Where are you hurt?"

She could only stare at him. Through him. She wondered briefly if this was madness and decided that this was certainly more welcome than the pain that was sure to follow.

"Kali, you are not the only person that lost their family tonight, please don't make me lose anyone else. Are you hurt?"

She blinked and sat up. Truthfully, she hurt everywhere, but she couldn't tell what pain was borne from injury and which was grief. She looked helplessly at her brother, and he seemed to understand.

"Here, stand up," he held out his hand and helped her to stand.

Her legs ached as they took her weight, feeling curiously like solid lead and liquid at the same time as she allowed William to check her over. She zoned out as he worked, unable to focus on anything. Everything was a contradiction – she felt like she was dying but she didn't feel hurt. Time seemed to be rushing by her, yet William moved in slow motion. Her exhaustion was beyond sleep.

"Your wounds seem relatively minor and I can't see any signs of poison," William announced eventually. "I'm pretty sure your left shoulder and collar bone are broken, but other than that your injuries don't seem too severe".

Kali stayed silent. He was telling her that she was okay, but nothing felt further from the truth.

"Kali, we need to go home," William began cautiously. "The Council need to know about what happened here, and Dad and Matt...they deserve a proper burial."

Kali struggled momentarily to understand what her brother was saying. Everything seemed to be happening out of sync, and words didn't hold as much meaning as they did before today in Kali's brain. She wanted to explain that they couldn't go back, not ever; that she couldn't face the Council and tell them what she was, admit that her very existence was a threat to their own, face the accusatory stares of the seraphs. She couldn't go back to their home and see the photographs, the laughing faces of the family she had torn apart and feel the weight of their absence in every room.

"But...we can't," was all she managed to say.

He looked at her, choosing his words carefully.

"Kal, we still have a duty to report demonic activity to the Council. This was practically an act of war."

The words from the prophecy rang in Kali's brain: *a war more terrible than the first…decided by a child with the blood of both seraph and demon…* Maybe it was best that she faced justice at the hands of the Council. Maybe they could make sure she could never hurt anyone else – she was prepared to die here on the battlefield, and it was no different really to die at the hands of the Council. There was even an honour to it, to willingly lay down her freedom and her life for the good of her kind (she quelled the voice in her head that spitefully pointed out they were only half her kind).

"You're right. We should go now," she glanced around, the unwelcome possibility that Liliana might return hanging uneasily in the air around them.

He nodded, surprised. He was evidently expecting more of an argument, but Kali was already turning away from him.

She contemplated the task of returning home to Domeneum. The duty of moving between destinations usually fell to her and her power of teleportation, but there were certain limitations on this ability. For instance, objects were harder to bring along than people. She had never tried to teleport with corpses before, and the thought nauseated her.

As always, William seemed to sense what she was thinking.

"We can go just the two of us and send reinforcements back if you'd prefer?"

She looked at him, appalled. "We can't leave them here, alone!"

Still, the thought of pulling the lifeless bodies of half of her family through empty space with her made her stomach turn. The events of the day caught up with her all at once, and she retched onto the grass beside her, vomiting despite the emptiness of her stomach.

She became acutely aware of how badly her shoulder ached, and of the heaviness in her limbs. She wanted to leave this place, this deceptively tranquil space that hosted the destruction of her entire world, and never return. Staggering slightly, she stood upright and marched towards her fallen brother and father, catching William's arm as she did so.

"Let's leave this Godforsaken place," she pulled him with her, and he nodded in agreement.

As soon as they reached the bodies, she lay a hand on each, with William holding her arm, and focused hard on the seraph capital, Domeneum, not pausing to look around, unwilling to see any more of the carnage around them.

* * * *

The seraph lands spanned across half the globe, running parallel to but out of sight of the human realm. Shared with the demons that inhabited the feral wilderness beyond their limits, the seraphs reinforced their borders with protective wards that ensured only those with seraphic blood could enter. Centuries old, the wards never failed, weakening only at the boundaries of the seraph territory, and rarely at that.

Those gifted with the ability to teleport, like Kali, could bypass the Inaustia – a series of gates that joined the human and seraph realm together – entirely, as could those traveling by portal, although the latter was expensive and required Council authorisation.

With their grief and slain family in tow, Kali brought them to Domeneum, the place they'd once called home and where the Council presided for most of the year. It was a magnificent city, built on the old architecture of the past with intricate art and stonework and the newer, sleeker buildings of glass and solid gold. Kali had always loved the atmosphere of the city, everyone rushing about their day, soldiers and artists alike leaving their impression on the streets. The ancestors buried in the sacred tombs below, never leaving, keeping an eternal watch on the city.

Today, its familiarity was a knife in the heart; to return like this, knowing what she knew, having lost what she had lost, it wasn't the return she so often dreamed of. It saddened her that her last look at the city would be this unsettling feeling of unbelonging in the place she always called home. The painful recognition that she was no longer a child playing soldiers with her brothers in the streets, but a harbourer of an insidious disease, an outsider, a threat, with the death of her family on her soul.

She brought them to their back garden first, to avoid prying eyes and to prevent causing alarm. The smell of the flowers was familiar, and it made Kali's gut twist wistfully. To be back here under any other circumstance would be a dream, today it was a nightmare.

They left their father and brother under an old oak tree that had stood for generations, looking over the family home. It felt wrong to leave them outside, but worse still to bring them inside, where they once lived and created memories, knowing they never would again. Kali avoided looking at them as they turned and made their way towards their house, feeling their empty, staring eyes on the back of her head.

Once inside, Kali and William each went to their respective bedrooms to shower and change clothes without uttering a word to each other, unable to muster the energy to speak. Kali longed for sleep, to sink into unknowing oblivion, but she knew that even if she had the chance, her dreams would likely be as bad as reality, or worse.

She hoped a hot shower would soothe her somewhat or clear her head, but it only served to aggravate the wounds she sustained fighting the demons. Blood, a mix of her own and the demons', turned the water brown-red as she tried her best to get clean without over-exerting her broken shoulder, but she reflected that she would probably never feel clean again. The impurity she wanted to rid herself of was on the inside, not outside, and no amount of showering would ever cure it.

She expected to cry, now that she was alone, to collapse under the weight of the grief not just for her family but for herself and the person she thought she would be, but still there was only pervasive emptiness. What was *wrong* with her, she wondered, that she couldn't even cry for the loss of her brother and father – was this her demonic nature? Cold and unfeeling? Her legs were shaking beneath her and she longed again for sleep, to just be able to rest.

Once dressed, she met her brother in the kitchen, which now seemed haunted and unfriendly; the entire house felt barren. She saw that William was dressed similarly to her in loose-fitting combat gear, which was standard attire for off-duty military personnel and their families. They both wore all black – a show of respect for the Council and of mourning for fallen loved ones or fellow soldiers. As she approached,

William looked up and handed her a bottle of white pills.

"Found these in a medicine cabinet upstairs, for your shoulder, should help with the pain. You'll still need to see a medic though."

She nodded and emptied two of the pills into her hand, before returning the bottle to him. As her brother turned away to put it in his kit with some other supplies, she stuffed them into her pocket; it felt like the pain was the only thing keeping her grounded and without it, she'd float away or stop existing altogether. She needed to stay focused if she was going to face the Council. Besides, demons and kin-killers didn't deserve pain relief, and she was both of those things.

Impatiently brushing off his attempt to put her arm in a sling, they set off on foot to the Council building – it was forbidden to enter by teleportation, and Kali was drained regardless – taking in the familiarity of the streets and commenting on how it had changed since they were last in the city. As the sky darkened, the stunted conversation faded into tired silence.

Kali turned her mind to how she would tell the Council everything without implicating her family. She was especially worried for William who might face punishment or excommunication if they found out that he had knowingly harboured a part-demon and kept her from their knowledge. She wondered how to do it without alerting him to her plan, too, when he knew her so well.

Her brain was sluggish and tired, and forming a plan was like trying to run through mud. Ultimately, she knew that her brother would need to do the majority of the talking as the oldest child, and she would need to take whatever opportunity she could to come clean to the Council without damaging her family's reputation, if possible.

It startled her to think of William as the oldest – that was always Mattias' role. The strict, eldest child with the family reputation on his shoulders, living up to the family name whilst the younger siblings snuck out to play pranks with the other children. They always laughed at his older brother-ness, and Kali couldn't remember the last time she told him that she loved him. She couldn't even remember the last thing she had said to him. They mocked him, she and William, as they walked back to camp whilst he and her father were attacked by demons. How unfair that she lived, and they had died.

She glanced guiltily at William, who seemed as lost in thought as she was, knowing she had robbed him of so many things. Their father would never see him start a career, find love, have a family. He would never get drunk and laugh with his brother again, never get to be the younger sibling, have his older brother to protect and fight beside him ever again. The guilt and pain crept into her bones and settled in her chest, seeping into the very centre of her, and although it was a relief to know that she could feel something again, it was at the least convenient time.

The Council building loomed before them, resplendent with its ancient stone pillars and artwork inlaid with gold. Guards lined the doors, armed with longswords and spears, and they nodded in acknowledgement as they climbed the steps to the main entrance. The guards at the main door spoke as they approached.

"Good evening, please declare your name and purpose!"

"William and Kali Robereun, children of General Malakai Robereun, come to inform the Council of demon activity in the human plane and of"— William faltered— "the death of our father and of our brother, Mattias Robereun."

A shocked murmur ran through the line of guards. Their father was well known amongst the seraphs, especially here in the capital, where many of the Guard likely served with him. Hearing it said aloud seemed to shatter Kali's personal bubble of grief and make it real. The pain in her chest felt heavier and drawing air into her lungs was becoming steadily more difficult.

The guard allowed them to proceed into the main hall of the building, where they were to wait for the Council to summon them. In the tense silence, every noise was magnified and echoed throughout the corridors. Neither of them spoke as they waited, until a voice punctured the silence.

"William?"

Her brother turned, and despite the circumstance, his face lit up.

"Amariel? I can't believe it! I thought you were stationed in Tereum? How *are* you?"

Her brother seemed delighted to see the man in front of him, who looked vaguely familiar to Kali and seemed equally as pleased to see her brother. It was jarring, but not unpleasant, to see her brother happy.

"Kali, you remember Amariel, don't you? You used to get jealous when we wouldn't spar with you because you were too little, and Dad would..." he trailed off. The grief in his eyes was unmistakable as he ran a hand through his hair, looking deflated.

"I've just heard the news. I am so sorry to hear about your father and Mattias, Will, Kali. I truly am. They were both truly great men and great warriors." Amariel touched William's shoulder lightly, and her brother smiled sadly at him.

Kali realised abruptly that she did recognise Amariel, although he was considerably older and distinctly more muscular than she remembered him. When they were younger, he was one of William's closest friends. In fact, if Kali recalled correctly, it was leaving Amariel behind that caused William to get into such a furious argument with their father about leaving Domeneum that she thought it would amount to physical violence. When she went to check on him, he'd shouted at her and told her to leave him alone. She couldn't understand why he was angry with her at the time, now of course that made sense.

There was a loud creak as the main door inside the hall opened, revealing the Council chambers and inside, a long wooden table at which the seven Council members were seated.

"Come forth, house of Robereun!"

Kali exchanged a nervous look with her brother; neither of them had ever interacted with the Council alone before, and the prospect of explaining the events of the past twenty-four hours was daunting. He squeezed her uninjured shoulder encouragingly despite looking as apprehensive as she felt and turned to Amariel.

"It was great to see you again, old friend, although I wish the circumstances were different. Perhaps when our business with the Council is done, we will meet again?"

Amariel smiled. "Yes, I would welcome a chance to reconnect! Good luck with the Council, it is best not to keep them waiting, and let me again express my sorrow at your loss – both of you," he inclined his head to them both, gave one last smile to William, then promptly departed the hall.

Kali met her brother's eye and wordlessly they entered the Council chambers to stand before the Council.

Chapter Five

The Council chamber was surprisingly bare in comparison to the rest of the building. There were no ornate furnishings, works of art or precious metals decorating the windowless room, and the most striking piece of furniture was the highly polished mahogany table at which the Council met for briefings. They sat there now, along one side of the table, facing Kali and William and watching them as they entered the room. All seven of them wore hooded robes of a dark, deep blue, and they lowered their hoods in unison as they approached. It was an aged woman at the centre of the table that spoke first.

"Welcome, children of house Robereun. You stand before the Council gathered, to relay talk of demonic activity and report the deaths of General Malakai Robereun and his eldest son, Mattias Robereun; is this the truth?"

"Yes, Lady Aequellus, I report with a heavy heart the deaths of my father and my brother, who were lost during an altercation with a faction of demons in the human realm. I come to report the events to you as is my duty as a child of the seraph,"

William's voice was steady, but his hands were shaking.

He'd met the Council on several occasions with their father, and he tried to emulate the way he remembered his father interacting with them. Kali thought his voice sounded stilted, and the unfamiliarity of it fuelled her nerves.

"Very grievous news, indeed. A true loss has befallen us this day. May the Council extend their condolences and blessings on your family." Lady Aequellus appeared genuinely saddened as the rest of the Council murmured their agreement.

"Yes, yes, and what of the demons, boy?" demanded a red-faced man to the left of Lady Aequellus.

Kali felt an instant dislike towards the man, who was leaning forward towards William as though prepared to pounce on whatever he said next.

"Lord Duris, my family and I despatched of the demons and their remains...but their leader escaped after she—*it* slew our father."

"And you know the identity of this demon?" Lady Aequellus asked, picking up on William's hesitation.

"Yes, my Lady, it was the demon that wears the face of General Liliana Robereun, our mother, that led the demons to attack."

The Council began talking amongst themselves for a moment, ignoring them. Kali shifted uncomfortably; this place made her nervous and her muscles ached. She wondered if she would ever see daylight again, or if they would take her straight from this chamber to a prison cell when they found out what she was.

"My boy, tell us everything," requested Lady Aequellus, not unkindly.

As she listened to her brother describe Liliana's attack, she grew increasingly more anxious. He was deliberately leaving out anything that could link her to the demon attack, or her family knowing of her additional powers or link to the prophecy and in doing so making it harder for her to come clean without outing him as a liar to the Council. He portrayed their stay in the woods as their father had – a trip to hone survival and navigation skills – and their mother's attack as a targeted attack on their father, leaving Kali out of it entirely, except for the fight itself.

"And you and your sister managed to survive this attack against thirty demons when your experienced father and older sibling could not? How…impressive." Her eyes flitted briefly to Kalı and then back to William, who barely managed to suppress an uncomfortable grimace.

"Yes, my Lady. We were most fortunate."

"Very well, the Council thanks you for your report and your valour. We will retire to deliberate our next actions. We will send a mourning party to collect your dead and prepare them for their final resting place. Have you any more for the Council to consider?"

Kali sensed her last opportunity and took a step forward, but before she could speak, she was interrupted by her brother.

"Yes, my Lady, my sister has sustained injuries and requires the attention of a medic at once." He shot her a look, and she stepped back.

"Yes, very well. You should both be checked by a medic to clear you of any signs of corruption. I will have one of the Council aides accompany you. If that is all, you may leave this Council to its deliberations."

William nodded then turned away from the Council, catching Kali's arm and steering her from the room.

As they entered the main hall, the door behind them closed and Kali began to protest.

"*Not here!*" William hissed at her, looking thunderous.

A side door Kali hadn't noticed before opened to her right and two robed figures stepped out. These robes were not the same dark blue as those worn by the Council, but rather a lighter blue, like the colour of the sky. Their faces were covered by their hoods and Kali couldn't tell which of them was speaking.

"Come with us, we will accompany you to the medic," one of them commanded.

They followed the pair in silence down a long corridor, and Kali briefly wondered if they were, in fact, being arrested. If the Council had sensed her brother's lies and they were about to be punished severely for it. She tried to catch her brother's eye, but he was regarding the pair in blue carefully and did not look her way.

The pair led them into a large room that was white, clinical, and occupied by a man and a woman each wearing green robes and large smiles. William let out a long breath, and Kali saw his shoulders relax.

"Hello, our dutiful blue friends, what have you brought for us today?" smiled the man good-naturedly.

The pair in blue did not return the pleasantries. "Two wounded from a battle with demons. The Council require you to check for corruption and provide a report, at once," one of them replied, stiff and formal.

"Of course, whatever the Council require we shall fulfil," the woman said and inclined her head, dismissing the pair in blue. They turned silently and left the room, keeping pace with one another without looking back or saying goodbye.

"They are a droll bunch those blue robes," laughed the man. "Alright, let's take a look, then! You with me"— he gestured to William— "you with her!" He pointed to Kali.

Kali obliged as the woman pulled a curtain around the two of them and instructed her to sit on one of the available beds.

She examined each of Kali's wounds, cleaning them out, stitching them where required and dressing them. She took notes as she worked and smiled when she noticed Kali trying to read them.

"Don't worry, your wounds show no sign of corruption, the Council just requires us to document all wounds and report on them ever since the re-emergence of the sickness. It's pretty much a non-occurrence though, the most recent case was years ago, and it seems to be a freak event!" she smiled reassuringly, and Kali did her best to return it, trying to think of anything else other than her mother's cold, black eyes.

Once the medic had finished with Kali's visible wounds, she got to work on her other injuries. Every so often the woman would ask Kali to move a certain way and report where it hurt; afterwards, she would place a hand on the area, eyes closed in concentration. It quickly became apparent that her power had something to do with detecting injuries and her choice of profession became obvious to Kali. She busied herself with slings and bandages, wrapping Kali up until she felt utterly ridiculous. After thirty minutes or so, the medic finally seemed satisfied.

"Okay: your collar bone and shoulder are broken –I expect that will take a few days to a week to heal. You have a fracture in one of your ribs but that should be fixed up in a couple of days, along with your cuts and scrapes. You've got some sprains and bruising dotted around but those should only bother you for another day or so. All in all, I would say there's nothing to worry about, but if you notice your wounds aren't healing or they are becoming discoloured then please do not hesitate to come back and see us!" She smiled warmly at Kali and pressed a bottle of white pills – the same kind that William had given her earlier – into her hands.

Kali thanked her and pulled the curtain back to reveal her brother waiting for her in a chair by the door. He raised an eyebrow as he observed the various slings and bandages the medic had forced upon her but remained silent.

As soon as they left the medic's office, Kali began removing the slings and bandages, keeping only the dressings for her cuts. William moved as if to stop her, and then seemed to accept defeat and waited for her to finish. She stuffed them into his bag hastily, desperate to leave the building and get some fresh air.

Night had fallen completely by the time they made it back outside, and they walked without much conversation. She knew her brother was as tired as she was, and that both of them just wanted to sleep, if sleep was even possible after all that had happened.

They reached home and saw the Council's squad had already visited, leaving a note on the front door to say that their father and brother's bodies would be returned to the tombs in the coming days. Kali felt guilty for the relief it brought, but she couldn't imagine sleeping knowing that they lay so close.

As they entered the house, they lingered awkwardly for a moment, unsure of what to do or say to each other. Kali started forward to go upstairs when William's voice stopped her.

"We need to be on the same page about what happened and what we do next."

"Will, I—"

"No, don't speak, just listen. I know what you were planning to do in there, and I will not allow the sacrifices this family have made for you to be undone by your sudden sense of martyrdom. Dad wanted us to keep you safe, but it's not just about you anymore, Kali. The second we decided to hide you from the Council we became enemies of them, and we put ourselves in danger. Don't think I didn't know you were going to try and pull some ridiculous, self-sacrificing bullshit if you got in front of the Council, despite the fact you'd have called out not only me but Dad and Matt as a liar too. I bet you didn't even think of us when—"

"Of *course* I—"

"Just LISTEN TO ME! You don't get to betray them like that, not when they gave up everything for you. You keep your head *down,* you keep the truth hidden and you don't breathe a word of any of this to *anyone.* We stick *together.* You stay here until we figure out what to do next and you act like the soldier Dad raised you to be instead of an emotional and impulsive *child! Realise all that is at stake here and grow up!* Do you understand me?"

Kali's blood felt like ice. "I'm sorry, I was just trying to do the right thing…"

"Well, why not ask Dad how that's worked out so far?"

She recoiled like he had slapped her, and he seemed to have realised that he'd gone too far. Guilt flickered momentarily across his features, but he made no move to apologise as she turned on her heel and walked numbly upstairs to her bedroom.

He was hurt, exhausted, and stressed; how could he not be? She knew better than anyone in that moment the sheer weight of the past twenty-four hours, but what hurt wasn't that he had thrown those words at her, but that she knew they were true.

She lost control and called the demons to them, and it led to Mattias' death. She challenged her mother and tried to take her own life in an act of defiance, and that had led to her father's death. If she confessed to the Council, she might have cost William his life, too. One impulsive, over-emotional decision after another, and it had cost them almost everything. Given the grief she had caused her brother, she wondered why he hadn't just thrown her to the Council to finally be rid of her. She felt wretched.

She sat on the end of her bed, thinking about the day's events, replaying it over and over in agonising detail until eventually, she heard William wearily climbing the stairs. He paused momentarily in the hall and Kali kept still, hoping he would think her already asleep. She heard him sigh and then move off towards his bedroom, closing the door behind him.

Kali lay on her bed, fully clothed, too tired to change. Sleep overcame her within a matter of minutes, but it was not peaceful. As predicted, her dreams were full of death and demons, some real memories and some imagined as they blurred into one awful sequence of horrors.

She was back in the clearing, but this time it was nightfall, and demons moved out in the dark. She called for her family, but nobody replied. She pushed forward, looking for them and saw Mattias lying in the grass, stirring slightly. She ran to him, hoping to save him, but by the time she reached him his body was bloated and blue, and his eyes bulged from his head. In horror, she turned and ran from him, only to find herself face to face with her father, blood streaming from his mouth every time he tried to speak to her.

He gripped her shoulders tightly, his eyes desperate and pleading. When she looked down, she saw that she was slowly pushing a dagger into his chest and her hands were covered in his blood. She cried out and heard demons laugh, unseen in the shadows; she backed away from her father and stumbled over something, falling to the ground. She landed beside the cause of her fall – it was William lying in the grass, choking for help as a demon hacked at him with razor-sharp blades. She crawled towards him, trying to fend off the demon, but he gagged in terror when she faced him and tried to get away from her.

Suddenly she was standing in her bathroom, her reflection in the mirror was not her own but her mother's. As she watched, her reflection began tearing at her face, peeling off skin in strips, blood pooling at her feet. She tried to scream but found she couldn't, and when she was done, the reflection in the mirror was now her own but her eyes were pupil-less, black and cruel, and a grin of sharp, fanged teeth was fixed on her face.

She woke with a start, breathing heavily and covered in sweat. Her shoulder ached where she had been thrashing around. Shakily, she stood up and threw open her window, gulping in the cool night air. She touched her face, remembering the sensation of her skin being stripped away to reveal a demon underneath and inhaled deeply, trying to breathe through the nausea it brought with it. She ached to speak to Mattias, who would have had something sensible to say, or to William who would offer comfort better than anyone and felt totally alone. One brother was gone and the other likely hated her, with good reason.

She rummaged around for the pills that the medic had given her, hoping they would take the edge off the pain rippling through her body to allow her to sleep more peacefully. She took two and felt relief almost instantly as she peeled off her clothes and got into bed, hoping for less traumatic dreams than before. The sky was lightening by the time she fell into a fitful sleep, filled with dreams of death and violence.

Chapter Six

When Kali awoke the next morning, her bedsheets were twisted around her, and she was drenched in sweat. Sighing, she extricated herself from the tangle and swung her legs out of bed, pushing her hair out of her face and wincing at the painful protest from her shoulder. The bruises and wounds from the previous day somehow ached more than they had yesterday, and she reached again for the pain relief issued by the medic.

Light filtered in from the window, illuminating her bedroom. She was surprised to find that it still felt like home to her, despite her time away from it. She scanned the familiar surroundings and her heart ached as she saw the framed photographs of her with her brothers, her father, and old friends adorning the furniture that lined the room, covered now in a thin layer of dust.

She stood, looking determinedly away from the smiling faces in the photographs, and began going through her old belongings. It had been years since she had worn any of her clothes, but she was pleasantly surprised to find that many of them still fit

– a relief, given that most of her belongings hadn't survived the fire and a shopping trip in the wake of so much death seemed ludicrous.

She picked out some fresh clothes, wrapped herself in a towel, and cautiously opened her bedroom door, listening for the sound of her brother's movements. She wasn't ready to face him yet, and she kept picturing the look on his face as he shouted at her on repeat in her mind. *"...ask Dad how that's worked out so far."* When she heard nothing, she crept along the hall to her preferred bathroom to shower. She let the warm water wash over her, trying to imagine it washing away everything from the last couple of days, erasing it all and neutralising the evil contamination inside of her. Maybe she could become normal through sheer force of will if she concentrated on it hard enough.

She tied her damp hair back from her face and reluctantly made her way downstairs. The large clock by the front door told her it was almost noon, so she expected William to be waiting for her in the kitchen. Instead, she found a note, hastily scrawled in her brother's handwriting.

"Called to meet with Council. Meeting Amariel afterwards. Be back around dinner time, go ahead and eat without me."

The note was accompanied by what she recognised as her father's wallet; she hadn't realised William had taken it from him but was thankful that he had. She looked around the empty kitchen, realising that a shopping trip was necessary after all if she wanted to eat. Absent-mindedly, she massaged her injured shoulder. The thought of going into the city again both thrilled her and filled her with anxiety – to be back home was wonderful, but to be back here with only half of her family and knowing she was some part-demon abomination filled her with a powerful sense of loneliness.

Suck it up, Kali, she admonished herself. William was right, it was time to stop acting like a self-indulgent child: her father raised her better than that. This was not the time for wallowing in grief or self-pity, she had to carry on as normal – whatever "normal" was now.

She snatched up the wallet from the table and strode to the front door. As she stepped outside, she found that it was a perfect sunny day, and the warm sun on her skin calmed her. It reminded her of the summers of her childhood, or of the days spent exploring in the human realm with her family, making their way through sun-beaten villages and seaside towns.

She slowed her pace as she wandered into the street, taking in the happy shouts of playing children, the *clack*s of wooden swords as teenagers sparred with their friends, the birds singing in the trees. The realisation that the world or indeed even the city had not come to a resounding, mournful stop in the wake of recent events was jarring to Kali; the grief she felt was so powerful she wondered how it was possible that everyone else continued as normal, unaware of it. How it hadn't rippled out of her, enveloping everyone in its path. It was disconcerting, but somehow reassuring to Kali, that even in the aftermath of something that was world-shattering to her, to her brother, that life outside of their bubble continued on, undisturbed. It made her feel less significant, less important, less of a threat.

She made her way down the wide, open paths from her suburban neighbourhood into the narrowing streets of the city centre. She felt a rush of warmth towards the city, noticing that the vibrancy she always loved had not changed in her absence. All around her people hurried through the streets between the old, pastel-coloured buildings of the Old Town, or made their way into the sleek, shiny buildings of the New Town. Kali preferred the historic modesty of the Old Town to the cool, haughty atmosphere of the New Town, and it was there that she walked to now, to the old food market.

From its centre, the market spanned a mile in all directions, filled with people selling brightly coloured fruits and vegetables; meat and fish; intricately decorated cakes; vats of hot, thick soup, oils, spices, wine, meads, and a variety of fabrics. It was a hub of the community and Kali always thought that it had a perpetual festival-like atmosphere to it. It was never devoid of laughter, happy cries of welcome, or of the music drifting into the crowds from the various live performers crammed into every free space available.

Kali inhaled deeply as she approached, smelling the usual mix of sweet and savoury food, the tang of spices, the heady smells of wine and mead, and the light touch of fragrances that intermingled throughout the market. The laughs and shouts of the crowd grew louder as she drew nearer, and she could hear snippets of song as the sound of music drifted lazily through the noise of the crowd.

Unexpectedly, the noise and the crowd became overwhelming, and Kali's breathing began to constrict. She darted down a quieter alley, sheltered from the sun and the throng of people, and tried to calm her breathing. *There is no threat, and this is still your home,* she silently repeated to herself over and over again, clinging to this new mantra.

She recalled how William had calmed her before and desperately began to take note of all the individual things she could see, hear, smell around her. Together, the combination of the sun's heat, the noises of laughing, shouting, music and the smells of the market were oppressive and over-powering – broken down individually, they were manageable, almost pleasant. Gradually, the panic coursing through her began to subside. She let out a deep breath and rolled her eyes at herself. *Yep, can't buy apples without freaking out but I'm meant to lead armies in some big, prophetic war – sounds about right.*

Trying not to draw any attention to herself, she emerged from the alley and entered the edge of the market. Nobody paid her any notice as she browsed the stalls, buying apples and oranges at one and a variety of vegetables from another. She eyed the meat stalls with distaste as she passed them; as an Empath with sway over animals, she had never been able to look at them as food. In fact, when her father told her as a child that was where meat came from, she cried and demanded that it be banned from the house. They pretended to agree, but she knew they would eat it when they thought she couldn't see.

She wandered over to the wines, looking at the different bottles of deep red and clear white-yellow liquids, and selected one she remembered her father enjoyed. It reminded her of their time in a place known by the humans as the "Mediterranean", where her father was as relaxed and happy as she had ever seen him. She smiled sadly to herself as she moved on.

As she approached a stall of spices, recognition flitted across the seller's face, and Kali did a double take.

"*Anissa?*"

"Kali!" the young woman in front of her squealed as her face lit up with delight.

Standing in front of Kali was her – former – best friend.

At once, Anissa threw her arms around Kali, hugging her and causing the ache in her collar bone to spike, but her smile was genuine as she drew back to face her old friend.

"When did you get back? It's so good to see you!" Anissa beamed at her, faltering slightly at the sight of her cuts and bruises.

"Uh, just yesterday actually," she replied, realising that news of her father hadn't yet spread.

She felt a stab of grief and wondered how to tell Anissa about her family's fate.

Anissa was a gentle soul, not at all like any of her brothers' Warrior friends. Gifted with the ability to feel what others were feeling, when Kali first met Anissa, she found it impossible to close her mind to the emotions of those around her. As she gained more control, her power made their friendship beautifully uncomplex. Anissa knew when something upset Kali, and Kali could never lie to her about it; their friendship was based on mutual respect and honesty. It was the simple and unburdened friendship reserved, it seemed sometimes to Kali, for childhood.

When Kali started to become aware of the darkness gnawing at her, subtle in its presence at first, she felt a sense of dread at Anissa feeling it too, without ever really knowing why. Even then, Kali sensed that something was different in her and that she mustn't tell anyone about it. So, the day Anissa announced she would no longer use her power on friends without permission was a relief to Kali. Anissa promised her she'd never invade her privacy that way, and it was one of the reasons Kali loved her so much.

Anissa was staring at her now, with a cautious expression. Kali realised that she was talking to her, but she hadn't taken in a word of it. She knew Anissa was sensing something was off, whether that was through power or perception she didn't know.

"Is everything okay?" Anissa eyed Kali's visible scrapes and bruising with concern.

Kali searched for the right words and the best way to tell Anissa about all that had happened but came up short.

"Ani…Dad and Matt are dead. Demons attacked us and they-they died, Ani. It's just me and William, now," tears stung at her eyes and her throat constricted as she spoke.

Anissa looked at her, aghast. She opened her mouth to speak, her eyes searching Kali as she tried to conjure words but shut it again quickly. She rushed forward, tears shining in her own eyes, and hugged Kali gently.

"Kali, I'm so sorry," she whispered.

Tears streaked both of their faces when they pulled away.

"Thanks, Ani," Kali sniffed and wiped her eyes with the back of her hand.

"If you want to talk…"

Kali considered for a moment. On one hand, it was far too raw, too fresh, to talk about openly, to even comprehend it. On the other, she had nobody else to talk to after her fight with William – she felt alone, and she couldn't stand it. It was like a black hole that was threatening to swallow her whole.

Anissa picked up on her hesitation.

"I'm about to hand the stall over to one of my mother's new employees anyway. Why don't we head into the New Town for a drink? We don't need to talk about anything you don't want to. I'm even meeting Tannick later, I know he would be thrilled to see you," she smiled encouragingly.

Kali smiled too. Tannick was Anissa's older brother, and they'd spent a lot of time together as children. Closer in age to Mattias and William, he initially spent most of his time trying to ditch his sister and her friend in favour of training with them and their friends. When Kali was finally allowed to spar and begin training with the older children, however, he went from simply being Anissa's older brother to a friend. Despite being older than William, he was one of the few older boys unrelated to her that would entertain the idea of sparring with her. Anissa would wait for them, reading a book under the huge oak in Kali's garden until they were finished, and then they'd all explore suburban Domeneum, pretending to fight demons along the way.

"That sounds great, Ani," she smiled warmly.

Anissa beamed at her.

"Great! I'll just finish up here and wait for Maria and then we can go. She should be here soon!"

She turned and busied herself with tidying up the stall, bending down to scrawl a note – Kali presumed it was to the aforementioned Maria – and then turned back to her, smiling nervously.

They waited around making casual conversation until Maria – a cheerful woman with a kind smile – arrived and fussed over Anissa before dismissing her from her duties and good-naturedly ordering them to have a drink on her behalf.

They strolled through the streets of Domeneum, Anissa chattering nervously as Kali remained silent, trying and failing to absorb everything she said. She gazed around at her surroundings, comforted by the things that had remained the same in her absence and thrown by all that was different. They made their way to the New Town, filled with chic looking restaurants and bars, a juxtaposition to the setting they'd just come from. It was here Kali truly noticed how much had changed since the last time she was in Domeneum. She felt oddly like a tourist in her own home, belonging and not belonging simultaneously – the effect was disconcerting.

"Kali? We're here!"

Kali realised with a start that Anissa had been talking to her again.

"Sorry, I was a million miles away," she apologised.

"That's okay, do you still want to come in?"

"Of course," Kali tried to arrange her facial expression into a smile, but it felt odd and unnatural and she stopped quickly.

Anissa held the door open for her, and they entered a simple but stylish bar, Anissa hurrying over to a booth in the back corner to claim it. There was a slightly awkward silence between them as they sat opposite each other, until a waiter came to take their order. As the wine began to flow, so did the conversation.

She couldn't bring herself to talk about her family, but she enjoyed hearing about Anissa's. She told Kali about how her mother bought the stall a couple of years ago after Tannick enlisted in the Guard with their father.

"She was stuck in the house all day and I was working in this awful restaurant, and she just decided *'why not?'*, you know?" Anissa chirped, taking a sip of wine.

"That's great, Ani."

"So, what about you and William? Do you think you'll stay here for long?" Anissa asked cautiously, as though afraid of upsetting her.

Kali sighed. "To be honest I haven't even thought that far ahead. A few days ago I didn't know if we'd ever come back and now we're here. I don't know what we do next."

She stared into her glass, the deep red liquid inside making her momentarily think of blood. She shuddered and took a deep breath, noticing that it caught somewhat in her throat as she did.

When she looked up, she saw Anissa was looking at her with pity in her eyes. She cleared her throat, a little uncomfortable.

"But it's a good question. I don't really know what to do with myself now I'm back here," she tried to sound more hopeful than she felt.

"You could open up a stall next to us at the market!" Anissa offered enthusiastically.

Kali pulled a face. "Work with people and the public? Hard pass."

Anissa looked faintly dejected but recovered quickly.

"What about the Guard?"

Kali considered for a moment.

"I mean I guess I always assumed my future was with the Guard but the timing...I don't know," Kali thought of all that she'd found out about herself in the past couple of days and wondered if it was safe for her to be somewhere so focused on demons and combat.

"You don't think your father would approve?" Anissa asked, her voice hushed.

Kali was temporarily confused, before understanding that Anissa knew nothing of the past couple of days and thought she was simply referring to her father and brother's death.

"I'm not sure, to be honest. We actually didn't talk about the future very often, not past where our next destination would be."

"What was it like, out there? What are humans like?" Anissa leaned forward in her seat, flushed from the wine.

"It was amazing, Ani," Kali jumped on the chance to talk about something else. "The world is such a beautiful place and the humans, they're so *weird!* They look just like us but they're so fragile and so...*temporary*. They don't even know about demons, not truly like we do – they're just scary stories told in the night for fun, every region of the world have their own versions, it's just...so different yet so similar," she gushed, remembering their travels fondly despite her periodic misgivings throughout them.

Anissa drank in every word as Kali detailed the landscapes of the human world, the vibrant pink and terracotta of seaside villages, the grandeur of the main cities, and the ferocious beauty of the wild countryside. They were enthralled in conversation when a familiar voice interrupted them.

"Kali Robereun, back in Domeneum – well I'll be damned!"

She looked up and saw Anissa's older brother standing just in front of their booth, looking surprised but pleased to see her.

"Tannick Bratheas, you're taller than I remember you," she laughed, standing to greet him as Anissa made room for him to sit down beside her.

"So, to what do we owe the honour? Finally get sick of travelling with those brothers of yours and want to return to civilisation?" he joked.

The smile faded from Anissa's face as she looked at Kali apprehensively. Kali began to tell him the reason she was back but found that the words stuck in her throat.

"Tannick...Malakai and Mattias...they're dead," Anissa came to her aid, her voice small.

Tannick looked shell-shocked.

"*No! Kali,* I'm so sorry I didn't know! When? How?"

"It's fine, don't worry about it. It just happened; you couldn't have known."

"Is William—?"

"He's fine. Well, he isn't hurt at least."

Tannick sat in stunned silence briefly before flagging down a passing waitress and ordering more drinks. When they arrived, he raised his solemnly.

"To Malakai and Mattias Robereun. The toughest guys I ever met."

The three of them drank, looking pensively into their empty glasses until Anissa broke the sombre silence.

"We were talking about where Kali wants to go next, Tannick. I suggested the Guard, but she isn't sure. What do you think?"

Tannick looked up and glanced over her.

"You been keeping up with your training?"

"Please, did you know my father?" she snorted. "Of course I have; I bet I could knock you on your ass," she replied with the hint of a smile, though her throat still burned with the effort it took not to cry.

"I'll take that challenge," he smirked, "when you don't look like shit," he added, eyeing the bandages and bruising decorating her.

"Always with the charm," she chuckled into her drink.

"Seriously though if it's something you're considering I'd be more than happy to help. The best thing I ever did was join the Guard. Besides"—he looked around and dropped his voice— "I might happen to know they're going to be recruiting soon. I can't say any more but trust me, *you* will want in on this."

She thought for a moment. It did make sense to Kali to join the Guard – realistically it was all she was really qualified for. It was all she ever trained for, and her family legacy was built on it. But what if she lost control again?

Tannick talked about the Guard for another solid thirty minutes until Kali eventually agreed to at least consider it. Afterwards, the conversation inevitably turned reminiscent about their childhood, and to catching up on what they'd missed in their time apart. Kali didn't realise it was dark outside until she saw Anissa stifle a yawn.

"I really need to get home before William sends a search party," she sighed.

"Oh, okay. Do you want us to walk you home?" Tannick looked vaguely disappointed.

"No, thank you. I appreciate it but I'm okay. I could actually use the time alone."

"Okay, if you're sure," he stood to hug her goodbye, and Anissa did the same beside him.

"It was so good to see you both," she hugged them both in turn, reluctant to leave them.

"You too, Kali," Anissa smiled. "Please, let us know if you need *anything!*"

"Yeah, anything we can do, we're there," echoed Tannick.

"Thanks, guys. That means a lot," she replied, grateful to know that maybe she wasn't completely alone in the world after all.

* * * *

When she arrived home, she found William waiting for her in the kitchen. His face was tight, and a muscle twitched in his jaw.

"Kali, where have you *been?*"

She looked pointedly at the bags of shopping she was carrying, raising an eyebrow at her brother.

"Uh...*shopping?*"

"This whole time? Kali, it's been hours!"

"I met Anissa and Tannick, and we got talking. You said you were out with Amariel tonight, so I didn't hurry back. Is it only you that's allowed to spend time with old friends?"

William narrowed his eyes slightly in response.

"I'm not the one with a sudden habit of suicidal recklessness and martyrdom, I thought you'd done something stupid."

"If you were really that concerned, I'm sure you wouldn't have left me alone to go into the city at all, don't get weird about it now when your concern has been notably absent today."

The argument from the night before hung between them, heavy and uncomfortable.

"I was summoned by the Council, I couldn't exactly refuse," he replied, but he didn't quite meet her eyes.

She walked past him without speaking and began to put away the items she had bought at the market.

"Look...I needed space. But what I said last night—"

"Was the truth. We don't need to discuss it any further." Kali made a point of not turning to look at her brother, but she heard him sigh.

"Kali..."

He sounded tired and, begrudgingly, she turned to face him.

"We need to decide what we're going to do next," she said, changing the subject. She saw no point in drawing out a long conversation about hurt feelings when other matters were so pressing. Truthfully, she wasn't sure she could stand to relive it all, anyway.

He hesitated, then nodded.

"Yeah, we do. Any thoughts on that particular front?"

"Actually, I did. There's only one thing that has ever made sense and I always assumed one day I'd end up there…tomorrow I'm going to report to the Council and request to be enlisted in the Guard."

He looked at her, stunned.

"Christ, Kali, the *military*? Really? You're supposed to fly *under* the radar, not jump directly into the one place you're most likely to be discovered!"

"I'm not arguing with you. I've trained my whole life to fight, there's nothing else I'd want to do, and our whole family legacy is built on protecting people by being part of the Guard. It just makes sense."

"Being in the Guard isn't a holiday camp, it's tough; what happens when someone upsets you and you lose control and set your whole squad on fire? What then?"

"I won't. But you're right, I need to learn control and the Guard can teach me that."

He stared blankly at her.

"You're actually serious about this?"

"Of course. We need actual jobs now; what exactly did you expect me to do, start selling all of our stuff at the market?"

"Fine, but I'll sign up with you and request to be in your Squad."

She rolled her eyes.

"How am I supposed to learn control if you're constantly coddling me? My whole life, you've all lied to me, I have no idea what I'm capable of or how to control it. Can't you see it's time to *stop?*"

"If you think I'm letting you walk straight into the most dangerous place you could possibly be right now then those demons must have knocked your brain loose," he looked at her, defiant.

"It's lucky for me then that I'm not asking for your permission."

She moved to leave, but he stood and blocked her path.

"You're making an impulsive, thoughtless decision like you always do, we're not done talking about this!"

"William, this is the least impulsive decision I've ever made, it just makes *sense.* All I've ever been trained for was to fight, you helped to do that, what did you think would happen when we came back? Now get out of my way."

"We taught you that to prepare you in case you ever needed it, not so you'd skip merrily off to battle for the people we've been trying to hide you from," William rested his hand against the wall, preventing her from passing.

"Did you expect us to bury Dad and Matt and then go back to the humans as if nothing had happened? Did you think when I learned the truth that I'd be happy to spend my life running? Get real! I'm doing this whether you want me to or not. You can do what you want. For the last time, *get out of my way!*"

Furious, William made to grab hold of her, but she stepped out of reach.

"What is your *problem?*" she spat.

"*You're* my problem!" he replied, his face flushed with anger.

"If you think you can stop me then you're welcome to try."

"You're still hurt."

"Then it should be close to a fair fight."

They glared at each other, each silently daring the other to make a move. Eventually, William sighed, his shoulders slumped, and he stepped to the side as he raised his hands in defeat.

"Do what you want. But you can't stop me from enlisting too."

"Fine!"

"Fine."

With the tension gone as quickly as it had come, they stood in awkward silence for a few moments.

"So...what did the Council want?" Kali asked, finally.

"They just wanted to confirm some details and let us know that the ceremony for...for Dad and Matt will be tomorrow," he swallowed hard, grief painted on his face.

Kali felt a pang of grief and sympathy for her brother; without saying anything, she drew him into a tight hug, ignoring the pain all over her body. At first, he resisted, standing perfectly still, but eventually she felt him relax and hug her back.

She released him, and he wiped at his eyes.

"How's the shoulder?"

"It's fine," she lied.

"Uh-huh," he regarded her sceptically. "Listen, Kali, with everything that's happened it's important that we stick together more now than ever."

She nodded. "I know. I've always got your back, you know that."

"So, if I enlisted with you...?"

She rolled her eyes again. "Then it would be pretty badass to fight demons with you, I guess."

He smiled at her, then turned to one of the cupboards behind him. "I don't know about you, kid, but I could use a drink right about now and I *think* Dad's secret stash of whisky is still right...about...*here!*" he pulled out a bottle of amber liquid and waved it triumphantly.

She watched as William set two glasses on the counter and poured a generous measure of whisky in each. He picked his up and raised it, solemn.

"To Dad and Matt."

Kali raised her glass. "To Dad and Matt," she echoed.

They threw back their drinks in one; William's eyes were red as he set his glass down, but he chuckled when he saw Kali's disgusted expression. She coughed as the whisky burned its way down her throat, eyes streaming. She grimaced and set her glass back on the counter.

Still chuckling, William re-filled both glasses, ignoring Kali's look of exasperation, and stared down at his glass.

"You know, when I was young and I first started training I was so scared that I would be the worst in the class, and that I would let Dad down. That I would let the memory of my mother down and be an embarrassment. The night before I couldn't sleep, and Mattias noticed. He practised with me long after we should have been asleep and told me that nothing I could ever do would make Dad less proud of me as long as I tried my best. That I was already a warrior regardless of how training went. And I believed him when he said I would be okay, and I believed in myself. I don't think I ever told him how much it meant to me."

As he took a long drink, Kali noticed his eyes were watery, and she felt a lump rising in her own throat.

"Do you remember that silly blazer he used to wear? The one he thought made him look like Dad. He wore it for *weeks* and wouldn't let anyone take it away, even to wash it," she smiled.

William grinned. "He marched around in that thing like he was the boss of everyone until the tutor finally got sick of him trying to take over lessons and challenged him to a sparring match. Man, he got his ass handed to him that day," he laughed. "I don't know what hurt worse after it, the bruised ribs or his ego."

They stayed like that for a time, laughing at old memories and reminiscing until the bottle was nearly empty.

"Will…I'm worried about tomorrow…the ceremony," Kali found herself admitting, searching for clear thoughts in her otherwise fuzzy brain.

William looked up as if about to say something encouraging, before visibly deflating.

"Me too, kid," was all he said.

They sat in silence for a moment, and Kali's eyes began to feel heavy. She fought the urge to close them, determined to stay awake. She knew if she went to sleep then her dreams would torment her, and when she woke, she would find no relief. If she fell asleep, then she would wake up and have to get ready to say goodbye to her father and Mattias, have to face the Council. William looked tired too, but he didn't seem to want to move either.

Kali thought back to when they were children; often, when one of them couldn't sleep, they would sneak into each other's rooms with their blankets and pillows and sleep on the floor. Sometimes, if their father was called away in the middle of the night to fight or strategize, the three of them would set up a fort in the living room and sleep there.

As they grew older, they stopped building forts, but still, if their father was called away, they would meet in the kitchen to sit up and talk – almost like they were doing now – before eventually settling down in the living room and falling asleep on the sofas. She smiled sadly at the memory.

"Hey, Will?"

"Yeah?"

"...Living room?"

He paused for a second before understanding; he nodded, grabbing the bottle of whisky as he stood and made his way out of the kitchen.

They left Mattias' favourite sofa empty but lying in the dark it was like their brother was with them, protecting them as he always did from the future and its uncertainty. It was then that it truly hit Kali she would never see him again. William had the good grace to pretend he couldn't hear her crying.

* * * *

The morning of the ceremony arrived too soon, and Kali awoke to find William standing over her, holding out a lukewarm cup of coffee. He was pale, with dark circles around his eyes, and his hair stood at angles as though he'd spent the night running his hands through it. Kali saw the empty bottle of whisky on the floor and wondered if he'd slept at all.

"I thought I'd let you sleep as long as possible, it's time to get up."

Kali nodded and took the coffee gratefully. She hadn't slept well either, although the nightmares that plagued her last night were thankfully lesser than the previous night.

She drank the coffee without really tasting it and noticed her hands were shaking. There was a knot of tension gnawing at her in her gut, and she felt oddly light and disconnected from her surroundings. She glanced at William, who was now sitting on the sofa opposite clutching his own mug of coffee and staring blankly in front of him.

She wished she knew what to say. She knew that neither of them wanted to burden the other with their grief, but all they had now was each other. She opened her mouth to speak words of encouragement but shut it again abruptly when she found that no sound would come out. William didn't even seem to notice.

They sat in silence for a few moments before the clock above the fireplace chimed, signalling that there was an hour to go before the ceremony. The noise roused each of them from their thoughts, and they stood up almost in unison. Kali climbed the stairs to her room, still strangely detached from the world. She showered and dressed numbly, simply going through the motions, trying to breathe deeply and ward off the nausea that hit her in waves.

She met William at the front door. She felt oddly formal in her black dress beside

William in his suit. It seemed strangely inappropriate to dress up as though in celebration for an occasion like this.

They agreed to walk to the ceremony, but they only got as far as the road outside before Kali stopped. The thought of walking through the streets, of people staring as they recognised their black clothes and began to murmur in curious sympathy, wondering how they survived and what happened to their brother and father was suddenly too much. It was like being part of an obscene parade, being put on display for everyone to ogle at.

"Will, can we teleport instead? Please?"

"Of course," he placed a hand on her shoulder, strong and reassuring.

She placed her own over it and tried to focus on their destination instead of the apprehension building inside of her. She closed her eyes, picturing the old amphitheatre to the west of the city, where the ceremony was to take place. She stumbled slightly as their feet hit the dusty ground, keeping hold of William to maintain her balance. People clad in black were already crowding around the entrances, and the sight of them all exacerbated Kali's anxiety.

People turned to them as they appeared, taking a moment to register their presence and recognise them. Kali had to stop herself from physically stepping back, away from the crowd. Truthfully, she found this to be entirely more intimidating than facing off against a swarm of demons.

She took a deep breath and looked at William who inclined his head, indicating they should continue into the building. As they passed, people called out to them in sympathy, but Kali could barely hear their words over the pounding of her heart in her head as they reached the stairs down into the centre of the theatre. She looked down and felt immediately winded.

Two coffins, draped in intricately detailed purple and black crape, lay at the centre of the amphitheatre, side by side. Kali tried to push the unwanted images of Mattias and her father lying dead, side by side, in that awful clearing to no avail. She heard her father's words in her head: *"I hope he's waiting for me."* She saw Mattias' glassy stare. Her breathing was painful and there was an aching burn in her throat as she tried to keep in her grief. The effort to remain dignified and to not make a scene was gargantuan and moving forward felt impossible.

She felt William place a hand reassuringly on her upper back, gently encouraging her forward. She deliberately didn't look at him, sensing that if she did, she would lose her composure entirely. She could feel his own hand trembling ever-so-slightly behind her.

They carried on down the stairs, and Kali thought they seemed endless as she made her way down on shaky legs. They were greeted at the bottom by the Council, who were also dressed in black, save for the fine blue embroidery that decorated their cloaks to mark them out as Council members.

Each of them bowed their heads to Kali and William as they approached, and they returned the gesture. Kali noticed Lady Aequellus watching her intently, her features a mix of curiosity and sympathy as they took their seats at the front. She couldn't stand to look at the coffins in front of her, and stared resolutely at the ground instead, trying to ignore the thousands of eyes on her as the crowd from outside steadily poured into the building.

She never really thought about her father's life before she and her brothers existed. To them, their father's life was always defined by before and after their mother's "death", separate and distinct from one another like he'd become a different man entirely. He hadn't, of course, and Kali knew she shouldn't be surprised by the turnout for him or Mattias despite the short notice of the ceremony. Her father was well-known and respected here. Mattias too was popular amongst his peers; he was expected to join the Guard and was regarded as someone with real promise. A vicious voice in Kali's head pointed out that it was her actions that snuffed that promise out.

She knew that she was the subject of curiosity here, too. Having left as a teenager, nobody quite knew what to expect of Malakai's only daughter. Answering that question was low on her priority list yet still she felt the pressure of living up to those expectations today. To be dignified and collected but appropriately grief-stricken; to be overtly emotional would be seen as weakness, to be too stoic would be seen as a callous disregard for her loss. Her head swam.

Ten minutes passed before the Council raised their hands in unison and the crowd fell silent. Kali lifted her head in response to the sudden hush and saw that William looked as anxious as she felt. She reached to give his hand a squeeze, which he returned without looking at her.

The Ceremony of Fallen Soldiers was always a particularly solemn affair. Kali knew of human funerals, but these paled in comparison to the seraphic mourning ceremony, reserved for members of the Guard who were lost in battle. It was the deepest level of grief, where the community came together to share the loss of their protectors and friends. It was a high honour, but selfishly Kali yearned for a private and quiet affair. Dead men didn't want honours, and Kali didn't want to be here or have an audience to her grief.

The Council began the ceremony with the official readings, but Kali scarcely paid attention. The coffins she was trying so hard not to look at before were now drawing her gaze. She felt compelled to look, unable to tear her eyes away. She thought of Mattias and her father lying inside them, just yards in front of them. It occurred to her that this was the last time they'd ever be this close to each other.

Tears obscured her vision and she bit hard on her tongue to stop from crying out loud; they spilled down her cheeks as she tried to focus on her breathing instead of the terribly sharp pain building in her chest. Her throat felt like she had swallowed glass. She glanced imperceptibly to her right, where William sat beside her and saw that his eyes were dry, but his jaw was set tight.

When she looked back to the front, the Council were finishing their readings. She knew the part she was dreading most loomed in front of them, imminent. Friends, colleagues, and teachers were invited up to speak for each her father and Mattias, telling stories that ranged from heroic to humorous. On any other day, Kali would love to hear these stories about Mattias and her father, but every word stung her, a reminder that there would be no new stories to tell from now on.

Eventually, Lady Aequellus stood and turned to face Kali and William, signalling the time had come for them to speak. William would be expected to speak first, then her. The thought of speaking in front of all these people – especially to uphold a lie that absolved her of the responsibility of their deaths – made her dizzy.

William walked to the nearest podium and began to talk, and Kali could tell the effort it took to keep his voice steady.

"Many of you knew my father as Malakai Robereun, soldier. I knew him, of course, as "Father." He was a fierce protector of me, and my siblings, as you can imagine. He taught us to stand tall, to fight for each other, the seraphs and for the good in the world. He was"—his voice cracked slightly— "a good man. One of the best. My brother would have made him proud. He *did* make him proud. He was everything my father wanted him to be and more, he was everything you could hope for in a brother and I'm genuinely sorry that we'll never get to see him reach his full potential, that some of you will never know him. Father, Mattias: we send you to watch with the Elders. Sleep well."

Hot tears flowed down Kali's face and she wiped them away impatiently before she stood to take her turn to speak. She was not alone, however – she noticed that many of those around her were crying now. She met William halfway between their seats and the podium, and they hugged each other briefly.

"You can do this," he whispered to her.

She walked to the podium and stared up at the hundreds, maybe thousands, of people watching her, waiting for her to speak. How to follow William, though? His speech was short but perfect, and she had nothing better to say. She looked back to where Mattias and her father lay, feeling a sudden determination to make them proud, to give them the recognition they deserved.

"Growing up, I was lucky," she began, her voice echoing around her. "I had not only one protector, but three of them. My father and my brothers have always been there for me, in ways I never even realised. Because that's who my father and Mattias were at their core. Protectors. My father risked his life repeatedly for our people, and I know nothing made him happier, except perhaps his children." Kali took a deep, somewhat shaky, breath.

"Mattias, too, could think of no greater honour in this life than keeping people safe from the darkness in the world. Together, they shone like a beacon of hope and goodness, lighting up the world around them without even trying. They were what the people in their lives needed them to be – a soldier, a protector, a confidant, a friend. Today, I can't help feeling that the light in the world shines a little dimmer without them, that we've lost some of that goodness. I can only ask that we keep their spirits alive, and vow to try and bring that light back as best I can. Father, Mattias: we send you to watch with the Elders; sleep well."

Kali resisted the urge to run back to her seat as the crowd stood as one. She made it back to William just as the Council stood, and a row of archers lined up behind where Mattias and Malakai lay, facing the crowd. Simultaneously, the Council members raised their right hand straight up into the air. The archers behind them loaded their bows in response, an aide in grey robes lighting the head of each arrow one by one.

There was a brief pause to allow the arrowheads to fully catch alight before the Council dropped their arms. At once, the archers released their arrows. They landed in an almost-perfect line between the coffins and the Council, and Kali was surprised to see that the parts of the arrowheads protruding from the ground were still aflame.

There was a great creaking noise and dust was cast up into the air as the platform on which the coffins stood began to sink into the ground, taking their father and brother to the tombs beneath the city. Kali watched on as they sank, trying to see through the haze of dirt and smoke from the arrows until eventually they were gone. Gone from the amphitheatre, gone from their lives, gone from the world.

Chapter Seven

Kali wanted to disappear as soon as Mattias and her father were gone, but she knew they were honour bound to address the Council. She turned to her brother, utterly drained, and saw the same tiredness lining his face. She rested her forehead on his shoulder for a few seconds before standing straight.

"That was tough," she muttered.

"Yeah, and it's not done yet," he replied, his voice hoarse. He cast his eyes in front of them, where the Council were approaching them.

As they approached, Kali inclined her head in thanks and respect, as did William. Only Lady Aequellus came to speak to them directly, the others hanging back, silent and solemn with their hoods now drawn up over their heads.

"We shall take our leave of you now. Should you need anything in this time of mourning, then please ask and we will provide assistance in any way we can," she reached out and clasped each of their hands in turn.

Her tone was sombre, and Kali was surprised by the kindness in her expression as she spoke to them. She always considered the Council members as emotionless, ancient and stiff, interested only in tradition and formality. Seeing the sincerity in Lady Aequellus now gave her the boost of courage she needed to address her directly.

"Lady Aequellus, my brother and I thank you. There is one thing we would like to request, with your permission."

"Go on, child."

"William and I would like to take this opportunity to offer our services to the Council for use in the Guard. With your blessing, we would like to start as soon as possible."

Lady Aequellus regarded her carefully. If she was shocked by this request then she didn't show it and in fact, Kali thought she saw the flicker of quiet pride pass over the older woman's features before she smiled politely.

"Well, you certainly come from good military stock. I knew your father rather well, and I can't think he would disapprove of this – warrior blood runs in House

Robereun, after all. It is unusual but not unheard of for Empaths to join the Guard, of course".

Kali blinked, impressed and taken-aback that she knew about her Revelare. Had she been researching her due to recent events or was it, as she had alluded to, due to a friendship with her father? She decided to take a risk.

"Yes, Lady Aequellus. Although I was designated as an Empath as a child, my father actually registered a second power that manifested after my Revelare ceremony."

She could sense William watching her carefully. Although it was the truth – their father did (reluctantly) formally register one of her powers at the Council so that she may use it freely – talking about the presence of additional powers was always a grey area in public for them, especially in front of Council members.

"Interesting. What may that be, child?"

"Teleportation, Lady Aequellus," Kali replied, although she suspected that she already knew the answer.

The woman considered her for a moment, before smiling and nodding.

"Of course, what a gift to be blessed with two powers. I am certain that you will both make fine soldiers, children of House Robereun. I shall lodge your interest formally upon my return."

"Thank you, Lady Aequellus," Kali and William replied together.

"Incidentally, in light of the troubling attack which befell your family, the Guard have organised additional recruitment events. You will, of course, be required to pass an entry test. Report to the Council Chambers at seven a.m. sharp tomorrow morning. I bid you farewell and good luck," she bowed her head and turned, walking away from them.

They looked at each other, not sure of what to do next. Everything was happening so fast. Less than a week ago they were relatively happy, travelling and laughing together and although suspicious about whatever her father was keeping from her, Kali knew nothing about her demon mother or contaminated soul. The future was open-ended, filled with possibility. Now, two of them were dead and the remaining two were about to join the Guard, burdened with a truth they could never tell. Kali looked back to the empty space her brother and father occupied only moments ago, and then turned away.

It was odd, but even through her grief, Kali was now filled with a burning determination. It felt like she now stood at a crossroads, in the wake of losing her family and finding out the truth about herself, and only she could determine which path she would take. It was her choice now to let it all consume her or to stand up and fight. And she was going to fight.

She would fight for her family, to make them proud. She made a silent vow to be strong, to fight the demons that threatened her home and the smothering darkness that clawed at her soul. Her hope was a fire burning bright inside of her, casting the shadows back and keeping them at bay. She would no longer be a helpless child, reliant on her brother's protection, she would be the soldier her father always knew she could be. She would make his memory proud. She would set William free from his lifelong obligation and most importantly, she would not succumb to darkness. She would live through this, she promised herself.

She broke free of her reverie as people began to filter down to them, and noticed William watching Amariel from across the room. Even as they greeted old friends of their father's, she noticed him stealing glances at him, only half-engaged in the conversation happening in front of him.

Finally, there was a lull in visitors and conversation, and Kali took her opportunity.

"Listen, Will, I'm really tired and if we have to report early tomorrow then I'd rather get out of here now before I get caught up talking with any more people. I'm going to head home."

He turned away from Amariel's general direction, distracted.

"Oh, okay. Let me say goodbye to some people and then I'll be ready."

"No, it's okay. You can stay. It's just…the last few days have been a lot to process and I feel like I need some time."

"Are you sure?" he looked hesitant.

"Totally sure. And Will?"

"Yeah?"

"You know a conversation with Amariel will be a lot easier if you actually, you know, speak to him, right?"

He threw her a look as she hugged him goodbye.

"Haha, funny. Listen, you know where I am if you need me, okay?"

She nodded and waved to her brother as she turned to go home. She tried to avoid eye contact with anyone, lest they draw her into another conversation laden with pity and nostalgia. She ducked in and out of groups, trying to pass by without attracting attention. She made it into a side room, sighing happily at the lack of people and the quiet. She collected herself for a moment then teleported back home.

She stood at the bottom of the main staircase, not knowing what to do with her time now she was here alone. The house being so empty and quiet unnerved her; it felt like people stood in the darkness just out of sight, like Mattias might come out from the kitchen any moment laughing. She started up the stairs to her bedroom, then stopped. The promise of the test tomorrow had her nerves peaked.

She wandered aimlessly into the kitchen, trying to find a distraction. She momentarily considered cooking something, limited in that capacity as she may be, but her appetite was virtually non-existent and it seemed wasteful. She drummed her fingers against the kitchen counter, massaging her collar bone gently with her other hand. She hoped her injuries wouldn't slow her down tomorrow; she hadn't counted on having to pass a test this soon, but she wasn't going to show weakness as her first impression to the Guard.

She left the kitchen and made her way instinctively to the armoury, which doubled as their training room. It was, without doubt, her favourite room in the house, and where she spent the most time as a child, coming in here to play or read even before she was allowed to hold real weapons. Something about it was soothing – it spoke of control and protection to Kali.

She began to cycle through the different weapons on offer, repeating the drills her father instilled in her from a young age, easing through the lingering pain in her shoulder. She wasn't aware of how much time had passed until she heard William's voice calling her name. Before she could answer, his head popped through the door.

"Might have known I would find you in here," he smiled, but it didn't quite reach his eyes.

"Maybe you should practice with me. I can't have you showing me up tomorrow. It would be embarrassing by association."

"I wouldn't worry about that," he laughed cockily, igniting a flame in his hand then extinguishing it.

"You need to show me how to do that one day," she watched him, envious of his control. Until a few days ago, she didn't know she possessed that power, and losing control of it cost her nearly everything.

"Not tonight. Not when you're still recovering and we have to report in the morning. We should eat something."

Kali made a face. "I'm not hungry, I'd rather get some practice in before tomorrow."

"One night isn't going to make or break your chances tomorrow, Kal."

"I know that, but it makes me feel better."

He sighed. "Okay. But only for a little while and only if you *tell* me when your injuries need a break," he removed his suit jacket and tie with a look she took to mean *I'm serious.*

"Promise!" she held up her uncrossed fingers to him.

It had been a while since they sparred like this, almost for the fun of it despite the test hanging over them, whatever that may be. Nobody was critiquing their form for the smallest hint of a mistake or forcing them to repeat something over and over until it was perfect. Kali barely noticed the pain from her injuries as muscle memory took over, and for a fleeting moment, she felt genuinely unburdened.

"That's enough, I'm done!" William said eventually, sweat shining on his forehead.

"No fun, old man," taunted Kali, but now they'd stopped she could feel the ache in her bones. "So...did you talk to Amariel?"

William's face reddened a little as he made a point of returning his weapons. He cleared his throat and tried to sound nonchalant.

"Yeah, I mean we chatted for ten minutes

just to be polite and show respect and you know, stuff."

"Uh-huh," she strained to keep a straight face. "And are you seeing him again?"

"Yeah, maybe. What about you, how are you feeling? You doing okay?" William quickly changed the subject.

Kali wasn't sure what it was about the question that hit her so hard; perhaps it was the incongruous nature of chatting about Amariel mere hours after they buried Mattias and their father, maybe it was simply everything catching up to her, but without the distraction of training Kali's mood shifted without warning. The weight of everything that had happened was palpable. She replaced her weapon wearily and leaned against the wall.

She didn't know how to answer her brother's question. *Was* she doing okay? Did she even know what "okay" was anymore? Would she ever be truly okay again? These questions seemed unanswerable to her.

William hesitated and then stood beside her.

"Hey, you okay? I know today was a lot. It was for me, too."

"It's just…how did life change this much in a matter of *days?* It doesn't feel real."

William looked at her as though trying to think of something to say, but in the end, remained silent, leaving Kali to wonder what their life looked like from this point onwards, wondering if they'd ever find their way back to the people they used to be or if this would change them irrevocably, forever.

Chapter Eight

They woke early the next morning and dressed in old military training gear – a gift from their father years beforehand. Seraph military gear changed depending on the intended use, ranging from heavily armoured vests and heavy boots to lightweight clothes and shoes. The training attire was the latter, suited for light sparring and ease of movement – they didn't know what the test would be, but they agreed it was best to assume it was physical and dress accordingly.

Neither of them had an appetite for breakfast, so they decided to leave early and run to the Council building, where they were to report. Kali enjoyed this time of the morning, where the sun wasn't quite risen yet and there was still a slight chill in the air. It was quiet and peaceful, and she enjoyed running, channelling some of her energy into physical activity instead of the chaos that seemed to now permanently reside in her brain.

They reached the Council building with fifteen minutes to spare and found a handful of people already waiting. Some stood together in groups laughing loudly, the sound of it cutting through the quiet morning, whilst some stood alone looking pale and nervous. Around them, people began to hurry in all directions, the city waking up in earnest as the sun rose fully and cast light across it.

Ten minutes passed before the door to the Council building opened, by which time a number of other hopefuls had arrived. A huge figure stepped through the door, cast an unreadable glance down at those gathered before him and walked down the stairs towards them.

"That's General Raikan, Leader of Squadron One!" William informed her, sounding awestruck.

Squadron One was renowned amongst the Guard as being the toughest unit, the elite that rushed to meet demons head-on whilst the rest fell back to protect the borders. She knew her father served with them very briefly before she was born, but she didn't know anyone who actively served with them. There was no immediate entry to Squadron One – a soldier had to serve for years, see active battle with demons, and pass an entrance test that was rumoured to be nigh impossible to complete before admission.

"Why is he here?" she queried, perplexed that a Squadron One Leader would bother with recruit selection.

William merely shrugged, but she was not the only one surprised by his presence. Excited murmurs ran through the crowd and people jostled to get closer to him as he descended the stairs.

As he reached them, he surveyed each of them in turn. His expression was neutral, but occasionally Kali thought she saw him suppress an eye roll or a wrinkled nose as he took in the recruits. His gaze shifted to her, but what he thought of her she couldn't tell.

General Raikan was an imposing man, and Kali couldn't help but think that he looked like he was carved from rock. She heard nervous whispers of some of the recruits behind her, some of whom looked barely eighteen.

"*I heard he ripped a demon's head off with his bare hands!*"

"*I heard once that a cadet was rude to him and he left him out beyond the borderlands alone for three days!*"

The clock on the Council building chimed to mark seven o'clock and General Raikan spoke immediately, not waiting for any stragglers that may be yet to arrive.

"*Attention,*" boomed Raikan's voice, and silence fell at once. "You will now follow me to the Guard district. Anyone who cannot keep pace, feel free to go home. The last ten to arrive will be dismissed. You may not use your powers."

A ripple of confusion ran through the crowd before Raikan turned and, with surprising speed given his hulking stature, ran to their left.

Kali began to run behind him, followed closely by William and a few other recruits. A number were slow to start, still not understanding or taken by surprise at the abrupt beginning of the exercise. Some were already playing dirty, tripping those on either side of them. Kali felt something at her foot, and she went sprawling. Using her momentum, she threw herself forward into a roll and stood, continuing to run. A man about her age looked back, grinning.

"Nothing personal!"

She growled and urged herself forward, ignoring the pain from her arm and shoulder, determined not to be in the last ten.

They ran for miles, and Kali was surprised that a good number of their group were already falling behind. Most recruits for the Guard came from military families that trained their entire lives; the news of recent demonic activity must have encouraged more people from various other backgrounds to enlist, she thought.

They took a sharp right turn and ahead of them loomed a formidable-looking obstacle course, equipped with a climbing wall, ropes, suspension rings, high beams, and tunnels. Looking at it made her shoulder ache, and she could tell she wasn't the only one worried by it. Some around her groaned audibly, and some slowed their pace as they sped towards it. Raikan gave no instruction as they approached, launching himself effortlessly up and over the first obstacle like it was nothing.

The group followed suit, nobody wanting to be left behind on the wrong side. It became immediately apparent to Kali which of the hopefuls were those from military families as one by one, members of their group fell to the hurdles. She pushed on through each of them, using her surge of adrenaline to drown out the pain and force herself onwards. This was everything she'd ever trained for, and she wasn't going to fail now.

The obstacle course acted as a kind of sieve, and by the time they made it to the end, their group had halved in size. But General Raikan didn't stop to notice, never breaking pace as he sailed through the course and kept running, the rest of them trying to hide the extent of their breathlessness from one another and keep up with him.

They ran for at least another two miles before finally Kali saw the beginning of a huge settlement clearly marked with the Guard colours of deep purple and black. She craned her neck back to see where she was in the pack; she was not too far from the front, a little behind William, and around twenty people ran behind her. As long as she stayed steady, she would make it. Raikan led them downhill, onto a narrow path surrounded by trees and large rocks.

 Kali sensed the movement before she saw it.

Soldiers – identifiable by their armour – began to pour from the trees, brandishing weapons. Kali saw that they wore demon masks and heard cries of shock behind her as people reacted to their presence. She looked to Raikan and saw that he never acknowledged the interruption, even as the soldiers infiltrated their pack as he ran past them.

The soldiers weren't using their weapons, she observed, they were simply tripping and wrestling with the runners. She saw one lunge for William at the same time one loomed beside her. She used her momentum as she did before, throwing herself into a forward roll out of the soldier's reach, trying to keep up with Raikan. She ran past the man who tripped her as he struggled on the ground against a soldier and stifled a smile. Ahead of her, William was still running.

She jumped over those that had fallen, and kept going, sprinting as fast as she could now to reach the camp when suddenly, someone tackled her to the ground.

"Hey, Kali!" laughed the soldier as he tried to pin her down. She recognised his voice through the crude demon mask he wore.

"*Tannick?*"

"Looks like *I'm* the one knocking *you* on your ass! Sorry, but I'm not going easy on you, better luck next time," Tannick laughed, muffled through the mask.

She struggled against his weight, assessing his form and trying to keep him from getting her on her back. His technique was good, but her father made her practise getting out of subduing holds over and over. She cursed him at the time, but now she silently thanked him.

"Sorry, Tannick," she grinned, elbowing him in the face and bringing her knee up to his stomach when his grip loosened. He let her go with an *oof*, and she pushed herself away from him, wasting no time in jumping up and running in the direction she last saw Raikan.

She dodged a few more masked soldiers, watching people being taken down all around her and gritting her teeth, urging herself to move faster. Finally, she saw the group ahead of her. Her heart leaping, she counted only four; she scanned the group for William and felt triumphant when she saw him in second place. She pushed herself forward as she saw the group coming to a stop at a large gate, reaching it only a few moments after them. The group was silent for a moment before bursting into nervous laughter, each of them breathing heavier than normal. Raikan regarded them coolly.

"Don't go congratulating yourselves yet. All you've done is manage to get here. Stand in a line, now. Single file. We'll see which of the rest join us."

They did as they were commanded at once, falling silent. They waited for five minutes or so as one by one, people arrived. Some were bleeding lightly from cuts and scrapes sustained in falls, and they looked relieved to see the group.

In total, Kali counted nine people. The man who tripped her was amongst them, and Kali felt a pang of annoyance that he'd managed to break through.

"Okay. I've waited long enough. Come with me," ordered General Raikan.

They followed him as he opened the gate with a key kept on a chain around his neck, locking it again as the last of the group passed through.

"Today, you will face a series of trials. Those of you that fail will not continue. Those of you that don't will embark on months of training. This training will test you, push you past your endurance. If you do not have an absolute commitment to this Guard, then this is the time for you to leave."

The group looked around at one another, but nobody moved.

"Good, now follow me."

They obliged, falling into step behind him. As they moved further into the camp, they passed tents and areas filled with soldiers who looked at them interestedly. They called out at the group as they passed, a mix of cheering and jeering; Kali saw the man who tripped her blush furiously in response.

Raikan led them to a makeshift arena in the middle of the camp, which Kali guessed was around fifty meters in diameter. Soldiers were already gathering to watch, and nerves began to bubble in Kali's stomach. She saw everyone else shift nervously, too.

"You will pass from one end of this arena to the other. In Round One, you'll be paired up – you may not use your powers. The winners from Round Two will try to get past me."

A current of panic ran through the group.

"Get past *you?*" cried one of the recruits, incredulous.

Raikan looked at her coolly. "Is that concept too confusing for you?"

She looked embarrassed. "No, Sir. Sorry, Sir."

"Get in the arena, now."

She looked terrified but obeyed his command without a word.

His eyes scanned the group, looking for her opponent. Eventually, he chose a scared-looking boy, one of the ones Kali thought could only barely be eighteen, and ordered him into the arena with her.

"You will take turns trying to stop the other from reaching your side of the arena. Only a complete but *temporary* incapacitation will be counted – I will call when I consider either side to be victorious. You will face a combination of your peers, so you will get multiple chances. The four with the highest score will proceed to Round Two. Does everyone understand?"

There were shouts of "*Yes, Sir!*" from the group.

Kali met William's eye and grinned nervously as Raikan instructed the two hopefuls in the arena and they squared off against each other. The fights began tentatively at first, before becoming more confident and in some cases, desperate, turning from weak sparring matches to brutal takedowns as the group warmed up. William looked at her shoulder with concern, gesturing for her to tell Raikan, but she shook her head. He rolled his eyes but didn't push, and Kali was thankful he didn't undermine her in front of the group.

It became rapidly apparent that William was the strongest of the group, and Kali noticed Raikan studying him intently as he took down all of his opponents easily.

Kali on the other hand was used to using her powers in combat; without them and with her injuries, she struggled more than she was used to. She took down the young recruit from the first fight without difficulty, but when paired with a man nearly twice her size she struggled to get past him. Her first attempt resulted in a blow to her face that left her spitting blood. When she tried again, he caught her by her shirt and threw her bodily to the ground, her ribs and shoulder reverberating with pain as she hit the dirt. She only just rolled over and got back to her feet in time to avoid him stomping down hard where her head had been only seconds before. She backed up cautiously as he bared down on her, her eyes never leaving him as she waited for him to pounce.

Frustrated, she thought back to her father's advice from early in her training:

"Chances are, your opponents will always be physically bigger than you, but you'll be faster. Use that to your advantage, never become predictable. They'll be used to fighting with strength, you need to adapt to your opponent."

Growing up with William and Mattias had given her ample opportunity to fight with those bigger than her. She was determined to win.

The man approached her and she moved forward, slow and patient, letting him come to her. When he was close enough to her, she feinted to the right. He lunged to catch her for the third time, arms outstretched, realising too late what she was doing and catching the kick she aimed at him square in the face. He recoiled, and she used the force from the kick to spin past him to the left, sprinting to the other end of the arena. When she turned, she saw blood streaming from his nose, and he looked incensed as he barrelled after her. Despite his size, he was fast – but Kali was faster. She reached the end of the arena with yards to spare, her heart thundering in her chest as she silently celebrated her victory.

When they met back in the centre of the arena, the anger was still clear on his face, but he looked confident. "You got lucky, but I hope you're ready for payback," he leered down at her.

She tried to ignore him, instead taking in his body language, his stance, and how he was carrying his weight – all things that predicted his next movements. She knew she would need to fight smart, but that she had his arrogance to her advantage.

Raikan blew his whistle and as she suspected, the man charged her instantly. She ducked low, causing him to dodge her in anticipation, jumping upwards instinctively. Now directly in front of him, she stood up and rammed her forearm into his throat with force, using both her own and his momentum against him. He made a gagging noise and brought his arms up as she swung round behind him, bent low and flipped him over her uninjured shoulder. He fell heavily onto his back, and before he could recover, Kali moved behind him and wrapped her legs around his throat. She caught his arms and brought them down behind his head, pinning them to the ground beside her.

He was strong, and Kali's injuries made it difficult to maintain her grip, but she held on, knowing she was strong enough to keep him pinned at this angle. She felt a sharp pain in her leg as she realised the man was *biting* her and responded by squeezing harder. Eventually, Raikan blew his whistle, signalling she was to release him.

She helped him up, and he accepted her hand with a resentful scowl. They walked back to the others without speaking, and he looked annoyed when they met her with polite applause.

In comparison, the other matches seemed easy. Kali bested a short, friendly-looking woman without incident and took glee in seeing the man that tripped her receive a broken nose from the woman from the first match.

By the time Raikan called time on Round One, everyone looked a little worse for wear. Kali noticed that some of the group stood looking faintly dazed, whilst others looked dejected or angry, not looking at the others. The energy was nervous again.

"Some of you were passable. Most of you need a lot of work," Raikan's expression was unreadable. "Robereun, Variez, Robereun, Saint – with me. The rest of you, you're dismissed."

There was a tense silence as everyone reacted to the list of names, each of them understanding in their own time what it meant for their hopes of joining the Guard. Those whose names had been called walked awkwardly away from the other half of the group, reluctant to hesitate and incur Raikan's temper. The man she'd taken down in the arena glared at her, as he and the remaining half of the group began to turn and walk away, some looking close to tears as they made their way through the dissipating crowd of onlookers.

Raikan turned to their group. "Wait here. I'll be back."

Without waiting for a response, he turned away from them and jogged down a path to their right.

Kali looked around her. William was, of course, standing with the group, and beside him was the woman from the first match. She was disappointed to see the man who'd tripped her was there too. He sensed her looking at him and shot her a grin.

"Saint," he said by way of greeting, holding out his hand to her.

Snorting, she shook his hand briefly. "If you say so."

"You're Malakai Robereun's daughter, right? And that's your brother?"

Kali winced slightly. "Yep."

"That must make you Variez!" he turned to the woman.

She looked him over appraisingly, her mouth turning up in a slight smile at the sight of the blood still staining his face.

"Emily. Emily Variez."

"Great. So, what are your powers?" he asked the group at large.

William raised his eyebrows at the question and looked at Kali, incredulous. "*Who is this guy?*" she could practically hear him thinking.

They were spared from answering by the return of Raikan, who was carrying something small and metallic. It looked to Kali like a weapon, glinting in the sunlight, but she soon saw that it was a medallion of some kind. Perplexed, she glanced at her brother only to see that he looked as confused as she was.

"Round Two," boomed Raikan, "on my whistle, you will take this amulet from me, and then make your way to the opposite side of the arena. If you cannot achieve this, then you go home. The use of your powers will be permitted."

The four of them looked around, seeming to wonder collectively how they were going to face off against Raikan, even with their powers. Kali didn't dare hope that it would be as simple as teleporting in and out.

"Robereun, you first," Raikan called.

Kali started, before realising that Raikan was commanding William, and not her. She thought she might have preferred to go first to get it over and done with, but at least now she'd be able to watch Raikan in action; William was going in completely unaware of what he was about to face.

They walked to the centre of the arena and faced each other. They exchanged words Kali couldn't hear before Raikan blew his whistle.

William moved at once upon hearing the whistle, raising his arm in one fluid motion as he shot fire at Raikan. Raikan moved out of reach with impressive speed, keeping his gaze focused on William as her brother charged him. She admired how there was no hesitation as William moved towards the much more experienced fighter in front of him. Hesitation in battle almost always meant death; their father drilled that into them from a young age.

Raikan easily dodged her brother, side-stepping without the need to counter with a defensive technique, and moving with a swiftness that defied his stature. Missing

150

his target, William flew past him wildly before forcing himself to stop and spin back towards the fight. Sensing he was off-balance, Raikan chose to strike as William was mid-turn. As his momentum carried him, William was unable to block as Raikan threw himself towards him, ramming his hand up into his face. Kali winced as blood instantly spurted from William's lip, and the force of it knocked him backwards. Beside her, Variez and Saint groaned in sympathy, although she noted there was a hint of glee in Saint's expression as he watched her brother hit the ground.

Raikan didn't give him time to recover, pouncing on him almost before he hit the ground, forcing him to roll hastily to the left and push himself to his feet. Although Kali could no longer see her brother's face, she could picture the angry determination she knew must be painted on it right now. William hated losing almost as much as she did. She silently willed him to land a significant hit, but she was struggling to find a weak point on Raikan – how could they possibly retrieve the amulet from him when he was so much more experienced?

Unexpectedly, Kali saw William's shoulders relax. For a moment, the two men faced each other, sizing each other up, and it seemed that nothing was happening. But then, Raikan gave a roar of pain and surprise, and William took his cue to leap forward. Realisation hit her as she caught sight of the amulet on Raikan's chest glowing red; William had used his power to heat the metal of the medallion and taken the opportunity of Raikan's distraction to grab it. She wasn't even aware he could do that, and she smiled with pride, barely resisting the urge to cheer in support as Variez and Saint looked on still confused.

William's hand closed over the amulet, barely flinching at the heat as he continued past Raikan, sprinting to the other side of the make-shift arena. Raikan tore after him, but Kali knew the battle was won. Try as he might, Raikan couldn't outrun her brother. This time, she cheered out loud as his hand touched the fencing on the other side, marking him safe.

Raikan's expression was inscrutable, but he didn't look displeased as he blew his whistle, signalling William's victory. William walked back over to Raikan, a careful smile on his face, and shook his hand. Raikan inclined his head to William, keeping his hand outstretched, and William dropped the amulet into his palm.

As he approached the group, they gave a smattering of applause and Kali shot him a grin. He looked triumphant.

"Other Robereun, you next!" barked Raikan, cutting through their congratulations.

Nerves churned in the pit of Kali's stomach as she walked towards the hulking figure in the centre of the arena. He surveyed her for a moment.

"You have injuries," he said. It was not a question.

"Uh, yes, sir," she replied.

"Why haven't you informed me before now?"

"It seemed irrelevant, sir. Either I pass the tests today or I don't. Sir."

He looked at her for a long moment, and Kali wasn't sure if she was in trouble. She tried not to shift nervously, holding his gaze with a confidence she wasn't convinced she actually felt.

He nodded and brought the whistle to his lips.

It was now or never she thought, as the whistle sung shrilly in her ears. She wasn't sure if Raikan knew what each of their powers were – she assumed he did – but without the element of surprise she didn't think she had a chance one-on-one against him. Not without using the powers she wasn't supposed to have and giving herself away. Without waiting to overthink it, she teleported towards him, grabbing the amulet as she appeared in front of him and then disappearing again before he could react. Before anyone had even noticed her moving, Kali stood at the other side of the arena.

There was an astonished silence before Raikan, looking half-angry and half-amused, blew the whistle. Disbelief flooded through Kali – it was over, she'd done it.

She teleported to the centre of the arena to where Raikan still stood. He looked down at her and she was almost sure that the hint of a smile played on the corner of his mouth as he held out his hand. She shook it and returned the amulet to him, before starting back towards the group.

As she approached, Saint's angry voice carried over to her.

"That's not fair, she *cheated!*" he raged. Beside him, Variez stayed silent but looked thunderous, and it was clear that she agreed.

"Coming from *you,*" sneered William, looking at him with distaste.

Saint rounded on him, furious. "What's that supposed to mean?"

"You literally tripped everyone around you just to get here," William scoffed at him.

Saint's retort was cut short as Raikan cleared his throat, and everyone fell silent.

"I specified two objectives: take the amulet from me and make it across the arena. The objectives have been completed; I'd thank you not to speak on my behalf again."

Variez and Saint looked mutinous but remained silent, glowering in her direction. Defiant, she continued towards them unflinching in the scrutiny of their gaze. Saint shot her a contemptuous look as she passed him, and Variez looked at the ground. William looked overjoyed.

"We did it!" he whispered to her, giving her a subtle fist bump as Saint was called into the arena.

She smiled, turning now to watch Saint face off against Raikan. She generally considered herself a kind person, in spite of the recent revelation about her parentage, but there was a spiky sense of resentment resting within her that longed to see Saint humbled now in the arena.

Her wish was granted almost instantly when Saint, still rattled by his sense of frustration, misjudged an attacking blow badly, resulting in not only a hard blow to the face but a total loss of balance as Raikan swept his legs from under him. He hit the ground with an *"umph"* and lay winded for a fraction of a second too long. As he began to recover, Raikan grabbed him by the throat, lifting him into the air and slamming him bodily to the ground. A ripple of shock went through the group at the brutality of it, as Raikan brought his foot to Saint's throat, pressing down on it with enough pressure that Kali could hear his choking from where she stood. Saint rained blows onto Raikan's leg with increasing desperation, until eventually tapping his leg in surrender.

Raikan's whistle blew, and he pulled a spluttering Saint to his feet. He pulled him in close, saying something they couldn't hear. Saint's shoulders slumped, and he turned without a word to Raikan. He stalked towards them – slowing pace only to ensure he bumped Kali hard with his shoulder – and then left without a backwards glance.

Almost automatically, Kali and William turned to look at Variez. The colour was drained from her face, but she looked determined. She didn't wait for Raikan's invitation before entering the arena, vaulting deftly over the fence, and making her way steadily towards him.

He blew the whistle as soon as she was in position in front of him.

Following suit of the others before her, she charged him as soon as the whistle sounded. Kali considered this a risky move – Raikan was two or three times heavier than her – but it became obvious why she'd done so. As she reached Raikan, she threw out a burst of energy that was just barely visible in its distortion of the air around it. The force of it knocked Raikan backwards, causing him to momentarily lose his footing and stumble. As he focused on staying upright, she stretched out her hand and the amulet flew towards her. By the time he recovered, she was flying by him in a furious sprint. He raced after her and they watched on, engrossed as he came within an inch of her before she reached the fence at the opposite end of the arena.

She turned, looking shocked and thrilled as Raikan blew his whistle. She handed him the amulet back, shaking his hand as William and Kali had done, and walked back to them, looking pleased.

Raikan approached them and for the first time all day, smiled.

"And then there were three! You all need work, but I would like to extend a formal offer to join the Guard to each of you."

He watched on, amused, as they each gave a little cheer and celebrated with each other, any animosity from before now gone.

His smile faded as he continued.

"Enrolment in the Guard is not to be considered lightly. You will face real danger. The training will be gruelling. You might watch friends die on the battlefield. You will be expected to lay down your lives for the good of your people if it is required. To accept is to swear an oath that your life is now secondary to the good of the seraphs. If you cannot accept this, I ask that you decline this offer."

He paused, as though waiting for them to speak. When they didn't, he turned to William.

"William Robereun, you are called to protect the seraphs. Do you heed the call and accept your place in the Guard?"

"I accept."

Raikan nodded and turned to Kali.

"Kali Robereun, you are called to protect the seraphs. Do you heed the call and accept your place in the Guard?"

"I accept," a thrill of excitement ran through her.

Finally, he turned to Variez.

"Emily Variez, you are called to protect the seraphs. Do you heed the call and accept your place in the Guard?"

"I accept."

They grinned at each other, now feeling bonded by an unseen force, a calling bigger than them. Raikan smiled at them with surprising warmth, addressing them all as he spoke.

"Congratulations and welcome to the Guard. Now that you've made it to Basic Training, I can tell you that we are in the middle of putting together two new tactical squadrons, of which you will be part of when you pass your training. You will be informed of your allocation in the coming days, after which your formal induction will take place."

"Will our training differ for these squadrons than for admission into standard squadrons, Sir?" William asked.

"All of you will train at the base here in Domeneum initially, with the rest of the recruits. You will then move onto Phase Two training, stationed in the borderlands camp of Alarium, where we've been witnessing increasing demonic activity. Once fully qualified, you and your sister squadron will formally join the soldiers already there to assist them in their fight to protect us. Any questions?"

"Who else will make up the squadrons, sir? Will you be leading them?" Variez took a small step forward.

"Recruits from existing soldiers here in Domeneum have been selected to make up the squadrons, as well as recruits like you from stations in Tereum and Belierel. You will also be assigned a dedicated medical team. I will oversee the running of the Alarium camp, but I will not directly lead your squadrons. The squadron leaders have already been chosen from existing members of the Guard."

Raikan's involvement in today was suddenly clear. They'd come today thinking this to be a general recruitment event, but this was never routine recruitment for the Guard. They were never going to stay in Domeneum. Kali thought of her home, now haunted by its emptiness, and was glad to know she wouldn't need to be there much longer. She wondered if William felt the same, or if he would be sad to leave his home behind once more. So much had changed in such a short time – nothing felt the same to Kali anymore, she thought that William must feel it too.

"What is required of us now, Sir?" she asked.

"Currently? Nothing. If you like, I can formally present you to those you will be deployed with?"

They looked at each other, then back to Raikan, eagerly. "Yes, sir!" they chorused.

"Very well. Shall I introduce you to your new family?"

"Lead the way, Sir," Kali grinned.

Chapter Nine

They followed Raikan to a large tent, the soldiers they passed shooting them curious glances as they followed closely behind him. The tent was full of people, and Kali recognised them as the soldiers from the woods, some of them still wearing their demon masks and laughing as they helped themselves to beer and wine. She saw Tannick and waved at him, which he returned looking sheepish but pleased.

Raikan cleared his throat, and the thrum of voices hushed.

"Squadrons Alpha and Beta: meet your newest recruits!" he gestured to the three of them.

A loud cheer went up from the soldiers as they rushed forward to meet and congratulate them. Kali introduced herself over and over until she found herself standing in front of Tannick.

"You did it!" he grinned.

"No thanks to you!" she laughed back.

"Oh, that? That was just some fun. Today's our day off and we wanted front row seats to the potential new recruits. Plus, Raikan thought it would be a funny way to see who can react to the unexpected," he chuckled.

"Glad our suffering is amusing to you," she smiled wryly.

"Some of you went down so easily, it was pretty hilarious."

Kali gave him a light punch on the arm, but she was smiling. For the first time in as long as she could remember, she felt a sense of elation: she'd done it! She was on the road to taking control back of herself, her powers and of her destiny. This was the start of a path that resisted the darkness inside her and rejected Kasandra's prophecy. She was her own person – not her father's secret or her mother's weapon – and she was going to prove it, starting here and now.

"Are you all in the new Squadrons, then?" she looked around the room at all the unfamiliar faces.

"Some of us are, some are Squadron Five soldiers on leave from Tereum; they plan on setting up similar teams out there in the next few months, so they wanted to be involved in our recruitment process."

Kali thought about the people from the group that hadn't made the cut today – maybe they would have their shot after all, once Tereum started recruiting. Although she quietly hoped she would never need to run into Saint again.

Raikan cleared his throat loudly, breaking her out of her thoughts and cutting through the loud chatter of the soldiers.

"Newbies: you'll have plenty of opportunities to chat later – let's move out!"

Kali gave Tannick an apologetic smile and bade him goodbye before moving to stand beside Raikan. When the three of them were ready, he guided them out of the tent and out towards a row of large buildings to the North of the camp.

"This will be your home for the next two to three months. You will eat, sleep, and train here until you are ready to travel to Alarium."

He stopped outside one of the buildings and gestured to it.

"This is the canteen. You will eat your meals here with your Squadrons at breakfast, lunch, and dinner. After dinner, you may go upstairs to use the library or lounge facilities. You may also use the Leisure Gym; this is not to be confused with the Training Gym which you are only permitted to use at set times as designated by your Squadron Leader."

Kali tried to take it all in, struck by the worry that they should be taking notes. Raikan continued walking, pointing out the gyms, the equipment, and weapons rooms, before stopping in front of the largest building of the complex.

"Here are the barracks. Since I am feeling uncharacteristically generous today, I can show you your rooms if you'd like."

Kali looked at her brother and Variez – both looked as eager to see their new living quarters as she was. He led them inside and up two flights of stairs into a long corridor, pointing out areas of interest as they strode down it, trying to keep up with him.

"That's the communal lounge area...in there is a small gym with a sauna...that's the communal shower and changing area – separate cubicles of course – there's the main bathroom, those are the toilets, and *these* will be your rooms."

He brought them to a halt outside two identical rooms facing opposite each other and allowed them to look around. In each one, a large main room was filled with five bunk beds, two large wardrobes, and several sets of drawers. A second door at the back of the main room led to a smaller room which contained private shower cubicles and toilets. The walls were painted a light green, the sheets on the bed in a matching shade. The floor was made of light-coloured wood. It was plain, but Kali thought it looked functional enough.

She looked to her left and saw Variez taking the room in, her face impassive. William simply shrugged his shoulders in an "*it-could-be-worse*" gesture.

"So, who takes which room?" Variez asked when they returned to Raikan in the corridor. "Do we just decide amongst ourselves, Sir?"

"Your rooms will be allocated by Squadron. Alpha"—he gestured to the room on his left— "and Beta," he gestured to his right. "Your allocations should come through soon; any issues or questions, don't direct them at me – go to your Squadron Leader."

As he led them back out of the building and dismissed them, Kali and William could hardly believe that their new life was beginning so quickly, both desperate to start it soon, and leave the events of the past few days behind.

* * * *

They waited for three days before news of their squadron allocations arrived. While they waited, they began to pack what they wanted to bring to camp with them which, as it transpired, was very little. The Guard would provide them with uniform and training gear and other than that, neither of them felt the need to bring many personal items with them. She worried that she might regret not bringing photographs or other mementoes, but right now they just brought with them a sense of anguish she wasn't ready to work through. This was a fresh start, and they decided to keep it so.

On the day their allocations came through, William called her downstairs in the midst of sorting through her old belongings. She threw an embarrassing and angsty teenage diary promptly into a black bag – silently vowing to burn it at the first opportunity – and followed his voice to the kitchen. She found him sitting at the table, gripping paper tightly in his hands.

"Well?" she raised her eyebrows at him.

"We report in two days…and we're in the same squadron!" he smiled and handed her the paper.

She scanned it and felt a rush of excitement as she looked over the list of names.

Squadron Alpha

Squadron Leader: Cael Fiden

Bratheas, Tannick

Faction, Jamael

Laeta, Clark

Macken, Gabriella

Regor, Meka

Robereun, Kali

Robereun, William

Sampson, Celeste

"Cool, we're in a squad with Tannick!" she said, looking up. She noticed William was distracted, looking over a second sheet of paper with surprising intensity.

"Will? You alright?"

"Huh? Oh, yeah. Sorry, what were you saying?"

"I said we're in the same squadron as Tannick. What's wrong?"

"Nothing!"

She looked at him, curious, and then held out her hand, gesturing for him to give her the paper.

Reluctantly, he handed it over and she grinned as she spotted the source of his distraction.

Squadron Beta

Squadron Leader: Amariel Beltura

William snatched the paper out of her hands as she doubled over, laughing.

"Shut up."

"This is amazing," she laughed.

"I don't even—whatever. It's good. He's a good friend."

"Yep. We all look at our friends the way you look at Amariel."

He scrunched the paper into a ball and threw it at her head. "I said shut *up!*"

She ducked out of the way, still laughing.

"Okay, I'll stop, I'll stop," she held up her hands placatingly. "So, are you going to go and talk to him about it?"

"I wasn't planning to, why?"

"To let him know that you're reporting for booty," she said mock-seriously, running from the kitchen laughing before he could aim anything else at her head.

They reported to the camp in Domeneum two days later, their house once again locked up and left behind them. Kali expected to feel sad about leaving it again but found herself wanting to get as far away as possible from it. She wasn't sure she would ever be able to get far enough away from the reminders of all that they'd lost recently but considered this a good start.

She was nervous, but not like she had been for the Ceremony of Fallen Soldiers. That, she reflected, was a roiling mess of chaos and panic; this was excitement, and an eagerness to get started. They smiled politely as they saw Variez again, the only face they really recognised in the collection of new squadron members other than Tannick. William greeted Tannick amicably, as the latter waved at her and looked poised to explode with excitement. In comparison to him, Kali felt almost calm.

They were greeted after a few moments by Amariel – William's cheeks turned pink – and a short, blonde-haired woman Kali didn't recognise, who introduced herself as their Squadron Leader, Cael.

They spent the afternoon touring the grounds and being issued with assorted bits of kit – training clothes, combat clothes, formal uniform, and weaponry like swords and daggers – Kali rather thought she would prefer to use her own but accepted them dutifully. After the tour came a series of cringe-worthy teambuilding exercises (Kali remained virtually monosyllabic during a "get-to-know-you" round).

Dinner provided a welcome interruption to the activities, and afterwards, they were given the night to do as they pleased. She was hoping to spend the night alone, preparing for the first day of training the following day, but Tannick successfully convinced her to join the others for what he dubbed "first night celebrations" which, as far as Kali could tell, consisted of getting drunk in the lounge area and little else.

When the third round of drinks went around, Kali refused, much to Tannick's disappointment.

"Kali, night one and you're already refusing to be a team player?" his tone was filled with mock disapproval.

"Come back to me at six a.m. tomorrow when you're hungover and crying your way through the first day of training," she laughed.

"We're made of tougher stuff than that, right, Will?" he grinned at her brother, who looked distracted. "Even Beltura and Fiden are joining us later!"

William's head snapped up. "They are?"

"This is bonding night, wouldn't be bonding without the Squadron Leaders now, would it?"

"Well, you enjoy yourselves, I'll stick to water," Kali said, expecting William to back her up. But an odd look had come over his face, and he threw back his drink in one.

Tannick gave a cheer and followed his lead as Kali rolled her eyes.

She expected things to calm down once Amariel and Cael arrived, but if anything, she found it grew increasingly rowdier after they joined the group. In fact, during one round of shots when Kali abstained, it was Cael that led the chant to make her drink it. She watched as one by one they went from tipsy to outright drunk, none of them wanting to be the first to give in and go home. The laughter was loud, and the discussion became more outrageous as the night wore on. William was as outgoing as Kali had ever seen him, laughing at embarrassing stories and telling some of his own. Much to her chagrin, when he ran out of his own stories, he began to tell embarrassing childhood stories about her instead. She swiftly shut him up with a drink and changed the subject, making a note to get revenge later.

Hours passed, and it was Amariel and Cael who left first despite their earlier enthusiasm (perhaps still duty-bound to encourage some sense of responsibility, Kali thought). Eventually, the others began to follow suit in small groups, heading back to their bunks whilst talking and chanting loudly.

She looked to Tannick expectantly, but he looked to be having the most fun out of all of them. He seemed relatively sober given the quantity of alcohol she'd seen him consume. She turned to her brother and saw him looking ahead vacantly, glassy-eyed. Even sitting down, he seemed to be swaying.

"Hey, are you alright?" she asked, amused.

"Hmmm?"

"I asked if you're alright."

"Me? I'm good. I'm good. Feel 'mazing," he slurred.

"Oh boy," she laughed. "I think it might be time to get you to bed, huh?"

"No 'cause I was just talking to Amariel and he's coming back, so I need to wait."

"Will, Amariel left like forty minutes ago. He's not coming back; you'll see him tomorrow."

William looked utterly perplexed by this information. "No, I need to wait," he repeated firmly.

Kali exhaled, caught somewhere between amusement and exasperation.

"Okay. Here's an idea: why don't we go find him? I'm sure we'll find him back at the barracks with everyone else."

William considered for a moment.

"Okay!" he stood up, and immediately fell back down.

Kali looked at him appraisingly as he giggled to himself. She looked around and gestured for Tannick's attention, beckoning him over when he looked her way.

He came over, incredibly steady on his feet compared to everyone else.

"What's happening over here?" he asked, his voice too loud in his drunkenness.

"William's drunk."

"We're all drunk!" he shouted, everyone joining him in a loud cheer.

"No, he's *drunk* drunk. Will you help me get him back to the barracks?"

Tannick looked at William and smiled.

"Hey man, did you go a bit too hard tonight?"

William simply gave him a half-hearted cheer, looking slightly dazed.

"Okay, let's get him back," Tannick looked over at her, biting his lip and trying not to laugh.

She sighed. "Thanks, Tannick".

"Any time," he smiled.

Together they helped William stand up, each of them taking an arm and draping it around their shoulder to support his weight. When they hit the cool night air, William sagged and stumbled as though it had physically struck him.

"Jesus, William," Kali huffed under her breath as his weight became painful to bear. Tannick merely chuckled on the opposite side of him.

They made slow progress. William shifted between talking incoherently about something neither of them could really understand and singing loudly, and very out of key. To her impatience, Tannick would join in each time he started singing, and the two of them evidently found it hilarious.

"I'm glad you're enjoying yourselves," she muttered. "I don't see how getting into this kind of state the night before training is of any use to anyone."

"Lighten up, Kal; it's tradition," Tannick replied whilst readjusting William's weight on his shoulder. "Everyone gets ridiculously drunk together on the first night and you bond over how mind-blowingly awful the first day of training is. Team-building and that sort of thing."

"Well, maybe I'm actually taking this seriously."

"Everyone here is taking it seriously. But come on, it's a lot. If you don't blow off steam together then you'll crack under the pressure."

Kali was saved from responding by William stopping suddenly. He looked at her, eyes wide, before staggering behind a nearby bush and vomiting loudly. He let out a pitiful groan as they approached him.

"Come on, buddy," Tannick said sympathetically as they half-carried him back to their bunk.

Once inside, they helped him awkwardly into bed; Kali was glad he'd chosen the bottom bunk. Tannick laughed as William flopped down onto his pillows without even removing his shoes, and then staggered to his own bed. Kali turned to leave, but William caught her arm.

"Kali. Did I throw up?"

"Yes, about ten minutes ago."

"Amariel...he didn't see me, did he?"

Kali suppressed a smile. "Nope, you're good. That show was reserved for Tannick and I."

He visibly relaxed. "Oh, that's good."

"Get some sleep, tomorrow is going to kick your ass."

"Hey Kal?"

"Yeah?"

"Do you think we're making them proud by doing this? Dad and Matt? Do you think we're making them happy?"

"Yeah, I think so," she answered.

He looked thoughtful for a moment.

"Can you feel it?"

"Feel what?" she took a slight step backwards in case he was sick again.

"The feeling that everything is about to change now," he muffled into his pillow as he rolled into a more comfortable position.

"Yeah. I do," she replied, but William was already sleeping.

* * * *

As predicted, most of them struggled through the first day of training. Despite Tannick's assurance that she was missing out on crucial bonding and a "funny story", one look at William's pale and clammy face made her grateful for her restraint the night before.

It wasn't just the first day they struggled through, though; months passed, and the training was as difficult – if not more so – than Raikan promised them it would be. The new recruits were separated from the existing soldiers in Squadrons Alpha and Beta to complete Basic Guard Training. It was tiring, but the routine of training was familiar to Kali. She enjoyed feeling tired because of physical exercise instead of the exhaustion of fighting her own secrets and grief. She enjoyed the ache in her muscles that told her she was getting stronger, instead of damage inflicted by demons. She enjoyed feeling in control of herself. She found that the constant exercise was an excellent channel for her pent-up energy, and it left little room for anything else for her to dwell on.

When Basic Training was complete, the group were allowed to re-join and train with their new Squadrons; Kali and William joined Tannick in Squadron Alpha with a handful of others, whilst Variez and the remaining recruits joined Amariel in Squadron Beta. Amariel looked determined to prove himself to Raikan as a newly appointed Squadron Leader, and she saw William casting him glances from the side of his eye when he thought no-one was looking. She smiled to herself when she saw Amariel doing the same to William.

It didn't take long for the camp at Domeneum to feel like home to Kali. She knew they could return to their house on their days off if they requested it, but neither she nor William ever broached the subject. It seemed they were both happy to leave that house and everything it represented far behind them, hoping they could outrun the memories of the past. Kali suspected there was a little more to it with William, who now spent increasing amounts of time in Amariel's company. She didn't mind, in fact, she often actively encouraged it. Her reasons for joining the Guard were not to spend more time with her brother, but to become more independent, and she could understand the draw of spending time with people familiar from childhood – she now spent most of her own spare time with Tannick.

Sometimes Anissa would be allowed to visit them at lunchtimes or weekends, and they'd spend the days happily reminiscing about their childhood and laughing at everything and anything. Kali loved those days – a reminder that amongst the battle lines drawn by good and evil there remained simple pleasures and carefree laughter.

The training picked up after they graduated from Basic Training and they joined the more senior members of their squadrons, but still Kali craved more. She felt more herself here and now than she had in a long time, and she buried herself in the drills, combat training, and all manner of activities that were thrust upon them. Her dedication was mirrored around her in the other recruits and sometimes she'd see Amariel and Cael watching them and nodding approvingly as they talked amongst themselves.

One morning, a few months after they'd enlisted and began training, General Raikan returned. The members of both squadrons gathered after breakfast in the training gymnasium's main hall to find him standing with Amariel and Cael on either side of him, standing rigidly straight to attention. He spoke in his usual booming voice and announced that they were to be sent to Alarium within the week. A ripple of excitement ran through the group and Kali glanced sideways at William and Tannick, who both grinned as Cael began to speak.

"Demons have been sighted moving closer to the borders than usual, so it is imperative that when we get there, we are prepared to assist the soldiers there without delay. It's a hilly, forest terrain, and there's nothing but wilderness for miles. This will not be like Domeneum – there are no permanent fixtures like this gym, it is a make-shift camp. It will get cold. It will get lonely. The demons pose a real threat to your safety," Cael's steady voice rang loudly through the empty gym.

"You will begin your training regimen the day after we arrive. This will include group patrols with experienced soldiers and likely facing demonic activity as a result," continued Amariel. He paused for a moment as murmurs hummed through the group.

"I appreciate the idea of seeing a demon for the first time may be daunting for many of you. But we are a team, and we will stick together. Does anyone have any prior experience with encountering or fighting demons?" he passed his gaze over Kali and William deliberately quickly.

Kali and William raised their hands, and Kali stared straight forward as she felt eyes on her. When she glanced around, she saw a handful of other soldiers also had their hands raised, existing members of the Guard like Tannick, but she and William were the only new recruits to do so, and people were looking curiously at them. Kali dropped her hand, her face growing warm.

"Great, so a there are a few of you," Cael smiled at them. "This will be difficult, it will be different from what most of you are used to, but we will stick together. Trust in each other, look out for each other, and most importantly work together. This isn't a vanity mission, you're not here to look good for the Council or Squadron One pre-selection – you're here to protect your people and that means each other, too."

"Yes, well said Squadron Leader Fiden," Raikan looked around at the group. "You will be met by the commanding officers in Alarium and by your designated medical team. Once you are familiar with the terrain you will be expected not simply to defend the border, but to go beyond it and take preventative action against any demons lurking within reach of our lands. Your units are trialling the use of smaller, tactical teams to prevent the demons attacking in larger numbers and eliminating the need for mass call outs for skirmishes. The wards are weak at Alarium, and it's our most vulnerable site; do not let us down."

"Yes, Sir!" the group shouted together.

He scanned the room for a moment, then dismissed them. "Take today to pack, you'll be leaving as soon as the Alarium camp is ready for you."

They filtered out in a buzz of excitement, and Tannick jumped around animatedly beside Kali, earning him a pointed look from William on the opposite side of her. Kali laughed and ignored her brother, finding Tannick's enthusiasm infectious as they made bets about who the first of them to kill a demon would be and raced to their bunks to pack.

Chapter Ten

The commanders at Alarium sent for them the very next day, Cael raising Kali and the rest of Squadron Alpha at dawn to tell them to eat breakfast quickly and be ready to leave by eight a.m. Kali rubbed her eyes sleepily as Tannick rushed around in a flurry of activity, wondering if it would ever be possible to bottle some of his energy. She rolled out of bed and saw William across the room, looking tired and frowning.

"Isn't there a sedative or something we can give him?" he inclined his head grouchily in Tannick's direction.

"You're so grumpy in the morning," she mumbled, stifling a yawn as she picked up clean clothes to change into and made her way into the bathroom.

William merely grunted in response, shooting Tannick another annoyed look as he rummaged around in his drawer for clothes.

They gathered at the canteen laden with their bags, all of them eager to set off on the journey to Alarium. They found themselves too nervous and excited to eat despite

Amariel and Cael's firm encouragement that they have a hearty breakfast to see them through the day.

"It's a long trip," Cael scolded them lightly, although Kali noticed she didn't seem to be eating very much either.

The trip was scheduled to take four days on foot. Their request to travel by portal was instantly denied, with Raikan reprimanding them for what Kali guessed was forty minutes on "taking the easy way" so early in their training. If they couldn't make it to Alarium on foot, how could they be prepared for life there or for combat? He'd thundered, a vein throbbing in his forehead.

They were sensible enough to never complain about the trip within earshot of him, Amariel or Cael after that.

Still, Kali wasn't overjoyed at the thought of trekking through wilderness for days on end, and she wasn't alone in that. The weather had turned cooler now, with a distinct chill in the air, and storms were unpredictable – both squadrons were less than enthused about the journey.

Alarium itself, however, was a different matter. Everyone was eager to leave Domeneum behind and see real combat, something they'd already spent each night discussing amongst each other in varying degrees of sincerity.

Some nights the conversations were jovial, mocking each other and placing bets about who the first to cry would be, the first to kill a demon would be, or who would be the first to give up and go home. On other nights, they talked about their fears; that they would freeze up in battle, that they would fail, that they would die, that they'd watch friends die. Although most of them had only known each other for a few months, it was hard not to form close relationships when you spent all day training together and were facing an impending sense of danger together. Kali came to consider them all as good friends far sooner than she expected.

When the call to leave went up from Amariel, each of them shared nervous smiles and stood, most of them still with full plates (something they would undoubtedly regret later, Kali supposed). Those around them addressed them with salutes and cheers as they left, something Kali had grown accustomed to here whenever a squadron was deployed. It embarrassed her a little now that it was finally their turn, but she appreciated the gesture.

They started in good spirits, chatting and laughing as they marched briskly out of the northern exit of the camp, through the city streets of Domeneum and into the waving, smiling faces of the public. Beyond the city limits, their interaction with other people dwindled as towns became villages and eventually buildings faded to old ruins that punctuated a wild landscape. They had been walking scarcely two hours before the rain started, torrential and sudden, dampening their spirits as well as their belongings. They began to quicken their pace before realising there was no shelter for them to run to and resigned themselves to their long walk ahead in the rain. They were grateful then, when Cael gave the order to stop several hours later, their clothes soaked, and their exposed skin numb from cold.

They took shelter as best they could underneath some trees and set about making fires and preparing lunch, everyone lingering as long as they could beside the flames, trying to heat up and dry off. Only Tannick seemed to have retained some of his earlier enthusiasm, sidling up next to her and sneaking her a chunk of chocolate with a cheerful look on his face.

"This is my own private supply of chocolate, a going-away present from Anissa. I *might* be inclined to keep sharing if you're nice to me," he joked.

"Oh really? What if I'm not?"

"Then my friend, it is disgusting ration pudding for you for the next few days."

"The horror!" she chuckled, accepting the chocolate and savouring the taste.

Tannick was right: when you forgot how chocolate actually tasted you could imagine the ration packs tasted fine, but it was no comparison to the real thing.

"Just don't spread it around that I have this, I don't have enough for everyone."

"Your secret will die with me," she gave him a mock salute.

He looked momentarily troubled, before giving a small shake of his head and smiling.

"I knew I could count on you, Robereun!"

William was walking a short way away from them, moving away from Amariel looking happy despite the wet and cold. He turned in response to hearing their last name, changing direction to meet them.

"Hey, what you guys talking about?"

"Nothing!" they said together, laughing at William's face as they exchanged conspiratorial winks.

"Okay…how you guys holding up? This weather is grim, I hope it isn't like this the whole time."

"Tell me about it," Kali muttered, moving closer to the fire and accepting a plate of food from Cael as she handed out lunch to her Squadron.

They ate in a hurry, reluctantly leaving the shelter of the trees behind to continue onwards to Alarium. The rain did not truly relent until well into the third day, and by then Kali had started to forget what it felt like to be warm and dry. Everything was sodden – the ground underfoot that was soft and slippery, their kits and spare clothes, and their morale – and they were relieved each night when they pitched their tents and had some brief respite from the elements.

By the time they reached Alarium, feeling distinctly weather-beaten, even Tannick's demeanour was more subdued than usual. Cael and Amariel had long since given up trying to encourage them, seeming almost as weary as they were. They'd done well though, Kali thought. In the cold and the damp, even the pettiest squabbles had the propensity to turn into something more, but the group never turned on each other. When they finally reached Alarium, Tannick gave up a sarcastic cheer and the group found themselves grinning at each other and chuckling despite their misery.

There was no rest for them once they reached Alarium, however. They were taken on a tour of the camp, debriefed on the situation there, the rules and the training expectations. The camp sprawled for miles, split up into different sections; the Living Quarters where their tents would be pitched and food was served; the Training Quadrant; the Base Command Centre; the Weapons Division; and the Medic Station.

They were surrounded by forest, but to the west of the camp lay a large, idyllic lake. Swimming alone was forbidden, as was swimming without permission, but they were assured that they would all get the chance to enjoy the lake once the weather was suitable. To the north of the camp, the border of the seraph lands lay approximately two miles from the edge of it; beyond this, there was no protection offered by the wards that protected Alarium.

After their tour, hardly able to take another step, they were ordered to meet with the medical team for evaluation before training began the next morning. They filed one by one into an impressively large, green tent; it was filled with people busying themselves around machines and equipment that seemed out of place to Kali this far into the wilderness. As she waited, she surveyed the medics as they hurried around the group. There were three of them, wearing clothes that were identical to their training gear aside from the fact they were green, like the tent. As she watched them, she realised with a start that she recognised one of them. The medic from the Council chambers after they'd reported the death of their father sat in the middle of the tent, taking Cael's blood pressure with a cheery smile. She nudged William and pointed her out to him.

"That's the woman that checked me over the day we saw the Council," she whispered, avoiding any mention of the reasons that brought them there that day.

"Is it?" he whispered back, sounding unsure.

"Definitely."

William looked troubled; he regarded the woman intently, brow furrowed as he watched her move around Cael.

"What's wrong?" she asked.

"You don't think...the Council couldn't have sent her here deliberately to watch us, could they?"

"What, like a spy?" Kali scoffed.

William looked serious and dropped his voice, so she had to strain to hear him even though she was standing next to him.

"It wouldn't take much for them to find holes in our story. It makes no sense that we got away when they killed Dad and Matt who were far more experienced fighters than us."

She considered for a moment, then shot a furtive glance in the woman's direction.

"So, what do we do?"

"I don't know. Keep an eye on her, I guess? But we'll need to be extra careful now that she's around."

"Oh well, there go my plans of revealing myself as the antichrist at dinner tonight," she remarked sarcastically.

William shot her a look. "Haha, you're hilarious. And stop saying that."

She ignored him, watching the woman as she waved Cael away and moved to work around Amariel instead. Could she really be a Council spy? She thought back to the good-natured woman that reassured her all those months ago and hoped William was wrong, that he was simply letting paranoia rule his thoughts. She couldn't help thinking he had a point, though.

She was nervous as she waited in line for her turn to face the woman. She wasn't even sure that the woman would recognise her; though Kali reflected that if she were a spy then she might pretend not to, anyway. When her turn finally came, she strode over to the woman hoping to appear nonchalant. The woman turned and instantly, her face lit up in recognition and a sincere smile spread across her face.

"It's you!" she beamed.

"Hello again," Kali smiled back.

"You look much better than the last time we met!" the woman said cheerfully, looking her over.

"Uh, yeah I bet I do," Kali replied, feeling a little awkward.

The medic checked the file in front of her. "Kali, is it? Let's get you checked out, shall we? I'm Lenaria, by the way – I'm Lead Medic here."

As before, Lenaria used her powers to assess Kali for any injuries. When she found none, she cheerfully made a note on Kali's file and started using various pieces of equipment to check her blood pressure, take her temperature and to check her vision. Kali watched her as she worked, wondering if it was possible this seemingly earnest woman was secretly here to spy on her for the Council. There was something about her that Kali couldn't help but trust.

Lenaria broke through her thoughts with a cheerful declaration of health and called out to her as she left.

"I'm really glad you're alright, Kali. I look forward to working with you." She smiled again, and Kali smiled back, hoping that Lenaria was as kind and as genuine as she appeared.

Chapter Eleven

Despite their earlier enthusiasm, it was the move to Alarium that really threw the new recruits. Kali often found herself so tired she could barely make it to her bunk before falling asleep each night. Indeed, it was not uncommon to see someone fall asleep whilst eating, so exhausted were the group.

The members of their squadrons with previous experience in the Guard fared only marginally better than they did; they were used to life in the military, but Kali overheard many of them complaining that this level of training seemed ridiculous. Amariel and Cael were relentless, but they led by example, which earned them unilateral respect amongst the squadrons. They would never ask anyone to do something they were not willing to do and were usually the first to rise every morning and the last to go to bed each night.

The patrols they were shadowing became particularly brutal as the weather turned intensely wintry, with ice making the ground beneath them solid and hard to pass and spontaneous blizzards bearing down on them without warning. Weeks passed without any tangible demon sightings, but occasionally they would find footprints in the frozen earth that let them know some were nearby. Such a discovery seemed to have the ability to drop the temperature several degrees lower and made the groups band tighter together.

The snow on the trees had a disorientating effect on them, and Kali was sure if she ever got separated from the group that she would wander out here for days before she found her way back to camp.

Eventually though, Kali's muscles stopped aching and the forest became less foreboding and unfamiliar as slowly, Alarium began to feel more like home. It took far longer than it did at Domeneum, but she could see it happening as people stopped falling asleep mid-sentence and started laughing with each other again. Interactions became full conversations instead of a series of monosyllabic grunts and everyone's mood seemed to shift. She was spending more time with Tannick and surprisingly, Lenaria, who seemed to have made it her personal mission to look after Kali's wellbeing. Even the weather began to thaw as Winter began to reluctantly give way to Spring.

They saw their first demons the day after the ice melted. They sprouted from the forest and came down on them in waves; despite Amariel and Cael's constant warnings otherwise, the group had admittedly become a little complacent after months of no activity. So, when the cry went up, they were all a little dazed, scrambling to take their positions and draw their weapons as the demons drew nearer.

The sudden appearance of the demons had a peculiar effect on time, which seemed to move both in slow motion and hyper speed as they followed Cael and the other squadron forward to meet them. For many of her group, this was their first encounter with demons. Kali and William had prior experience but at that moment it didn't feel like an advantage. All Kali pictured when she looked at them was Liliana in the clearing, Mattias dead and her father dying. She was breathing hard by the time they were finished but she wasn't entirely sure if that was down to the physical strain or the memories that haunted her.

That night was the first in weeks that nightmares stalked her dreams, the visions of demons and murder that she was becoming too acquainted with plaguing her each time she closed her eyes. Accepting that she wasn't likely to get much sleep, she crept out of her tent and decided to go for a walk in the cool night air.

She passed William's tent, listening for any signs that he was also awake; she was worried that he too might have been thrown by their first encounter with demons since that day. As she tiptoed nearer, she heard hushed voices and muffled laughter coming from inside his tent. Recognising Amariel's voice, she hurried in the opposite direction, not wanting to intrude and feeling strangely alone.

As the weeks continued to slip by, she noticed William and Amariel spending yet more and more time together, sneaking around in private when they thought nobody was looking. Kali knew that if she was noticing it then surely others would be too and started to grow concerned that someone might take issue with a Squadron Leader sneaking around with a subordinate. She wondered how to broach the subject with her brother when suddenly, it stopped being her main concern about their relationship.

As their two squadrons began to patrol together without the Alarium soldiers, she noticed Amariel watching her intently.

Often, she would turn, feeling his eyes on the back of her head, only to see him hurriedly looking away. She began to feel as she had as a child – the now-familiar gazes she'd seen her brothers fix her with growing up adorning Amariel's features – the sinking unease that he knew something about her, and he didn't want her to know.

It came to a head when one day, just after a patrol, she found Amariel and William in an intense discussion at the edge of the camp. They stopped abruptly as she approached them, looking guilty. A familiar rage roiled inside of her as she stared at them, now convinced that William had shared the truth with Amariel without her knowledge. When, through gritted teeth, she asked her brother to speak in private, Amariel avoided her eye as he dismissed himself, leaving them alone and awkwardly bidding William goodbye.

"You told Amariel about me, didn't you?" she rounded on him as soon as Amariel was out of earshot, her hands balling into fists at her side.

His face reddened and he spluttered, unable to articulate a response. She looked away from him, betrayed.

"How *could* you?" she cried.

"Kal, I'm *sorry!*" William exclaimed, finally finding his voice. "I was going to tell you, but I didn't want to upset you!"

"Pretty sure-fire way of not upsetting me is not to tell *my* secret to any random person you find attractive," she spat.

"He isn't some random person, Kal. I trust him!" William looked equal parts angry and guilty.

"Great, so tell him *your* secrets then!"

"This is my secret too; it doesn't just affect you! And I didn't mean to tell him, I just started talking about stuff and it sort of…came out."

"Whatever," she glared at him and turned to walk away. She stopped briefly, talking in a low voice over her shoulder, shaking with anger. "It's not *our* secret, Will. Nobody's out to get *you,* are they? I'm sorry I'm such a burden on you but don't dare think we share this equally."

She walked away and was glad when he didn't follow her. As she walked back towards her tent, her anger turned to sadness, and worst of all – loneliness. She could understand William wanting to tell Amariel the truth, to have someone to confide in, because she desperately wanted that too.

Somewhat contradictory to that, at that moment she would be happy to never speak to William ever again. She went straight to her tent, declining the offer of dinner when Lenaria popped her head in to ask. She didn't feel up to seeing William right now, or Amariel for that matter. Amariel, who knew the truth about her, who watched her from a distance. She wondered what he thought of her; the idea of it made her chest feel tight.

Her resolve not to interact with her brother held for most of the week, and he eventually gave up on trying to apologise to her or engage her in small talk. Every time she came close to forgiving him, she'd see him and Amariel hunched together deep in conversation and get angry all over again.

Her silent streak came to an end one early afternoon after a particularly eventful patrol deep into the woods around Alarium. They'd been scouting the woods with Squadron Beta since before dawn, and they were exhausted. The rain had arrived a few hours into their patrol, which made visibility all the more difficult as the wind whipped the cold rain into their faces like angry shards of glass. Kali drew the hood of her jacket up over her head, though it offered little protection for her face, and re-tightened her grip on her sword as her hands became increasingly numb. They were well beyond the wards and Cael and Amariel maintained a steady stream of encouragement and warnings to them as they continued along their allocated path.

The group were minutes from their scheduled return time when the scene around them erupted unexpectedly. Tens of demons burst out of the trees around them, small groups of them breaking off to target each member of the group as they rushed forward to mount a defence.

Kali swore under her breath, bringing her sword up to counter the demon nearest her as it lunged towards her. She fought off the demons surrounding her and looked around to see which of her friends needed help the most. Shouts echoed all around her, reverberating back towards her as they bounced off the dense forest that encased them.

To her alarm, she saw that demons were encircling the group to her left and that William had been separated from them, caught alone in between a group of around ten demons. She teleported into the centre of them just as they began to attack, and he looked grateful for the assistance. The wind howled ferociously as it grew in intensity, mocking them as they battled the demons. Her hood flew back, and loose strands of hair whipped at her face as she threw herself towards the attacking demons.

After her third kill, an uneasiness crept over her as she noticed that these demons were almost effortless to take down, most of them barely putting up a fight as she moved towards them. In fact, even as she watched, two of them backed away from her and retreated towards the trees rather than engage in fighting with her.

It didn't make sense to Kali and it didn't sit well with her. All fights kept to a certain logic; none were so clear cut as those with demons, whose sole purpose was to cause pain and death. They did not falter, and they did not waver in their mission to inflict suffering. They did not fear death in battle. So why were they backing away from her?

She stared after them for a moment, then turned to drive down a fatal blow on the demon nearest to her when she heard William call out to her. In the midst of her distraction, a demon had crept up behind her; it was too far for William to reach in time, and she was about to catch its axe in her back. She turned as it began to strike and watched, mouth hanging open, as it saw her face and recoiled away from her. A sense of horrified recognition seemed to flit across its features as it drew back instantly and stumbled backwards.

Shaken, she drove her sword through its head and turned to William, who had killed the last of the demons near him and was looking at her in astonishment.

"What was *that* about?" she asked him, her vow of silence now entirely forgotten.

"I have absolutely no idea," he replied, a line of confusion creasing his forehead.

They looked around at the rest of the group. Most of them were now making short work of the remaining demons, nobody sparing them a second glance. Nobody appeared to have noticed the demon's hesitation.

"It looked...it looked like it recognised me," she said, remembering the expression on the demon's face as it shrank back from her.

"Is that even possible?"

"I don't know. But maybe it's…I don't know."

"Maybe it's what?"

"…family resemblance?"

Understanding registered on William's face, before being replaced again with confusion.

"But that's never stopped them before. You don't think she's told them not to hurt you, do you?"

Kali bit her lip, trying to think. Before she could reply, Amariel rushed over to them.

"Are you both alright?" his voice was filled with concern and his eyes looked urgent as he searched William's face.

His face flooded with embarrassment as he met Kali's eye. The tension Kali had momentarily forgotten about came rushing back, and she took a small step backwards.

"I'm fine," she said coldly. "*Sir.*"

He blinked at her, flushed, then regained his composure.

"We need to talk. After dinner," he commanded.

The physical restraint it took Kali not to roll her eyes at a superior officer was immense, and she could sense William awaiting her reaction. She nodded curtly, not trusting herself to speak as Cael approached them.

"Is anyone hurt?" she studied them, eyeing the bruising already purpling beneath the skin and the blood oozing from superficial wounds neither of them had even yet noticed.

"All good here, ma'am," Kali replied, looking away from Amariel and William.

"I want you all to report to your medical team. Beltura, we need to inform General Raikan about this. This didn't feel random – it felt planned, it was like they were lying in wait for us. They must have been watching us for a while, knowing we would come this way."

"I agree," Amariel sighed heavily.

"We can't leave now! What if there are more of them?" Kali exclaimed, thinking about the demons who'd managed to escape.

Cael raised an eyebrow. "Did you suddenly become the leader of this Squadron, Robereun?"

Kali looked at her, defiant. She considered challenging Cael but bit back her retort when she caught Amariel's eye.

"No, ma'am," she said coolly.

Cael smiled. "Okay then. We head back now."

Sullen, Kali made her way back to the group. She didn't wait on William, leaving him to walk awkwardly behind her as Amariel and Cael began an intense discussion. The group was subdued and on edge as they walked back to camp. Every whisper of wind through the trees, every rustle of small animals moving along the forest floor, breaking branches as they scurried was enough to send adrenaline pumping round their bodies, envisioning a second attack. There was an almost audible sigh as they finally crossed back within the protective wards of the camp. Shoulders slumped, they made their way wearily to the medical tent.

Lenaria's face briefly flickered with shock as they filed in, some more bloodied than others, but she quickly launched into action, becoming business-like and ordering the other medics to their appropriate positions.

Kali wasn't hurt, but she could see Lenaria's eyes flitting to her often. They were seen in order of severity, so Kali hung back with William. When Lenaria eventually got to her, she looked worried.

"Lenaria, I'm fine; I promise!" Kali shrugged off her concern.

"Well, there's no harm in letting *me* establish that, is there?" she pulled a curtain around them as Kali sat on a clinical-looking bed.

When Lenaria was satisfied that Kali was indeed fine, she smiled and gestured that she could go. Kali stretched her muscles out and yawned before standing, trying to stall her return to the events of the day.

"I have a few more people to check over and then I'll join you for dinner?" Lenaria called to her as she rummaged through various drawers and pulled out fresh strips of gauze and bandages.

"Yeah, no problem," Kali replied, pulling on her jumper and jacket in preparation for the cold outside.

She braced herself and emerged from the warm, dry tent into the cold wind. The rain, thankfully, had stopped but there was still an unseasonable chill in the air as she made her way to dinner. She saw William sitting alone at one of the long, wooden tables in the large canvas structure where they ate their meals (colloquially referred to as the "mess tent") and made a point to sit as far away from him as she could.

She knew she was being petty, but she couldn't help it; every single time she looked at his face, she felt betrayed. More than that, it brought up the same feelings she'd experienced the day she found out her family had been lying to her for her entire life, the day their family secrets literally came back to destroy them. Of everything that was lost to her since that day, the one thing she counted on, even when they fought, was that William would be there to watch out for her. Knowing that he'd betrayed her trust the way he had felt like too much to forgive.

Tannick appeared beside her, looking questioningly between her and William, who appeared to notice Kali sitting far away from him and was scowling in between glances at her. When she offered no explanation, Tannick merely shrugged and sat down beside her, turning his attention to his dinner and devouring it like it might escape him at any minute. Kali merely stared at her food, unable to stop thinking about the demons.

She'd never heard of a demon reacting like that before and she could have *sworn* it recognised her as it backed away from her. How did it know her? More importantly, why did it recoil mid-attack? Why were the other demons so reluctant to attack her? Something was amiss and she hated the uncertainty of not knowing why.

She sat for several moments, lost in thought, and jumped when she felt a hand on her arm. She turned to find Lenaria smiling kindly at her. Lenaria: yet another source of uncertainty. Was she as sincere as she seemed or was she, as William originally suggested, a spy sent by the Council to watch them? Kali silently lamented the fact that nothing in her life was ever simple.

"Kali?"

She blinked. "Sorry, Lenaria; I was completely distracted."

"That's okay," Lenaria replied warmly. "Leader Beltura asked me to tell you to report to his tent once you're finished with dinner."

Great, she thought; just what she needed, an argument with Amariel and her brother.

"Ooooh, Robereun's in *trouble,"* Tannick sang tauntingly. She gave him a half-hearted shove as he laughed.

Seeing no point in delaying the inevitable, Kali excused herself from the table and made her way to Amariel's tent. She saw William watching her as she left, and thought it was odd that he wasn't joining her. She assumed whatever Amariel was going to say to her involved William either directly or indirectly.

Amariel's tent was near the Squadron Alpha/Beta camp in the Living Quarters, but as a ranking officer, his tent was significantly larger than the rest of the squad. The canvas was a pleasant burnt orange instead of her own pale beige and was almost double the size. She looked at it resentfully, then called to Amariel to let her know she was outside.

"Uh…Am—Sir? It's Kali. Lenaria said you sent for me?"

Amariel's face appeared at the opening of the tent. He didn't look angry, but there was a strange determination on his face. She wasn't sure what she was about to be faced with. Had he decided to turn her in to the Council? Was this why William wasn't here?

"Kali, good. We need to talk," Amariel said in his usual steady manner. "Come in from the cold," he motioned for her to come inside.

She obliged, half-expecting an ambush, but the tent was empty.

"Tea?" Amariel gestured to a small kettle that sat on a portable heater.

"Uh, no thanks."

"Something stronger?" Amariel bent down into a bag and brought out a bottle of whisky.

Kali hesitated. She sensed that wherever this conversation was going, that it wouldn't be an easy one.

"Yeah, sure. Thanks. Sir."

"Stop calling me "Sir", Kali, we're not in the field," his tone was not unkind. He measured two glasses of whisky and handed her one.

He raised his glass to her, and she copied before taking a sip. Like the night she sat in the kitchen with William before the

Ceremony of Fallen Soldiers, the whisky burned and made her want to gag, but she forced her face to remain impassive. She met Amariel's gaze, waiting for him to speak first.

"Obviously we need to talk. This tension isn't healthy for the team dynamic, or for you and your brother."

"Did he ask you to speak to me?"

"No. But as a Squadron Leader, it's my business to know what's going on both in my own team and in your team."

Kali couldn't help raising an eyebrow. "And William has nothing to do with it, then?"

Amariel looked like he was choosing his next words very carefully.

"Your brother is a very dear friend to me, and I care about him. I do not want to be the reason your relationship has become so strained."

Kali noticed his slight hesitation on the word "friend."

"I wouldn't worry about that, Amariel," she said, draining her glass and suppressing a cough. "You're not the reason for that, he is."

"Because of what he told me?" he asked softly.

Kali met his eye, suddenly feeling very vulnerable. Nobody else knew her secret, nobody that wasn't a blood-relation, and here she stood facing the first person outside of her family ever to know. She wondered what he saw when he looked at her. Did he see a monster? An abomination? She folded her arms across her chest protectively, as though she could hide her soul from him.

"And what exactly did he tell you?" Kali tried to keep her voice steady, indifferent.

Amariel re-filled her glass and then his own, taking his time before he answered.

"That your mother turned whilst pregnant with you. That you're...different because of it," he said in a low voice.

"Did he tell you what happened the day our father and Mattias died?" she was surprised to find that her voice was barely above a whisper and her hands were trembling.

She took a long drink from her glass. It felt surreal to be discussing this openly with Amariel, a commander in the Guard, when the need for secrecy had been sewn into every fibre of her life.

He looked at her, and she saw the hint of sadness in his eyes. "Yes."

She felt her eyes burn and finished her drink, trying to replace the sensation with something stronger. She was beginning to enjoy the way the whisky burned her throat and warmed her body. Knowing that Amariel knew their deaths were her fault made her feel empty and cold inside, and the whisky felt like the antidote to his searching gaze. She looked at him, wanting to reply but not having the words.

"So, what are you going to do?" she finally managed to ask.

"Do?"

"With me. Are you going to report me?"

"Report you? No, Kali: I want to teach you."

Chapter Twelve

Kali stared at Amariel blankly. "Teach me?" she echoed.

"William said you have issues controlling your powers. That maybe you don't even know which powers you have. I'd like to help with that."

Of all the scenarios Kali was playing out in her mind as she walked to Amariel's tent, there was never one in which she imagined him offering to train her. She was utterly bemused.

"No offence or anything, but how much experience have you got teaching half-demons how to use their powers?" she asked, unable to keep the snark out of her tone.

He smiled. "Granted, none. But I've got a long history of training people throughout my career in the Guard; how do you think I got to be leading this squadron at such a young age?"

She looked at him hesitantly.

"I really think I can help you, Kali," he encouraged, earnest.

Kali considered it. Was this not exactly what she was looking for when she joined the Guard – a way to control her powers? How could she turn down an offer like this when it was exactly what she needed? Especially when it was so easy to trust Amariel? She still felt a pit of resentment towards William for sharing her secret without her permission, but she could see it more clearly now, how one might feel compelled to share their troubles and darkest burdens with Amariel. He emitted an aura of measured calm that was effortlessly soothing and overtly trustworthy. It was hard not to be drawn in by it.

"Okay," she nodded slowly.

"A word before you agree though. We do this in secret, at night. We don't tell anyone. During the day I am nothing more than Squadron Leader Beltura to you. During our lessons, I expect the same commitment and effort from you as I would from any other training. I will not waste my time with this if I don't think you're taking it seriously."

"Of course, absolutely," she agreed.

"Good. Then we'll toast to it. Then we'll go find your brother before he explodes from not knowing what we're talking about," he quipped, the corners of his mouth twitching upwards.

They toasted with another glass of whisky – Kali was rather light-headed by this point – and left to find William. As they walked, Kali thought to herself that it wasn't just the alcohol that was buoying her up, but a newfound sense of hope, and the feeling that she was finally moving in the right direction again.

* * * *

Amariel's training sessions began the next night, the two of them meeting in a clearing by the lake after the rest of the camp were asleep, and it became readily apparent that he was going to be a tough teacher. Kali wrongly assumed they would spend this time working on her powers, but Amariel instead dedicated hours to honing standard combat skills, explaining that he wanted to ensure they had the right foundation for moving forward.

"Your powers just now, namely the teleporting, you can't rely on them all the time in combat. Those seconds before you teleport – in which you're concentrating on where you want to go – and those after where you adjust to where you've landed, those are opportunities during which you are vulnerable to attack. If you're taking other people with you, those windows of opportunity increase exponentially," he explained as he led her through a warm-up exercise.

"But it isn't just teleporting that leaves you vulnerable; all powers come with a side of risk. It takes far more energy to use a power than it does to engage in hand-to-hand combat. You won't run out of power, but you'll tire faster. You'll make mistakes, you'll get slower. Over-reliance on powers is a death sentence if you don't have the right techniques in battle. Powers should always be used to give you an advantage over your opponent or as a last resort."

Kali listened intently, although she'd heard a similar speech from her father years previously. Her gut twisted painfully as she thought about how much she missed him, before she forced herself to push it down and focus on Amariel instead.

They spent most of the night training, Amariel assessing her capabilities and occasionally correcting her stance or positioning. She noted that he really did seem to have a knack for training, always explaining clearly why a certain stance was preferable, or where a weakness lay. By the end, her eyes were heavy, and she was desperate for sleep, but she felt like she'd accomplished something. She was pleasantly surprised to find that Amariel looked pleased with their work, too.

They met four times a week for the next few weeks, and Kali could barely keep up. The days not spent on patrol were spent on training, and then she'd spend a couple of nights training, too. Yet on their relief days off, she longed to do more. She was making a lot of progress under Amariel's instruction, and she'd never been so optimistic about her control over her powers. It was oddly addictive, even if she had started dozing off at mealtimes again.

The more time she spent with Amariel, and with Amariel occasionally pleading his case to her in between training sessions, Kali gradually forgave William. He promised that he would never keep anything from her again, and although she wasn't sure she believed him it was nice to be on speaking terms with her brother again.

She was tired but happier than she'd felt in a long time, and she found herself warming quickly to Amariel. Between sneaking away at night with her twice a week, and sneaking away with William the remaining nights, Kali often wondered how he found time for sleep. He seemed almost impervious to the fatigue that plagued her, never slowing down in battle during the day or during their nightly training sessions.

In fact, Kali was just getting used to their schedule when the frequency of their training increased dramatically. After several occasions on patrol where demons reacted in the same strange manner as before, avoiding her in battle at all costs, they grew increasingly concerned. Together, all three of them discussed in hushed whispers what this odd behaviour could possibly mean. The most worrying implication to Kali was that Liliana knew she was there and wanted her alive. With Kali seemingly in Liliana's sights, Amariel increased their schedule to four nights of the week, William occasionally joining them (he claimed brotherly concern, but Kali suspected it had more to do with watching Amariel fight shirtless).

Knowing her biggest problem was losing control of her emotions, Amariel made her practise a form of meditation over and over again. He showed her grounding techniques and calming techniques, and when she complained she would much rather pummel something with her sword, he retorted that that was one of her problems, and made her start from scratch.

When she finally convinced him that she possessed the ability to remain calm during battle, he began teaching her on accessing her other powers.

"Close your eyes," he instructed her one night, as the moon illuminated the clearing around them and danced on the surface of the lake. It was quiet, peaceful. She was in control.

"Without actually using it, let your mind find the place inside of you where your power – powers – rest. Feel them lying dormant, ready to be called upon. Feel them brewing just beneath the surface. Feel their potential, not yet realised. Feel each one, and recognise their distinctive sensations, each one a separate entity within you; part of you, but not bigger than you. An extension of yourself, of your energy. Even the ones that are nameless right now, feel their energy, and let them tell you what they are."

Kali stood perfectly still, trying to follow his instructions. He was right, she could feel her powers; she sensed the ones she knew well by now but beyond that lay others. As she pushed past the known, she entered a sea of potential, hovering over each power and hearing them call to her, getting a taste of each of them. *Teleportation; Zoopathy; Telekinesis; Pyrokinesis;* she pushed further, noticing as she did so that these powers had a different energy to them; *Sickness. Suffering. Destruction. Death.* She wanted to flinch back from them, but something pulled her back. A feeling of wanting to know more. When Amariel's voice brought her back to reality, she was shocked at how tired she was. Amariel simply smiled.

"I told you powers tire you out quicker than combat," he remarked.

Amariel made her practise finding the potential for each of her powers, what he called the "E Point" – that moment between building the energy for an attack and using it – over and over during their sessions before he finally let her use them. The day she successfully conjured fire, she was thrilled and William (who was on standby with a bucket of water from the lake) gave her a cheer, looking ecstatic.

At last, she felt in control. As Spring became Summer, Kali laughed freely and more often, and noticed the tension in William's shoulders was almost entirely gone. Amariel watched him affectionately and Kali observed that he too seemed lighter. Their good mood was contagious, and they spent many nights between dinner and bedtime sitting with Tannick and Lenaria telling stories, playing around and laughing. For the first time in what felt like forever, Kali felt genuinely and effortlessly happy.

Excitement too was growing for the Guard's annual Summer Festival, where the full-time members of the Guard were given leave to spend time with their families. In built-up cities like Domeneum, this usually meant going home, but for Alarium, it meant families visiting the camp. A separate camp had started being prepared for the family members scheduled to visit, along with the reserve relief team sent to cover the basics for the festival's two-day duration. With nobody to visit them, Kali wasn't particularly excited about it until Tannick excitedly informed her one day at breakfast that Anissa was coming.

"Did I forget to tell you she was thinking about it?" he laughed at her expression as he tore a large chunk from his bread with his teeth and re-filled his coffee.

"Yes! I'm so excited to see her!" Kali beamed at him. "Is she staying for the full festival?"

"Yep! My mother is heading to see my father, so Anissa thought she'd come to see us instead!"

"How is your father, Tannick? What's life at Tereum like?" William asked.

Kali zoned out of the conversation as William and Tannick began talking in-depth about where Tannick's father was stationed and what the demon activity was like there. The thought of seeing Anissa again was filling her with greater joy than she would have expected.

Anissa was perhaps the last person in her life unsullied by the violence that seemed to now follow her around. She didn't spend her days thinking about or fighting demons, they weren't bonded in anything sinister, she was just a good friend and a good person. The prospect of seeing her again made Kali realise how important their friendship was to her. As they finished breakfast and set off for another difficult patrol, the thought of Anissa's visit lifted Kali's spirits, and she reflected that it was nice to once again have something to look forward to.

* * * *

The days leading up to the festival flew by quicker than Kali could have anticipated, time a blur lost to the hours spent training and patrolling. The lake was officially opened to them, and she spent most of her free days with Tannick swimming or bathing in the sun on its shores. William and Amariel joined them occasionally, but she knew the struggle of hiding their now well-established relationship from the eyes of others meant that they preferred to spend as much time alone together as they could.

Lenaria had also taken to spending most of her free time with them, although she preferred to sit in the shade with a book to splashing around in the lake. She fussed over Kali often – was she eating enough? was she sleeping enough? – and Kali trusted her despite the nagging doubt about William's initial suspicions of her. She'd never discussed it further with her brother,

her attention taken up by other matters, but even when she remembered, it wasn't something she wanted to talk about. Lenaria was her friend, and she didn't want to question that. She hoped it wasn't something she'd come to regret.

The night before the festival formally began was a flurry of activity, making sure that the camps for the visiting families and reserve soldiers were complete and that there were sufficient supplies for everyone. As Squadrons Alpha and Beta returned from patrol, they returned their camp-issued weapons and headed to the Mess Tent, weaving their way through the crowd. Safe in the knowledge they had the next few days off from active duty, they enjoyed a long dinner together, everyone in high spirits as the sun finally set, casting an orange glow over the camp.

As darkness settled in, they peeled off in groups; William and Amariel creating a small fire as Kali, Tannick, and Lenaria watched on. Laughter peppered the calm night and shadows cast by the fire danced lazily on the trees beside them.

She closed her eyes, leaning back and letting the sound of her friends' conversations drift by her. Their voices, so uncharacteristically carefree, were soothing to Kali; so soothing that she was soon waking to William gently shaking her, despite being unaware she'd even fallen asleep. The fire was out, and the others were gone. She yawned and stretched, the muscles in her legs seized and stiff.

"You looked peaceful, so we didn't want to wake you. Well except for the drooling, that was pretty disgusting."

"Uh, shut up," Kali groaned, still groggy.

William laughed and helped her up from the ground.

"How long have I been asleep?"

"Maybe an hour or so? I'm not sure."

"Ugh. Did I miss anything?"

"Oh yeah, big time. Demons stormed the camp and Tannick took them on one by one with just a big stick. He has Raikan's job now," William remarked.

Kali snorted, for once too tired to think of any sort of retort to her brother.

They walked in silence, Kali's mind on how much she was looking forward to reaching her bed and little else. She wondered briefly if her brother would go to

Amariel's tent or his own after he'd walked her to hers. She realised Amariel hadn't mentioned whether his family was coming to visit tomorrow. She considered asking her brother about it but decided against it. Amariel didn't talk much about his family and she sensed a tension there.

"So, you and Amariel seem especially close these days," she glanced at him, casually.

As expected, William turned faintly pink, but he didn't look unhappy.

"Yeah," a small smile played on his lips.

"My brother, the wordsmith," she laughed when he didn't elaborate.

He smiled sheepishly at her. They reached her tent, William still wearing a guarded smile.

"Thanks for walking me!"

"No problem, I'll see you tomorrow," he started to walk away.

"Will!" Kali called him back; he stopped and turned back towards her. "It's nice to see you happy."

"Thanks, Kal. Get some sleep."

"Night," she called, retiring to her tent and hoping her brother's newfound happiness would last.

She awoke the next morning to families arriving for the festival, the camp transformed from the dreary, isolated place she'd known when they first arrived into a beautiful and scenic one filled with reunited family. Shouts of delight punctured the air frequently as loved ones recognised each other and embraced. Children ran around excitedly, playing and laughing with each other.

Kali watched it all in a confusing mix of joy and grief; she imagined her father and Mattias in the throng of visitors, coming to wish them well, and it made her stomach hurt. She saw movement to her left and looked to see William standing beside her. He gave her a knowing look and patted her on the shoulder. She smiled sadly at him and began to turn away when she heard a voice calling her name.

"Kali! *Kali!*"

She turned back in response and saw Anissa hurrying towards her, a wide smile on her face. She threw herself at Kali as she reached her, embracing her tightly.

"My *goodness,* Kali! You feel so strong!" she stared in amazement at her, gently prodding the muscles in Kali's arms as she drew back.

"Uh…thanks?" Kali laughed, exceptionally happy to see Anissa again. William greeted her with a polite smile, as Tannick flew into their line of sight.

"ANI! You made it!" he bellowed, gesturing wildly with his arms and earning some amused looks from those around them. Kali laughed again and shook her head as he skidded to a halt in front of them and hugged his sister, who gave a startled cry in response before laughing, too.

"How are things at home? How's the stall? How was your trip?" Tannick barely drew breath. "Oh, we need to give you the tour!" he exclaimed excitedly.

"Tannick, let her breathe," Kali pulled him away, chuckling.

Anissa gave her a grateful look and smiled. "Okay, where to first?"

"I'll show you your tent allocation now," Tannick replied, grabbing his sister's bags, "and then we *have* to show you the lake!"

Tannick was already moving at speed past them as he spoke. Kali and Anissa giggled, and William stared after him in disbelief.

"He's like a one-man tornado," he said, stunned.

"Are you coming with us?" Kali asked him, trying to keep one eye on Tannick lest he be lost to the crowd.

"Nah," William shook his head, "I'm going to go find Amar—uh, Squadron Leader Beltura," he blushed, his eyes darting to Anissa who seemed entirely oblivious.

"Okay. Well tell *Squadron Leader Beltura* I said hi," Kali smirked, linking arms with Anissa and hurrying after Tannick.

The next couple of days passed in a haze of bliss for Kali. Their duties were suspended, and their days were filled instead with live music, games, eating, and drinking. Kali and Tannick introduced Anissa to Lenaria early on the first day and the two instantly hit it off; William and Amariel joined them later, both looking pleased with themselves and sitting very close to one another. Kali thought it looked like it physically pained them to not be touching and wondered how the same person that ran her into the ground each training session could also be wearing the goofy, love-drunk expression now painted on Amariel's face.

They spent their last night lazing down by the lake, a fire crackling loudly and sending little plumes of smoke into the air as they lay beside the water. Kali rested her head on Tannick's leg as she watched the sun set and turn the blue sky into a magnificent red before fading gradually to pink. A slight chill in the air brought them closer to the fire as the sky turned a purple-toned blue that gave way to night. They passed a bottle of Amariel's whisky round between them, pointing out shapes in the stars before the conversation suddenly turned competitive.

"You know, you guys think you're so tough," Anissa giggled, "but I bet Lenaria and I could beat you back to camp from here – training or no training."

"Ani, I've seen you run. It would be fairer if we were starting from the bottom of the lake," Tannick snickered. He dodged the twig Anissa aimed at him and laughed.

"I would be interested to see how you fare when you're so…chemically disadvantaged," Lenaria smiled, glancing at the near-empty bottle in Tannick's hand.

"Oh, fighting talk," he laughed. "Beltura's a Squadron Leader, you really think you're beating him?"

Amariel's eyes moved from William for the first time all night.

"What's this?" he asked.

"We're racing," Kali grinned, sitting up.

"Ha! Are you forgetting she can teleport?" William inclined his head in Kali's direction.

"We probably should head back though, it's later than I realised," Amariel said, his voice tinged with reluctance.

"Great! We can race back!" Anissa stood enthusiastically.

"Okay, well, you're not going anywhere alone!" Tannick said to his sister.

"Why don't we go in teams?" Kali suggested. "Lenaria and Anissa, Amariel and William, Me and Tannick?"

"This sounds exciting!" Lenaria replied, looking to Anissa who beamed at her.

"No powers, though!" Anissa insisted.

"Alright. And since we're being generous, we'll give you two a head-start," Tannick teased.

"Accepted! Let's go, Anissa!" shouted Lenaria, and the two of them ran giggling into the forest back towards the Living Quarters.

"I will bet you a year's supply of whisky they get lost within five minutes," Tannick laughed.

"Well," Kali stood up, "I bet *you* a year's supply of chocolate that *I* can beat all of you back to camp." She ran into the forest, laughing as she heard Tannick chasing after her.

Chapter Thirteen

Kali sprinted into the forest with the sound of Tannick's shouts behind her. He was catching up to her, laughing.

"If I catch you, you need to forfeit!" he shouted after her.

She stopped running and turned to face him. He wasn't far behind her; she stuck her tongue out at him.

"Fine, I'll be up there," she laughed, pointing to a tree near the top of a hill to their left. Just before he reached her, she teleported to the top of it.

A few minutes later, he entered her line of sight again; he was smiling as he used tree branches to pull himself up the hill. Kali smiled as she watched him. It had been a perfect two days, away from the world, away from training and fighting demons. Away from grief, violence, and worry. It was like she was living a life she knew in a dream once but had forgotten. She felt not just distracted, but like she was genuinely content in her own skin.

Tannick reached her, still smiling broadly, radiating excitement and hyperactive energy. She loved to see him like this, so different from seeing the nervous tension in his shoulders before a fight, accompanied by anxious checks of weapons and a desire to throw himself in head-first, just as long as he didn't need to *wait.*

He came to rest on the ground below her, watching her, appearing thoughtful.

"Okay, you won. I think you cheated though," he said finally.

She rolled her eyes at him, laughing, and climbed down from the tree. At the bottom, she turned and found herself almost face to face with him. She jumped slightly, then laughed again.

He didn't laugh with her; instead, he was looking at her with a kind of intensity she'd never seen him wear before. It threw her off balance.

And suddenly, his face was even closer, just inches from her own. She didn't know what was happening, and then his mouth was on hers. His lips touched hers softly at first, the kiss becoming more intense as he leaned into her, backing her up into the base of the tree.

Shock seemed to dictate all her thought processes, and all she seemed to be able to do was kiss him back, numb and detached, as her brain shouted at her that this was all wrong. She didn't think of Tannick this way. She didn't think of *anyone* this way.

The rustling of nearby foliage and laughing voices broke through to her, alerting her to the presence of other people, but Tannick seemed oblivious. His hands moved from her face to round behind her back, and he brought one up into her hair as the kiss grew more urgent. A branch snapped beside them, the sound of it seeming to waken him from a stupor, and he sprang away from her.

Amariel and William stood in front of them, looking awkward. Amariel seemed amused and embarrassed, like he'd been beaten to his favourite game, and William was turning a curious shade of scarlet.

"Hi! Uh you were-we were, so we thought we'd come find...you," William's voice was unusually loud. Beside him, Amariel was barely hiding a grin as he tugged on William's sleeve, bringing him past them towards the camp.

"We'll meet you back at camp?" he asked.

Kali nodded, flustered, and Amariel half-dragged her brother away.

Tannick looked like he'd been awoken from a spell. He grinned at her, looking almost groggy, and she smiled back, wondering if he could pick up on her awkwardness. She supposed that even if he did, he might assume it was due to the sudden arrival of her older brother. She resisted the urge to groan in embarrassment.

"We should probably get back to camp, it's getting late."

He nodded silently, looking pleased with himself.

She was relieved that he didn't try to kiss her again or initiate any contact between them on the walk back. She racked her brain to determine if she'd ever given him the wrong signals, if she'd ever accidentally led him on, but she couldn't think of where this was coming from. She'd known Tannick for a long time, sparred as children and fought as adults, and could never remember a time where there was ever anything romantic between them.

Especially not now, not since Kali found out the truth about herself. She spent so much energy trying to keep the darkness in check that she couldn't even imagine giving so much of herself to someone that way. Her focus over the past year had been training, finding herself again, forging new family, finding people she'd die for. Not this. She wanted to be whole again on her own, not give a part of herself to someone else.

Almost in spite of herself, she let her mind wander to what it would be like, to be that way with Tannick. She knew it could never work. For one, she didn't want Tannick to ever know the real her. She didn't want him to see her tainted blood, her deficiencies, to ever catch him looking at her like a ruined thing. To lose his friendship to that would be heart-breaking, and it wasn't worth the risk.

She saw Amariel's tent up ahead and made a beeline for it.

"I'm going to go check on the guys...maybe you could go find Ani and Lenaria?" she said to Tannick.

"Sure," he smiled at her, before walking away further into the camp.

She shook the entrance to Amariel's tent vigorously a couple of times to warn them of her presence before ducking inside.

"Kali! Hey!" William's smile was plastered unnaturally onto his face.

"Hi."

"So, I didn't know you and Tannick were, uh, a thing. Tea?" he asked too-brightly, gesturing to a teapot, steam rising from the spout. Amariel was watching him, shaking his head affectionately and smiling.

"We're not."

"Oh…okay then. Did you want tea?" The odd smile was still fixed on his face as he clumsily fetched a cup from one of Amariel's packs.

"No. Stop being weird."

"I'm not being weird."

"Shut up, yes you are, and I need help. I don't know what just happened back there."

Amariel and William looked at each other, and William shrugged and shook his head. Amariel turned to face her, choosing his words carefully.

"Well, Kali: when someone has romantic or sexual"—William visibly cringed—"feelings for another person, sometimes they—"

"No, not like *that!*" Kali interrupted, exasperated. She heard William mutter something that sounded suspiciously like *"thank God"* to Kali as Amariel too looked relieved. She gestured behind her wildly.

"Tannick! Tannick! It's Tannick!"

"Yes, we've been acquainted, thanks. Not quite on your level though, of course," smirked William, now clearly finding humour in the situation and her frustration.

She threw a pillow at him.

"This is *serious!* We fight together, we work together and train together – what am I going to do?"

"I assume you don't return Tannick's uh, *enthusiasm?"* Amariel asked, measuredly.

"No! I love him as a friend, but I don't have *feelings* for him. I don't even know where that came from! But I don't want to hurt him."

"Perhaps you should tell him you don't reciprocate his feelings, plain and simple, get it over and done with?" suggested Amariel.

"What if he wants an explanation or something? What do I say?"

"Keep it simple. Be honest."

"What am I meant to say, Am? Yeah, I'll just tell him 'Sorry I don't have feelings for you! But don't take it personally because actually, I'm secretly a half-demon that spends all my time making sure I don't end the world with my weird powers I can't control, and I might never feel that way about anybody! Oh also, my demon dictator mother wants to recruit me and if I start a relationship with you then she'll probably kill you anyway!' Sounds great! I'm sure he'll understand."

William snorted, and even Amariel chuckled lightly. But the expressions died quickly on their faces, turning from amusement to shock as they looked past her to the opening of the tent.

A horrible sense of dread seeped through her as she turned. In the opening of the tent stood Tannick, a dark look on his face.

Behind her, William half-rose from his chair but Tannick had already turned on his heel and marched from the tent.

"Shit," William muttered.

Kali raced out of the tent after Tannick. He was moving fast; it was as if the shock of her revelation had sobered him up. He was just a shadow in the darkness as she hurried to catch up to him.

She called his name as she drew closer, but he ignored her and walked faster, almost breaking into a run to escape her.

"Tannick! Tannick, please! Let me explain!"

He whirled round to face her. "Explain what, Kali? That you think I'm a joke? That you ran and told your *brother* about me, about us, and you all sat making up amusing ways to make fun of me?"

"Tannick, it's not like that!"

"Don't lie to me, Kali! I heard you!"

"What are you talking about?"

"I heard you! Making up ridiculous reasons to tell me you don't *like* me and laughing about them! Am I not even worth the truth to you?" he looked genuinely hurt.

"Tannick, I…"

"Forget it, Kali. Forget any of this even happened. I was foolish to think—just forget it. Leave me alone."

Initially relieved that Tannick didn't believe any of what he'd heard to be true, she almost sighed in relief. But as she saw the distress in Tannick's face, she faltered; she couldn't stand to see her friend in pain, least of all because of her. A voice in her head told her to leave it alone, that Tannick's wounded pride would heal, but she just couldn't bear to be the source of his hurt. Didn't want these perfect couple of days to end this way. The whisky from before and the kiss had her brain all confused, and he was already turning away from her. She took a deep breath.

"Tannick, I promise we weren't making fun of you! What I said, it was true. Liliana is alive, it was her that killed Mattias and my father. She's a demon. I'm…she was pregnant with me when she turned. I promise you that we don't think you're a joke. I don't think you're a joke. You're my best friend. Please believe me," she implored.

He stopped, standing dead still. Slowly, he turned to face her, a look of blank shock on his face.

"You…?"

"I'm not a demon. But I'm—I don't know what I am. I have more powers but they're…different."

"I—you're lying," he challenged, but he didn't sound sure.

Shaking, she bent down and placed a palm on the ground, feeling the grass tickling her arm as she did. She closed her eyes and imagined drawing energy from the life around her, replacing it instead with a darkness, a sickness. She heard Tannick cry out and opened her eyes. In a perfect circle around her, the grass was dead, and the earth blackened. She stood up, watching Tannick carefully.

"I've hated lying to you Tannick, but I only found out last year and I didn't know who to trust with it, who to burden with it. I'm so sorry, please forgive me. You're not a joke to me at all, you're my *best friend,*" she repeated.

Tannick didn't look at her, staring instead at the dead grass around her in shock. He looked faintly ill.

Finally, he looked up at her. She met his eye and saw nothing but disgust. It was like being physically struck.

"*Demon,*" he spat.

"Tannick, no, I—". Her head was spinning. This was all wrong.

"I have to tell Raikan. I have to tell the Council. This whole time you've been amongst us, a traitor. Are you a spy? Is William one too?"

"Tannick, listen to me—" she took a step forward, and he recoiled away from her.

"*Get back!*" he hissed at her so venomously she actually took a step backwards.

He looked at her with an unreserved revulsion that made her feel smaller than she'd ever felt.

"Stay away from me and stay away from my sister! Oh God…Ani! What have you done with her? Where is she?"

"Tannick, I haven't done anything to her. She's my *friend. You're* my friend," she replied in a small voice.

Tears welled in her eyes and silently spilled over, some dropping heavily onto the ground beneath her and some trickling slowly down her face. She couldn't believe this was happening. But then…what did she expect? What did she think the outcome of telling Tannick would be? This was exactly what she'd feared. Not everyone would react like level-headed Amariel, and Tannick was always the reactive type. More likely to leap with his heart than think with his head. She'd made a mistake in telling him the truth and now she couldn't take it back.

He was taking steps back now, backing up away from her as though afraid to take his eyes off her. Waiting for her to strike. She'd finally shown him her real self, and all he'd seen was a monster.

Behind her, William and Amariel arrived. William looked tense as he looked from Tannick to Kali and finally to the dead earth around her. Amariel was watching Tannick cautiously.

"Hey, guys…everything okay?" William asked with forced neutrality.

"You and your traitor bitch of a sister better stay away from me!" Tannick shouted at him.

William's lip curled in anger, but before he could reply, Tannick rounded on Amariel.

"And *you!* How could you? A Squadron Leader! We all look the other way with your relationship with a lower-ranking soldier out of respect for you and this whole time you were hiding a *demon!*" He filled the last word with so much hatred it made the breath hitch in Kali's throat. "You're a disgrace to the Guard and to the seraphs, you disgust me!"

William moved forward, standing in front of Kali so he was facing Tannick. The muscles in his arms jumped threateningly.

"You've insulted two people I love tonight; would you like to push me any further?" he snarled, flames springing to life in each palm.

Tannick eyed the flames warily, before narrowing his eyes at William.

"Let's see if you're this brave when the Council come for you," he threw them one more contemptuous look before turning on his heel and running away from them, down the hill in front of them and out of sight.

William swore and turned to her.

"William, I'm sorry, I thought if I told him the truth it would be okay," she cried.

He looked annoyed, but she must have looked pathetic enough because the annoyance dissolved almost immediately from his face.

He hugged her briefly, looking at Amariel over her head.

"We leave now," he said.

Amariel nodded, and Kali looked up, confused.

"Leave? What do you mean?"

"We prepared for this. Well rather, Dad prepared for this. I'll explain on the way. We have to go."

"We can't just *leave!*" she stared at him, incredulous. She looked to Amariel for support, but he looked away, somewhat apologetically.

"Kali, he just said he's getting the Council. He's probably telling Raikan as we speak!"

"But they won't believe him; it doesn't even sound real! We'll tell them he's making it up, or we played a joke on him!"

"Kali, look at the ground you're standing on."

She faltered slightly, looking at the sickened and dead ground around her.

"We can say you did it with your fire, or—"

"Kali, we cannot take that risk. Amariel and I are in on this now, too. They'll imprison us, or they'll test us to see if we're like you. And...I don't even know what they'd do to you."

"Experimentation, weaponisation, neutralisation, probably," Amariel offered, earning a stern look from William.

"Yes, *thank you,* Amariel. Look, we've already waited too long, we have to go!"

"Will—"

"I mean it, Kali!"

"No, *Will!* Someone's coming – listen!"

Kali could hear voices – female – and the sound of people running towards them from the same direction Tannick had run in.

Stricken, she grabbed William and Amariel, pulling them behind some nearby bushes. Recognition washed over her as Anissa and Lenaria came into view, shouting her name cautiously into the darkness.

"Kali! Kali? Kali are you okay?"

"*Kali!*"

Kali started forward, but William's hand on her upper arm kept her firmly in place.

"What are you doing?" he whispered.

"I want to see them; I want to explain…to say goodbye."

"Are you out of your mind?" he hissed back. "It's probably a trap!"

"I don't think they'd do that."

"Did you think Tannick would turn you over to the Council the second he found out?"

She looked back at Lenaria and Anissa, who were now moving past their hiding spot. Her instinct told her she could trust them; she took a leap of faith.

"Anissa! Lenaria!" she shouted. They turned, and an exasperated William released his grip to let her stand up.

"You will literally be the death of me, Kali Robereun," he muttered, looking around for signs of a trap.

The three of them emerged from their hiding place, and a frantic Anissa ran to them, followed closely by Lenaria.

"Kali!" Anissa hugged her. "What happened? We saw Tannick, he wasn't making any sense, he told me to stay away from you and that he's telling Raikan to have you arrested for being a traitor!"

"Kali, we don't have time for this, we have to go *now,*" William's voice was urgent as he began to pull her away.

"Go where?" Lenaria looked concerned. "Will someone tell us what is going on?"

"We don't have time to explain, but we need to go. Kali is in danger. We all are."

"Then we're coming too!" exclaimed Anissa. Lenaria nodded in agreement.

"No, you can't. This isn't a road trip, Anissa, this is serious," William said impatiently.

Anissa looked insulted. She opened her mouth to reply when a loud bang rang through the air, followed by an explosion of red in the sky.

"A security alert flare…" Lenaria looked at Kali slowly. "*What* is going on?"

But William was already pulling her away, trying to run towards the forest, and even as Kali looked on, a burst of green sparks lit up the sky accompanied by a second loud bang.

Lenaria and Anissa followed them.

"A medical alert," muttered Lenaria almost to herself, sounding utterly perplexed.

William turned to Kali and the others.

"Time's up. Kali, get us into the forest, past the wards. Take them if you need to, but we need to GO!" he shouted as the noise from the main camp began to build, shouts and the clanging of steel as they responded to the flares.

She nodded and turned to Anissa and Lenaria.

"If you come with us, you won't be safe. They'll hunt you; you need to stay here. I'm sorry, goodbye," the words tumbled from her mouth in a garbled rush.

She turned to leave but Lenaria stopped her, looking apprehensive but resolute.

"We are your friends, and whatever danger you are in, we want to help."

She looked helplessly at William. She couldn't drag them into this mess, not when they didn't know what they were signing up for.

"Make a decision and make it fast!" he commanded them, looking into the darkness for approaching soldiers.

She looked at Lenaria and Anissa, hesitant.

"Everyone, grab hold," she instructed, holding out her right arm. As soon as she was sure everyone was holding her, she willed them to move from the camp deep into the tree line, beyond the border.

They materialised into a clearing they'd scouted months before; she knew it was at least an hour's hike to here from the main camp. She'd bought them time, but not a lot of it.

Anissa looked unsteady on her feet as they arrived. She closed her eyes and sat down, placing her face in her hands, and Lenaria jumped into medic-mode at once, fussing over her.

"I'm fine," came Anissa's muffled voice, "just my first experience with teleporting."

"You get used to it," William said, sympathetically.

Lenaria helped Anissa stand, and they both turned to Kali.

"Will you tell us what's going on now?" Lenaria asked her.

She looked at William, but he simply threw his hands up – his meaning was clear: *do what you want.*

"Amariel, help me set up and check the perimeter. We're exposed out here and I don't want any surprises," he turned to his boyfriend.

Amariel nodded, springing to action. They left the clearing, leaving Kali alone with her friends.

She looked at them, wondering how to tell them everything. She thought of Tannick looking at her in disgust and words failed her. She couldn't tell them, she *couldn't*...but she had dragged them out here into the wilderness, at night, out past where the wards kept them safe. She owed them the truth.

She started at the beginning – her beginning, the day Mattias and her father died. The day she found out what she was. She told them about the fire, about her father finally telling her the truth, about what William told her, and how Liliana had arrived to take her with her before killing Malakai. She told them how they'd kept her secret this past year, working with Amariel at night to learn to control her powers so she never lost control again.

They listened, entirely silent and looking mildly horrified; Kali prepared herself for them to turn against her the way Tannick had. She was shaking by the time she was finished, waiting for them to see her for the monster she was. Recounting and reliving the past year made her tired in ways she couldn't explain. There was a heaviness in her and it weighed on her now, crushing and exhausting.

"If you want to leave now, I'll take you back. I'll understand if you want nothing to do with me…if you think I'm a monster," her voice cracked on the last word, and she cleared her throat impatiently.

She watched her friends, waiting for them to demand to be taken back to camp, to look at her with the same blatant revulsion and terror Tannick had. They simply sat silent for a moment, as though incapable of taking it all in.

It was Anissa, tears in her eyes, who spoke first.

"Oh Kali, I'm so sorry," she breathed. She looked at her uncertainly, inching closer to her as she spoke. "May I try something?"

Kali agreed, feeling apprehensive. Anissa approached her, raising her hand and placing it lightly on her forehead.

She spoke over her shoulder to Lenaria. "I told you about my power, but I didn't really explain it properly. I've been practising it, and I can *feel* people. Not just their emotions at the time but *them.* Who they are, what kind of person they are," she looked at Kali now, "I'll be able to tell if what Kali told us is the truth."

A fear like Kali had never experienced before lanced through her, and her breathing became faster. She couldn't let Anissa in like that. She couldn't let Anissa see the darkness. The darkness that even as a child she knew must never be shared with anyone, must be protected from Anissa at all costs.

Panic rolled off her in waves and she could tell that Anissa was feeling it. She took Kali's hand in her free hand and squeezed it reassuringly. Anissa looked her in the eye, holding her gaze and quietly searching her. She raised an eyebrow in a silent question: *are you ready?*

Kali exhaled a shaky breath and nodded, and Anissa closed her eyes in concentration.

A few seconds went by before Anissa's grip on her hand became vice-tight, and she opened her eyes, wide. She looked at Kali, and her face was a mask of grief and pain, and something Kali couldn't identify. She stood still for a few moments before throwing her arms around Kali and hugging her tightly. When she drew back, both of their eyes were wet. Anissa called over to Lenaria.

"She's telling the truth. I...I trust her," she gave Kali a watery smile.

Lenaria looked relieved and stood up to hug Kali at once.

Kali's heart sung. She was so sure they would reject her but Anissa, finally accessing the hidden parts of her, chose instead to stay with her. It was everything she'd never dared to hope for. An acceptance she never thought she could have.

"Thank you," she half-sobbed.

"We've got your back," Lenaria assured her.

"What do we do, though?" Anissa bit her lip. "They've taken Tannick's claims seriously enough to mount a security response against Kali."

"It is the green flare that concerns me," said Lenaria grimly. "I imagine the prevailing theory right now is that you have been infected like your mother was all those years ago. I remember the fear when it was reported the sickness was still out there, virulent, and capable of infecting and transforming one of our strongest. That kind of abject panic can have curious effects on even the most rational of people."

"What do you mean? Why would a medical flare be a bad thing? Isn't it just to make sure nobody is hurt?" asked Anissa.

"Truthfully, I fear the medical flare has more worrying connotations than the red. There is no cure to the corruption, and it carries with it the kind of terror you are too young to know of. It will be easy to dispel any idea of sickness with an examination, but the paranoia will not end there. Especially not now that you've fled; forgive me, but you now look very guilty, Kali."

"But I still don't understand why it's so bad! They'll check Kali doesn't have the sickness and then they'll assume Tannick made a mistake," Anissa's brow was furrowed in concern and confusion.

Kali looked at Lenaria, and there was sadness in her eyes. Kali knew exactly what waited for her underground in the Council's medical chambers, and it made her skin prickle uncomfortably.

"There are various tests they could run on Kali under the umbrella of "precautionary medical checks" to look for any signs of corruption. The first of course would be the standard examination. When they don't find any proof of corruption, they'll likely dig deeper," Lenaria cast a cautious look at Anissa before continuing.

"They'll perform tests of varying invasiveness to check the claims. Any irregularities in Kali's blood, physiology, anything – which I would expect them to find given what Kali has told us about her powers – it will only fuel their search. They might try and force a reaction, provoke her into using her other powers by using pain or fear as a stimulus to prove Tannick's claims. They won't care what they subject her to if they think she has any form of corruption. Anissa, there is a very real chance that if we returned now, we would be surrendering Kali for what would essentially be Council-sanctioned torture."

The word "torture" hung heinously in the air around them. Kali shivered as Anissa looked between them, aghast.

"The Council would never do that!"

"Ani, I'm one person. Do you think there's a limit on what they'd do to one person if they thought it meant saving everyone?"

Anissa stayed silent for a moment. Kali and Lenaria glanced at each other.

"Why would Tannick *do* this?" she finally exclaimed, kicking out at the ground and casting dirt into the air.

"He was scared," Kali replied, hugging herself as the scene replayed in her head. "Scared…and hurt. He, uh, he kissed me, and he caught me telling Amariel and William that I didn't like him back that way."

Anissa looked thunderous.

"He's done this because you hurt his *feelings?*" she half-shouted, dropping her voice to a whisper and looking around her when she remembered they were outside of the seraphs' protective wards. "I am going to kill him!"

"Yeah, well. No point dwelling on it now is there?" Kali sighed gloomily.

A noise from the trees behind her made them all start, and Kali instinctively drove Lenaria and Anissa behind her, placing herself between them and the source of the noise. Something was moving at speed towards them. Behind her, Anissa inhaled sharply. Kali drew her sword – thankful she stayed armed throughout the festival – and prepared to defend them from whatever creature burst through the trees at them.

William and Amariel sped into view, and Kali sensed instantly that something was wrong. Anissa and Lenaria sagged with relief, but the expressions on their face and the way they moved screamed urgency to Kali.

"What is it?" she asked.

"Demons," Amariel answered. "Maybe hundreds of them, heading towards the camp."

Chapter Fourteen

Kali swore.

"We need to go and warn them," she re-sheathed her sword and looked to her brother.

The expression on his face was pained. She knew that within him a conflict was raging; he couldn't bring Kali back to the camp, but he couldn't let the soldiers walk into an ambush either.

"Kali, we can't go back! They'll hurt you!" Anissa said, aghast.

"Ani, I'm still a soldier. I'm not leaving my friends and my people to be slaughtered. That includes your brother."

Amariel looked at her as though seeing her properly for the first time, and it made her feel quite exposed. She looked away from him quickly.

"Listen, it's not even a choice. We'll deal with whatever may come later. Right now, we have to warn them."

Amariel nodded in agreement, watching William. Eventually, William closed his eyes and nodded, too.

"Okay, let's go," she held her arm out, waiting for the group to grab hold.

"Hold on, shouldn't we get our stories straight first?" asked Lenaria.

"Our stories?" Amariel looked at her, puzzled.

"Well, if we return now, they will arrest Kali and potentially all of us on sight. They won't listen to anything we have to say. We need to place enough doubt that they're prepared to listen to us even until the morning."

"She's right," William frowned.

"Then we tell the truth – at least, half of it," Kali urged. "We say Tannick got too drunk, we played a prank on him that he didn't take well and then he kissed me and I rejected him. Frame it like he's hurt, angry, and confused. We can say we went out looking for him and that's why we've been away, and then we saw the demons. We pretend like we don't know anything is even happening. It won't buy us much time, but it will give us enough."

Everyone nodded.

"Don't get too specific. Be vague and generic if you can. Don't tie yourself up in details you won't remember when asked a second or third time," advised Amariel.

Kali couldn't help but notice that he spoke primarily to Anissa.

They all nodded, suddenly nervous. Kali held out her arm once more, and they each took hold of it.

"On three," she said, trying to avoid thinking about facing Tannick again and instead on General Raikan's tent as apprehension took root inside her. "One, two, three."

They arrived just outside Raikan's tent, which to their disappointment was empty.

"He'll be at Main Command by now," said Amariel.

"Yeah, he and half a dozen others prepared to arrest us on sight, no doubt," William replied.

"We have to go, demons move fast. They can't be that far away," Kali turned and ran towards the Main Command tent, the others following her lead.

William and Amariel kept pace easily, but she noticed Anissa was lagging behind, Lenaria somewhere in the middle, reluctant to leave her. As they approached the tent, they noticed more and more soldiers busying themselves, and once or twice she saw recognition on their faces as she sped past them. She thought she heard voices call out to them as they passed, but they pressed on.

They reached the Main Command tent, and Kali flew inside without hesitation. General Raikan was standing in the middle, a stony-faced Tannick beside him, and they were accompanied by four other soldiers, two of whom Kali recognised as Squadron Leaders.

All except Raikan appeared startled by her sudden interruption, and she took advantage of their surprise to speak first.

"General, Sir! We come with urgent news. We were out beyond the border and saw demons coming this way. We need to get ready to fight."

"She's lying!" protested Tannick immediately. "This is a distraction. She's one of them!"

Anissa made an angry sound at the back of her throat and Tannick looked at her as if only just noticing her. He looked stricken to see her with them.

William ignored him, addressing Raikan directly.

"It's true, Sir. Amariel and I saw them – there are tens, maybe hundreds of them heading in the direction of the camp."

Raikan surveyed them for a moment and then turned to Kali.

"You stand accused of being a traitor, Robereun. There are claims against you that you have been infected with corruption. How do we know this isn't simply a trick?"

"The timing is certainly peculiar," nodded one of the Squadron Leaders Kali recognised – Kali was sure her name was Eleya – as she looked over the group suspiciously.

Kali feigned surprise, arranging her face into what she hoped was a passable expression of shock.

"Sir, I don't know what Tannick told you or what it is you think I might be, and I will happily dispel any doubt afterwards, but I know what my brother and Amariel saw is the truth. We are in danger, we're all in danger. We need to get ready."

"The wards will protect us if what you're saying is true," one of the soldiers Kali didn't recognise replied, hanging over the word "if" and looking at her with a scowl.

"If she is corrupted then this could be a trap," said another, cautiously. "We should detain them and then verify these claims."

"There are simple tests that can be done to prove Kali isn't infected with corruption," Lenaria interrupted the wave of suspicion being cast their way. "I will happily administer them myself, but I suggest we protect ourselves first as a matter of urgency."

Silence momentarily fell amongst them as the soldiers looked between each other, struggling to decide what to believe.

"I'm not a demon," Kali addressed all of them but focused primarily on Tannick, who had the decency to look away. He looked somewhat ashamed now, shooting furtive glances at his sister and avoiding Kali's eye. "If I were a demon, I wouldn't have been able to come back through the wards into Camp."

"Why were you out beyond the wards in any case? Why did you leave, unauthorised?" asked Raikan.

A look of triumph momentarily flitted across Tannick's features. Kali tried to ignore it, but the anger she felt towards him gave her the conviction to tell her next lie.

"Honestly, Sir…we were looking for Tannick," she feigned embarrassment. "We all took the festivities a little too seriously tonight and we…well, we thought it would be funny to play a joke on him, and then he kissed me and I rejected him and he…he didn't take it very well, Sir. He ran off and we were worried about him." Kali tried to get the balance of sincerity and mock embarrassment in her tone just right, trying not to over-sell it.

A murmur ran through the group as they cast a now scarlet-faced Tannick dubious looks. He spluttered but seemed rendered speechless by rage or embarrassment – Kali couldn't tell which.

Raikan rounded on Tannick.

"Is this true?"

"No! Well—yes, but not—"

"Enough." Raikan's voice was dangerously quiet, and Tannick stopped talking at once.

"If you've lied to us all over a lover's quarrel then there will be serious consequences!" chimed one of the Squadron Leaders.

"But I have proof!" Tannick looked desperately between the Squadron Leaders.

"The girl is standing right in front of us, she doesn't look infected to me," countered one of the soldiers, impatience and doubt now replacing any of the earlier suspicions.

Tannick shrank back.

"We don't have time for this!" Kali cried. "The demons know that the camp is protected, but the wards are weakest out here. If they are heading here in numbers, then this must be a significant attack. We can't risk them breaking through!"

Everyone was silent. A nerve in Kali's leg twitched as she willed them to come to a decision.

"Surely it is best to err on the side of caution in a situation such as this, Sir?" urged Amariel.

Raikan considered for a moment and heaved a sigh.

"We've already mounted a security response," he looked contemptuously at Tannick. "We are as prepared as we could be for an attack. You two"— he gestured at William and Amariel— "debrief the Squadrons on what you saw. You"—he gestured to Kali— "with me."

Kali felt William tense beside her. "Sir, I—"

"I don't recall asking for your input, Robereun," Raikan retorted.

She turned to William. "It's fine. I'll meet you later," she forced a smile and turned back to Raikan, nodding at him.

"Whatever you need from me, Sir."

"You, you better stay too," he gestured to Lenaria.

Anissa hugged herself nervously, looking around them all. Kali gave her a small smile she hoped was reassuring.

"May I take my sister to safety, Sir? She is merely here for the festivities and shouldn't be caught up in this," Tannick looked at his sister, resolutely avoiding eye contact with Kali.

"Very well. The families have been evacuated back to their camp; you may join the soldiers there."

Tannick huffed a relieved sigh and rushed to Anissa's side. She scowled at him and moved out of his grasp when he tried to catch her arm, marching defiantly ahead of him instead, casting a hopeless look back at the group as she went.

"Sir, we should take our leave now too," Eleya said, as the other three nodded in agreement.

"Very well. Take Robereun and Beltura with you," he inclined his head towards William and Amariel.

William cast Kali a quick, apprehensive glance. *"I'll be fine,"* she mouthed at him. He grimaced, his face taut with strain, and followed the four soldiers and Amariel out of the tent.

Kali steeled herself and turned back to General Raikan. The fear of what might happen to her friends if she was discovered was roiling in her gut, fear for herself a secondary consideration.

Neither of them spoke, and Lenaria shifted her weight beside her in the uncomfortable silence.

It was Raikan that broke the silence.

"So, am I to believe that a prank gone wrong and some wounded pride is the source of Bratheas' claims that you are in fact, a demon?"

"Yes, Sir."

"Quite a reaction to a joke and a spurned kiss, wouldn't you think?" he considered her, an eyebrow raised.

"The alternative is that I'm a demon and as you can see, I'm not. Sir," she gestured to herself.

He looked at her, appraisingly.

"Kali, is there anything you want to tell me now when you still have the chance?"

Kali paused for a moment. The use of her first name threw her, and she wondered for a moment if she should just tell him the truth. If it would be better to come clean now and get ahead of it.

"No, Sir."

He sighed.

"Very well. I need to go give the task forces new orders. Half of the Guard is drunk, this couldn't have come at a worse time…" he trailed off, eyes narrowed in concentration. He looked at her for a moment, a sudden realisation on his face. "Your father: it was your mother that slew him, was it not?"

Kali winced.

"Yes, Sir," she stared at him, mouth open, as the same realisation hit her. "And she was in the Guard…"

"Then this wasn't random. Someone knew exactly how vulnerable we'd be tonight. And possibly that you and your brother are currently stationed here."

They regarded each other for a moment, a quiet understanding passing between them. The danger here was far beyond some demons looking for a fight. This *was* co-ordinated, and it was almost certainly co-ordinated by Liliana.

"You: check her for corruption," he barked at Lenaria suddenly. He turned to Kali. "If you're cleared, meet us at Weapons Distribution. If not…" he trailed off again, looking at her with a tinge of sadness. The sword hanging at his side glinted menacingly at her. He left without finishing his sentence, leaving Kali and Lenaria alone.

"We have to find the others and get out of here!" cried Lenaria at once, scrambling towards her.

"Shhh...I know, but we need to help here first."

Lenaria looked at her doubtfully, worry etching every line on her face.

"How long should this examination take, exactly?" Kali asked.

"About forty minutes?"

"We don't have that long!" she yelped.

"I don't think we have a choice, Kali."

"Fine...go through the motions, make it quick."

Lenaria flew through her exam in twenty minutes, by which time Kali was practically jumping out of her seat. When Lenaria gave her the all-clear, she was standing with her sword in hand before the medic was finished speaking.

"Okay, I'm going to find Raikan. You go to the families camp and find Anissa; you'll be safe there!"

Lenaria nodded and they hurried out of the tent. They had only gone a few yards when the hair on the back of Kali's neck began to stand on end. Something was now eerie about the camp, but Kali couldn't place what it was. She re-adjusted her grip on her sword instinctively as they continued forward.

"It's so quiet," breathed Lenaria.

And so it was. Kali realised this was the source of her unease. The camp was never this quiet, and right now it should be buzzing with activity.

"Lenaria, stay behind me and stay alert," she said in a low voice.

They crept towards the main camp, making their way to the weapons station, barely daring to breathe. For a few moments, they saw nothing, saw no-one.

Then, up ahead in the darkness, a dark shape was visible, huddled on the ground. Kali threw her hand up, silent, commanding Lenaria to stop. She looked around for any signs of movement, searching for danger, but the night was still.

Slowly, they moved towards the shape and found that it was one of the soldiers from Main Command, lying face down in the grass. Kali hurried over to him, gently turning him over. She fell back in horror as she looked at him. His face was ravaged, bloodied and unrecognisable, and someone – *something* – had all but torn him apart. Pieces of him had fallen away when she disturbed him, and Kali could barely look at him. Behind her, Lenaria gagged in terror, and Kali vainly searched for a whole piece of skin to look for a pulse.

When she found none, she gestured to Lenaria to continue onwards, wanting to put as much distance between them as possible, knowing they were likely getting closer to whatever killed him. She couldn't shake the feeling they were being watched.

As they made their way through the main camp, they found more bodies. This time, they didn't stop to check for survivors, checking instead to make sure none of the dead were their friends. Kali's heart thudded in her chest every time she turned one of them over, convinced she would see familiar eyes staring back, empty and unseeing. Blood smeared the canvas of the tents around them, and Kali suppressed a shiver.

Eventually, the crushing silence was permeated by the noise of shouting, growing louder as they drew nearer. Ahead of them, they saw heavily armed soldiers running to their left, towards the Family Camp. A chilling scream pierced the air. A howl of anguish and fear.

"Come on!" she called to Lenaria, as she ran after them, adrenaline beginning to surge through her.

They approached the camp and were met with chaos. Dozens of fires burned through the camp as people ran in all directions, trying to escape. The soldiers were no longer visible, obscured by smoke and enveloped by the crowd, but Kali could hear the clanging of steel and the tell-tale snarls of demons.

She turned to Lenaria.

"Lenaria, you need to stay right behind me. We help who we can, and we find Anissa and Tannick; are you ready?"

Lenaria nodded, looking queasy but resolute.

"Okay, let's go," Kali raised her sword out in front of them, trying to keep her friend shielded behind her.

They made their way through the smog, shadows distorted by the flames lurking menacingly around them. Even at the edge of the camp, the smoke was nearly overpowering. Each of them brought their shirts up over their mouth and nose, already coughing. Kali's eyes stung and watered, but she tried desperately to keep them open, looking for demons, or anyone who might need help. They came to a fork in the path and Kali decided to take the left, taking them further into the temporary camp.

"*Anissa?*" she whispered into the darkness, uncovering her face briefly.

Without warning, something barrelled into her, knocking her over. She rolled over with the force of it, losing grip on her sword as she did.

Lenaria screamed before Kali could focus on the shape looming over her. It snapped its head round in her direction in response and rounded on Lenaria with alarming speed. Lenaria began to panic, backing away in terror from the figure. Kali jumped up, grabbing her sword as she moved, and aimed a kick at the figure's back. It stumbled forward and turned, and Kali finally saw its face.

The demon standing before her was unlike those she'd seen before. Its features were monstrous, even by demonic standards, and it looked maddened with rage and bloodlust. It snapped at her with sharp teeth and lunged forward, forcing Kali to dodge out of the way.

As she spun back around to face it, it charged at her again – but this time she was ready. She held her sword back, waiting until it was within reach. Using all her force, she swung the sword round and in one fluid swipe, cut the creature in half.

Lenaria whimpered in relief, but Kali gestured for her to stay back as she drove her sword through its skull.

The sounds of hideous screeching punctured the night around them and screams of pain followed. Whatever was happening, they were approaching the centre of it.

"Let's go," she whispered to Lenaria, who walked past the demon without looking at it, as if scared her gaze would wake it from death.

The smoke was thickest here, and it was becoming too difficult to continue. Lenaria coughed painfully, and Kali too was finding it hard to breathe. She was considering turning back when up ahead, they saw something moving in the shadows. Kali held her sword up, walking slowly and deliberately, ears pricked for any sudden movement.

She heard the whimpering first, the sounds of sniffling and coughing, and she quickened her pace. She could see the silhouette in front of them was small, about waist height, and it was crying.

"Hello?" she called, making Lenaria jump.

"H-hello?" the figure coughed back in a child's voice.

Kali sheathed her sword and raced forward, hoping this wasn't a trap. In front of her stood a little boy, rubbing his eyes with the back of his arm, covered in ash. Tears carved a path down his soot-stained face, and he looked terrified. When he saw Kali, he flinched back from her before seeing her clearly through the smoke. Recognition flickered over his face as he took in her clothes, the black and purple uniform of the Guard, and he hurried to meet her.

The screaming around them was growing louder, closer, and Kali knew they had to get the little boy out of here. But she couldn't stop searching for Anissa. Time was running out.

She picked the boy up and turned, walking hurriedly back in the direction they'd just come from. Away from the screaming and away from the thickest smoke, Lenaria following closely behind her.

"Where is your family?" she asked the child, keeping her eyes and ears open for any indicator of an oncoming attack.

"I lost them," he said tearfully. "Everyone was running, and I got lost and then the smoke made it hard to see."

"It's okay, you're safe now," she soothed, but her mind was still on Anissa.

They hurried along the path and stopped just before where the demon had attacked them before.

Kali turned to Lenaria.

"You have to get him out of here."

Lenaria paled. "I don't think we should split up," her eyes darted around them as though expecting demons to leap out at them from the dark.

"We don't have time to go back and then return for Anissa and Tannick. Besides, it's safest for you to go back with him."

Kali shifted the boy's weight, revealing the sheath for her daggers.

"Take him, run as fast as you can and don't stop until you find safety – try and find Will. Take one of my daggers; do not engage in any hand-to-hand fighting unless you have no other option. Aim for the eyes, the throat, and the head. Kick at pressure points, the knees, and do not let anything get you on your back. Do you understand?"

She tried to keep her voice as quiet and as calm as possible so as not to scare the little boy.

Lenaria's eyes were wide as she nodded and withdrew one of Kali's daggers. She placed it carefully in one hand, blade facing away from her, and then motioned to Kali to give her the child. Kali handed him over, hoping she was doing the right thing. Every second that went by, the smoke was getting thicker, and the only thing more alarming to Kali than the screaming around them was the sudden silence falling in its place.

"I'll see you soon," she promised Lenaria.

Lenaria took a deep breath that hitched in her throat and nodded. Then she turned, and Kali watched her run back the way they'd come before for a second before pressing on into the centre of the camp.

Without Lenaria with her and with time escaping her, Kali abandoned all caution. She sprinted through the haze, occasionally pausing to check fallen bodies on the ground, checking for survivors and hoping, guiltily, that none of the faces would belong to Anissa or Tannick. She ran for a few minutes, never encountering a living soul, eyes streaming and throat burning as she listened intently for the sounds of fighting or any sound that might indicate life.

Eventually, she heard shouting up ahead to her right, and she raced down the path towards it. She came to an abrupt halt as the path gave way to a clearing between the many tents which housed a scene of total carnage. Bodies lay strewn amongst those still fighting, both soldiers and civilians, and Kali tried not to look at their faces, some of them heartbreakingly young. Her heart leapt as she saw Tannick battling demons with a handful of other soldiers, then sank again when she couldn't find Anissa.

"Anissa!" she called out, earning a few hungry glances from nearby demons as they abandoned their task of mutilating the dying and turned towards her instead.

She didn't have time for this, she thought impatiently: she had to find Anissa and get back to William and Amariel. She thought of Lenaria and hoped she had successfully made it out of the camp. She wasn't sure what she would find once she did would be any better than here, though.

Frustrated, Kali teleported amongst the demons, wounding and beheading them before they realised she'd moved. Her presence seemed to have emboldened the tired soldiers, and they beat the demons back with renewed vigour. She cut her way through the demons until she was beside Tannick.

He raised his sword reflexively at the sight of her and she caught his eye, wondering if he was about to attack her, but after a moment's deliberation, he nodded curtly at her and threw himself once more towards the demons. She followed his lead. Despite the tragedy around them, fighting side-by-side with Tannick like this almost felt like the way things were before, but she couldn't suppress her growing panic for Anissa.

Eventually, the demons – at least those in their immediate vicinity – were all dead. She spun to Tannick, who looked briefly alarmed at her intensity before it turned to shame.

"Look, Kali—"

"We don't have time for this!" she snapped. "Where is Anissa?"

"I sent her away with a group of survivors about five minutes ago, I figured she would be safer away from here. I told her to head to the Main Camp and find some soldiers."

Kali's face must have betrayed her fear because Tannick was on her at once.

"What? What's wrong?"

Kali shook her head, trying to drive the images of the dead she'd seen along the way from her mind.

"I've just come through there, it's not safe. We have to find her," the urgency in Kali's voice made Tannick's face lose all colour as he realised that he'd made a mistake sending his sister out into the camp alone.

They sprinted in the direction Tannick saw Anissa last, both with their weapons drawn. Their feet thudded loudly as they ran, kicking up ash and dirt behind them. The effect of the clouds of ash and oppressive walls of smoke was claustrophobic. They called Anissa's name as they ran, hoping to hear her call back and that the sound of their voices would draw any demonic attention to them instead of those remaining in the camp.

Tannick tripped over a body on the ground, and Kali caught him, helping him regain his balance. He nodded in thanks, then turned his gaze to it – a young woman, her hair long and dark, lying unmoving face down in a pool of blood. They exchanged glances, unspeaking, but their fear was plain on their faces. Tannick reached out with a trembling hand and painfully slowly, turned the woman round. A mix of sadness and relief washed over Kali – it was not Anissa. But this woman had been someone, before tonight. Someone who laughed, who smiled and loved; now she lay with her throat torn out, a casualty of a battle she should never have been part of.

"May the Elders receive your spirit," she whispered to the woman, briefly closing her eyes. They turned away from her, continuing their search for Anissa, their calls becoming increasingly desperate.

A cry of pain followed by screams came from their left, and they changed course, racing towards the sound. They flew down paths created by the tents left behind by the dead and fleeing families until they came across a group of around twenty, a demon bearing down on them as they backed up, unarmed and terrified. At the centre of them stood Anissa. Relief flooded Kali, and she turned to Tannick. He was staring at his sister with unbridled joy and relief. He sprinted towards her, never taking his eyes off the group.

"*Anissa!*" he called, causing her to spin round. Her face changed from joy to fear as she saw what Tannick couldn't and Kali watched in horror as a demon, hidden by the smoke and shadows around them, lunged at Tannick from the left, swinging a sword in the direction of his neck. Kali knew there was no way he could dodge it now, as he saw the movement and began to turn to look, only just registering the danger.

She moved instinctively, teleporting between the two of them. She landed facing away from Tannick, using all her force to push him back whilst trying to dodge the sword. She didn't quite manage to avoid the arc of it as it swung round, the top of it cutting a gash in the side of her face. Hot blood ran down her cheek as she snarled at the demon, and Tannick whirled round to face it.

"Go! Help the others!" she instructed, her eyes never leaving the demon as it leered at her. She felt Tannick hesitate before running towards the group, sword raised.

The demon raised its sword tauntingly, and Kali saw that the tip was stained red with a light coating of her blood.

"You're going to regret that," she snarled, rage building inside of her.

She thought of the children lying lifeless in the clearing where she found Tannick, their tiny arms still reaching out towards their slain guardians. She thought of the woman they feared was Anissa, lying alone in the dirt. She thought of the countless others they'd passed on the way. A cry of anger escaped her, low in her throat as she felt the urge to kill take over. She couldn't bring the dead back to life, but she could avenge them; this is what she was trained to do. What she was born to do.

She used her powers, focussing them on the demon. Its arms snapped up out of its control, bending back painfully as her lip curled in rage. Next, its legs snapped sideways, hit by an unseen force, and then its head was forced backwards. It stood immobile, howling in fury at her. She approached it, never looking away from its monstrous face. She looked at its cruel features, seeing the faintest flicker of fear in its eyes, and she relished it. She stopped when she was face to face with the demon; it snapped its sharp teeth at her, unable to move and reach her.

"This? This is what I'm going to do to each and every one of you," she hissed, grabbing it by the throat and turning its head to look her in the eyes with one hand, and drawing her sword down its torso with the other. It roared in pain, and Kali cut its cry short by spinning and carving her sword in a circle around her, decapitating it in one motion.

She let the body fall, both it and the demon's head hitting the ground with a dull thump. She turned, breathing heavily, and looked to the group. They were out of immediate danger; Anissa tended to the wounded, hurrying around them all and comforting the shaken as she went. Tannick was perfectly still, watching her. She couldn't tell what he was thinking, but she realised she no longer cared. Tannick's mind was made up, and changing it wasn't on her current list of priorities.

She jogged over to the group, and Tannick's sword hand twitched as she reached them. She raised her eyebrows at him, and his face flushed. He looked at her cheek, where blood still flowed from the cut sustained protecting him, and he looked grateful.

"Kali, I—thank you," he said sincerely.

"Don't mention it."

Anissa turned at the sound of her voice and ran to her, throwing her arms around her. Kali only just had enough time to point her sword away from her friend to avoid running her through with it.

"Ani, be careful!" Tannick admonished.

Anissa rounded on him. "*You* can keep your mouth shut! I don't care if you think Kali is dangerous, she's my friend and she just saved your *life!*"

Tannick opened his mouth as though to speak and then closed it again a moment later, looking conflicted. Kali watched them, vaguely amused.

"Uh, Ani? I think he meant because of this," she held her sword up and waved it in front of Anissa's face.

"Oh."

"Look, we can do all the family drama we want later. We have to get back to Main Camp and find Raikan and my brother," she moved past the group towards Main Camp.

"Can they travel?" she heard Tannick ask Anissa.

"I think so," came Anissa's uncertain reply.

Kali's senses were urging her forward. It was like she was moving on autopilot, having to fight against her muscles to wait on the group. All she wanted now was to find her brother and Amariel. She hoped desperately that Lenaria and the little boy made it to safety, if anywhere here was safe now.

"Guys, we need to move!" she called impatiently over her shoulder.

Kali's muscles twitched as she waited for them. She paced back and forth, unable to stand still. Tannick came to stand beside her.

"What's wrong?" he asked.

"Besides the obvious?" she laughed humourlessly.

"There's something else bothering you."

"Tannick...the demons we saw in the forest were still at *least* forty minutes away. They should only just be getting here. That means there are still more to come, like this was all some kind of distraction or something. It's too well planned, and I think...I think this is going to be a massacre. I don't know what we're about to walk into."

Tannick looked troubled, but their conversation was cut short by the arrival of the survivors behind them, and Kali turned to him.

"I'll go first, you flank. Make sure any stragglers keep up," she instructed. He obeyed despite his seniority to her and moved to stand near Anissa.

"Stay sharp, stay fast, and stay quiet," she commanded the group.

She led them down path after path back towards the main camp, despatching any demons they came across as quickly and quietly as she could. After about ten minutes, the path they were on finally spat them out into the Main Camp, and they stopped.

The scene around them was pandemonium, a new wave of demons just beginning to pour from the trees as Kali predicted, soldiers everywhere trying to stem the flow and push them back.

She turned bleakly to the group.

"Those of you able to fight, find a weapon. Find shelter. Stay together. Do not engage the demons unless it is your only option. If you can run, get as far away from here as possible. Find a portal. Send for help if you can."

They looked at her in disbelief.

"You're the Guard! You're supposed to help us!"

She gestured around her. "Look around you! Our hands are a little full right now!" she barked at the man who had spoken.

Tannick ran a hand through his hair, taking in the mayhem in front of them. They looked at each other, the question of what to do with Anissa unspoken between them.

"Anissa, you should go with them," Tannick said begrudgingly.

"Like Hell I am! I split up from you already and it didn't work out so well!"

"She has a point," Kali looked at Tannick as he opened his mouth to argue. "Decide what you're doing and find me, I'm going to find William."

"We're coming!" Anissa followed at once, reluctant to be left behind. Tannick moved closely behind her.

"Okay, let's go."

They hurled themselves into the chaos, having no choice but to leave the survivors behind, their joint focus on keeping Anissa safe and finding their friends. All around them, the demons kept coming. The soldiers were struggling to contain them.

They ran towards the weapons tent, where Raikan told Kali to meet him, killing demons as they went.

The weapons tent was a hundred meters in front of them when they saw the flames.

"The demons have set fires here too, then," Tannick's shoulders slumped as he took in the scene before them.

Kali was about to turn around and head to Main Command when she heard her name.

"Robereun, here!" boomed Raikan's voice.

She looked in the direction of his voice and was thankful to see William and Amariel fighting beside him. Behind them, a shaken Lenaria treated wounded soldiers. The little boy was nowhere to be seen and Kali hoped with all her heart he was safe, away from here.

"Will!" she ran to her brother, smiling despite the devastation around them.

"Are you okay? You're hurt!" he fussed over her, trying to examine her blood-stained face.

"It's fine, it's shallow."

"What if it's poisoned?"

"I'd know by now," she shrugged out of his grasp, trying not to think of how quickly the poison affected their brother when the demon struck him down almost a year ago.

"Robereun, what's the status at the Family Camp? The medic tells us it was over-run, how badly?" Raikan demanded.

She looked up at him, wishing she was delivering better news.

"Limited survivors, Sir. We got twenty or so out, but I don't know about anyone else. There were a lot of bodies, Sir – it doesn't look good."

Raikan swore.

"What about here?" she spoke to William and Amariel.

"They just keep coming. I've never seen anything like it. The wards aren't having any effect," Amariel panted from the effort of keeping the demons away from the wounded. "They appear to have strange sigils carved into their skin," he added, sounding appalled.

"Liliana knew the families would be here and that the demons could penetrate the wards. We've been sitting ducks this whole time," Kali met her brother's eye, dumbfounded.

She turned to Raikan. "What do we do, Sir?"

"You do what you're expected to do, wards or not. You kill the demons, or you die trying."

"Yes, Sir."

"All of you, go. We need to move the survivors away from here, they're too exposed. Try to drive the demons back into the treeline and we'll move behind you!" he commanded to the soldiers around him.

Anissa now stood with Lenaria as the medical team prepared to move the wounded. The soldiers in the area moved into place around them.

She looked at William and Amariel, then to Tannick. There was a strange burn of excitement building in her. She enjoyed the fight. It was the waiting around that shredded her nerves, something she and Tannick shared. She caught his eye and grinned, in spite of the situation.

"If we're going to die, let's at least try to look really cool doing it," she shrugged to the group, twirling the sword round in her hands, trying to sound more confident than she felt.

Tannick laughed and shook his head, as the others prepared to fight.

"Forward on my count!" barked Raikan. "Three, two, *move!*"

They flung themselves forward on his mark and came up against a wall of demons, fighting their way through them only to find more behind them. Around Kali, soldiers fell with shouts of pain to frenzied attacks by demons, but still they pushed on. Their progress was slow, but eventually, painstakingly, they cut their way through the demons and made it to the treeline.

She turned just in time to catch a demon lunging at her from the side, ducking low and throwing it over her shoulder. Tannick killed it before it even hit the ground.

"Now we're even," he smiled cautiously.

"Not even close," she shot back, but she was smiling too.

She heard William give a shout and turned in response to see him on the ground, a demon on top of him. He held it back with both hands, but it seemed impervious to the flames he was casting against its skin. William struggled against its weight, his power seemingly useless; Amariel was locked in battle with two demons, unable to help.

Kali ran to them, jumping on the demon's back with force and grabbing it by the neck, rolling away from her brother and dragging it with her. She landed on her back with the demon on top of her. It rammed an elbow hard into her ribs, winding her; she coughed but felt the demon's weight lessen on her as William's face came into view. He slit the demon's throat so brutally that he severed its neck, hot, black blood hitting Kali in the face and drenching her chest.

William dragged the demon's corpse and threw it bodily off of her, helping her stand.

"That…was…disgusting," she rasped, wiping the demon blood from her face with the back of her arm.

"You good?" William asked sharply, and she nodded.

They sprang back into the main fight. It seemed to rage forever, the ground becoming almost impassable as the bodies of demons and soldiers began to accumulate.

Around her, the soldiers still fighting were bloodied and bruised. She saw Amariel catch a slash from a demon's sword before he knocked it down and crushed its skull underfoot. Beside her, William received a nasty blow to the head from a demon, and Tannick – whose nose was streaming blood from an earlier altercation – helped him unsteadily to his feet as Kali destroyed it. All around them, the demons were closing in, impossible numbers of them coming in wave after wave from beyond the trees. They were outnumbered.

A ripple of hesitation ran through the soldiers and the demons, sensing weakness, pounced on them. Soldiers fell all around Kali as she tried to fight through and get to Anissa and Lenaria, who were now largely unprotected.

Raikan's voice thundered over the din of the fighting, filled with sadness and regret, giving the order to retreat.

"The Camp is lost. Retreat! Your orders are to get survivors to safety. Retreat! Find a portal! Retreat!"

Calls of "*retreat!*" ran through the line of fighting soldiers, but Kali realised it was too late. They were all but surrounded. There was nowhere to retreat to.

Some soldiers stayed to fight, but most of them turned back, running in earnest away from the onslaught. If it was chaos before, then this was Hell. Demons struck down as many fleeing soldiers as escaped the horde, the ones still fighting eventually succumbing to the numbers.

Desperate, Kali did something she'd never tried before. Something reckless.

She closed her eyes, drawing on all her power and feeling it course through her like Amariel showed her once before. She pushed even further, feeling it build until it was almost unbearable, burning through her and desperate to escape. She heard someone shout her name, and when she opened her eyes, the veins visible at the surface of her skin were dark and bulging.

She imagined striking down every demon near her as she let go of the energy building inside of her. She watched as one by one the demons around her clutched at their insides, blood spurting from every orifice as they fell. She felt the steady drip-drip-drip of blood from her nose hitting her lip as dizziness took over her and she fell to her knees, closing her eyes again to stop the world from spinning.

But despite the dizziness, something else rose above the physical sensation of it; a delicious and dark sense of power as she willed the demons dead one-by-one. It spread roots inside her, and she didn't want to let go of it, the exhilarating sense of falling into freedom. Every life snuffed out only added to it: excitement and a sense of peace all at once that called to her on a level she'd never experienced before. She wanted to dive deeper, the feeling was so inviting – no more uncertainty, no pain, no fear, just a feeling of being absolutely and terribly complete. It wrapped itself around her core, whispering to her to keep going, to go even further, and she silently agreed, wanting it to take hold of her and burn out everything else. There lay a thrill in this darkness, and she wanted to explore it.

But something was interrupting her now. How inconvenient, she thought as she tried to push it to one side, only to find it increasing in its insistence. Something was forcing its way through to her, a sound. A voice. Her brother's voice, calling her name. She tried to resist it, but there was a familiarity to it, like trying to remember the details of a particularly comforting forgotten dream.

It broke through to her and brought with it reality – the noise of the battle, the smell of burning and blood – and Kali felt like she was surfacing from icy water. She gasped for air, opening her eyes and seeing William's anxious face in front of her. Her upper lip was uncomfortably wet and when she wiped it with the back of her hand, it came away with slick with blood. Her vision was hazy and when she wiped her eyes, her hand came away bloodied again. William was paler than she'd ever seen him as he stared at her, speechless.

There was a deathly silence all around her, and she realised that everyone who'd remained behind to fight was staring at her. Dead demons littered the ground, one or two still making an awful gurgling sound where they lay. She was still on her knees, and she staggered when she tried to stand.

A strong hand – Amariel's hand – caught her and kept her upright as William too stood up, still staring at her.

Whispers hissed at her from every direction as the remaining soldiers watched her, unmoving.

She turned, seeing Tannick, Lenaria and Anissa watching her, awestruck and uncertain. Behind them, Raikan looked on, a terrible expression on his face.

"William, we have to go," she said in a low voice, never taking her eyes off Raikan, realisation setting in.

"Agreed. There's a place we can go, I was trying to tell you earlier. An old safehouse the Guard took off their books years ago – Dad and Matt converted it just in case…"

Just in case this happened, she thought.

"Give me the coordinates, I'll get us there," she gestured to her brother, watching Raikan finally begin to make his way towards her.

"Are you sure you're up to it?" William looked her up and down doubtfully.

"We don't have a choice!"

"Fine, here," he handed her a piece of paper with random numbers and letters scrawled in it in familiar handwriting, accompanied with a small description of the house.

She memorised it and burned it in her palm, noticing that the calm sense of power was yet to leave her entirely. She momentarily imagined the small flame becoming a blaze that razed what remained of the camp, destroying everything in her path and letting her rebuild as she envisioned, and forced the thought from her mind.

They all made the same fatal flaw in the wake of Kali's outburst.

Not a single person looked beyond the trees, every eye either on Kali or Raikan as the pair faced off against each other, each unsure of the other. Nobody saw the next wave of demons flowing towards them until it was too late. The screams of those closest to them as they were slaughtered sounded the alarm, and it was like time was instantly reversed, like Kali's massacre never happened, and once again they found themselves outnumbered and surrounded.

Kali looked on helpless as soldier after soldier fell to the demons, everyone running now, their former conviction long abandoned.

"Kali, we have to go!" cried William.

"But—"

"We can't help here, it's over, we lost! We need to go!"

She looked at Raikan, who was the only one who looked determined to get through the demons. He was hacking a path towards her, every blow a promise that he would get her, no matter what it took.

"Fine!" she reached for him, and then for the others, but Tannick held back.

"Tannick, please."

Anissa turned at the sound of Kali's voice, only now noticing her brother wasn't with them.

"Tannick! Come on!" she urged.

He looked at them sadly.

"I can't…I just—I'm not coming," he said firmly. "Take care of her," he spoke directly to Kali now.

"No! Kali, tell him," Anissa cried.

But Kali could tell there was no changing his mind. "Look after yourself, Tannick," was all she said, trying to swallow the lump in her throat that burned at the thought of leaving him behind.

"Kali, *now!*" shouted William as demons began to encircle them.

She grabbed hold of Anissa, who was holding onto Lenaria; Amariel held onto William. She thought of the coordinates on the piece of paper William gave her earlier and left the slaughter behind them.

Chapter Fifteen

They arrived outside of a large wooden house, hidden from the town that lay just beyond them by a copse of trees. A large fence ran along the perimeter, and seraphic runes were painted on almost every surface – anti-intruder wards, anti-demon wards, protective wards. Her heart leapt as she recognised her father and Mattias' handwriting amongst some of them.

She was swaying on her feet, and a headache was beginning to throb along her temples. She looked around the group; William and Amariel appeared as bloodied and bruised as she was, and whilst William, Amariel, and Lenaria observed the house appreciatively, Anissa was quietly sobbing.

"Anissa, are you alright?" Amariel sheathed his sword and reached out to her.

"We have to go back! We have to save Tannick!" she cried, her sobs growing louder. "Please, Kali, you can go and bring him back," she seized Kali's wrists, her nails digging into her skin painfully, her eyes wide and pleading.

Kali took a small step backwards but didn't try to break free of her grasp, tears pricking at the back of her eyes.

"Anissa, look at her! We all need rest, going back now would be suicide! I'm sorry, but Tannick made his choice," William's unsympathetic tone seemed to make Anissa cry harder.

"How can you *say* that?" she sobbed.

"Tannick's a grown man; he was in charge of his own choices when he betrayed us, and he was in charge of them when he chose to stay behind. We could never trust him out here with us!"

Anissa shrank back, the truth in his words sinking in as she released Kali and covered her face with her hands.

Lenaria cast William a sharp look. "Come on, Ani. Let's get you inside. It's okay, it will be okay."

William shrugged unapologetically and tossed Lenaria the key to the house, sighing tiredly. Kali watched them go, a dull ache in her chest.

"We abandoned our post," she said forlornly.

William and Amariel looked at her, looking as equally dejected.

"The orders were to retreat, Kal. The Camp was already lost, we did everything we could."

"Yeah, I know. It still doesn't make me feel better about it," she sighed.

"What concerns me is the nature of those demons. How did they get past the wards and how could they resist William's power?" Amariel wondered aloud.

"Liliana," Kali and William said in unison.

The thought of Liliana experimenting on demons and weaponising them even further chilled Kali, and she shivered. She wondered if the same fate awaited her if Liliana ever got her hands on her.

"She must have been planning this for months," William stared blankly at the ground in front of him, sounding horrified.

The thought disturbed them, and they looked around them nervously.

"Are we safe here?" Kali asked William after a moment's silence. She longed to find somewhere to sleep, tiredness bearing down on her relentlessly.

"It's an old Guard safehouse, modified by Dad and Matt. I'd wager it's one of the safest places on the planet. I never really knew what to expect, he just told me it was a last resort. A "use in case of emergencies" type thing. Looks decent enough, though. I was imagining a squalid little cabin or something."

"Where are we? Won't the Guard or the Council find us?" Amariel queried.

"I'm not totally sure, I just know we're somewhere in the human plane," answered William. "The Guard have hundreds of these abandoned outposts that aren't even on record anymore, plus we have the anti-intruder wards, my father made sure we were protected."

"Even still, we should promote caution."

Kali was barely listening, but an uneasy thought came to her.

"If Dad knew about this place, did Liliana?"

"I don't think he'd have taken that risk but…it's possible. But we have the anti-demon wards up too."

"So did Alarium," Kali replied bluntly.

An uncomfortable silence hung over them, before Amariel spoke.

"We'll just need to be vigilant. For now, it is imperative that we rest," he took William's arm gently and led him towards the house.

Kali stumbled on the steps leading to the front door and practically fell through the threshold, hardly able to lift her feet off the floor. Lenaria had left the key in the lock, and William locked the door behind them. Too tired to speak, they grunted "good night" at each other and went their separate ways.

William and Amariel took a bedroom towards the front of the house, but Kali wandered deeper inside, putting distance between her and the front door. She came across a set of stairs leading down and made a note to investigate later.

She passed a closed door, hearing muffled voices on the other side of it, just audible; she considered knocking but hesitated and decided against it. She felt like she would be the last person Anissa would want to see right now.

She moved on down the hall, finding a spacious room with a comfortable looking bed. It was dark, but familiarity tugged at the corner of her mind as she sank onto the bottom of the bed, falling into a deep sleep almost immediately.

* * * *

Kali awoke abruptly the next morning, momentarily unsure of where she was before she remembered the previous day. She ran her hands through her hair, groaning at the ache in her muscles, and stood up. She took in her surroundings and was hit with instant realisation as she understood now where the sense of familiarity the night before was coming from.

The room she was in was an almost exact replica of her bedroom when she was twelve years old. She thought of her father meticulously recreating her room out here with Mattias all those years ago and smiled. It was unbearable how much she missed them sometimes. She knew Will felt it too – a memory unexpectedly hitting him in response to a sound or smell. She wandered around the room, taking in each detail, wishing they were still here.

There was a knock on the door. She opened it to find Lenaria, already showered and dressed.

"Good morning. I like your choice of room, it's very…purple."

"Thanks, Lenaria. Is everything okay?"

"Yes. We're going into town for supplies and wondered if you had a preference for breakfast."

"You're going into town?" Kali asked, shocked. "Is that safe?"

"There is no food in the house, it is a necessary risk. Amariel is joining Anissa and I, I assure you we will be safe."

"Okay, if you're sure…do you want me to come with you?"

Lenaria considered her, her eyes travelling the length of her body.

"I think your current appearance may cause the humans alarm. We can manage ourselves," she smiled reassuringly.

"Uh, okay…pancakes, then," Kali's stomach growled on cue as she realised how hungry she was.

"Pancakes, great," Lenaria repeated. "Also, I'd like to do a quick exam on you all later to make sure you're not injured too seriously from the fight."

Kali shook her head and laughed. "Lenaria, I'm fine."

"Well, just to be safe. After breakfast."

"Okay, whatever you say."

Lenaria returned down the hall and Kali closed the door behind her, eager to continue examining her new bedroom. She was pleased to discover that it had a private bathroom attached, complete with a shower and bath. Feeling distinctly grimy between the layers of dirt and blood, she decided to go try out the shower as a matter of priority.

She walked into the bathroom, stopping short when she caught sight of herself in the mirror. No wonder Lenaria had commented on her appearance, she realised; most of her face and chest was covered in dried blood, both the brown-red of her own and the inky-black blood of demons. The whites of her eyes were interrupted by angry red specks of burst blood vessels and the cut along the side of her face stood out angrily, now healed over but inflamed and red.

"Jesus, I look like a nightmare," she muttered to herself.

She searched around for towels, finding them in the wardrobe nearest the bathroom, and padded back across the cold tiles.

She peeled off her clothes and started the shower, waiting until the water was warm enough before getting under it. The hot water felt incredible, and she scrubbed her skin, revitalised by the hot, soapy water as it cleansed her, the water turning from red to pink before finally running clear.

She hopped out, wrapping herself up in a big, fluffy towel and wrapping her hair up in another smaller one, happy to be clean again. She wandered into the bedroom and realised she had no clean clothes to change into. She opened a second, larger wardrobe doubtfully, and was pleasantly surprised to find clothes in a range of sizes, from child-sized combat and loungewear up to her current size and beyond. She touched the fabric of the children's clothes fondly; it seemed like a thousand years ago that she was ever that small. Life was so much simpler back then – not perfect, but simpler – and she sometimes wished she could go back.

Sighing, she picked out some dark-grey loungewear, looking for underwear and finding drawers positively stuffed full of undergarments in what appeared to be every conceivable shape, size, and style. She laughed out loud as she pictured her father awkwardly trying to cover every scenario that she might be here under. It seemed to her that he'd chosen to buy everything in the hopes something would fit. She made a mental note to sort through it all as she selected items in her size, and shoved the over-flowing drawers shut with some difficulty.

She dried herself and got dressed, brushing her hair back out of her face. She left her dirty clothes in a pile on the bathroom floor, telling herself she'd get them later, and set about finding her way to the kitchen through the unfamiliar house. She took several wrong turns into various rooms on her way, coming across a small library, a laundry room, and another bedroom before eventually finding the kitchen. William was already there, drinking a cup of black coffee.

"What, no food in the house but Dad made sure we had coffee?" Kali remarked.

"The man had his priorities," William looked up and raised his cup in mock salute. His eyes lingered on her face for a moment, and Kali could tell he was taking in not only the healing scar on her cheek but the flecks of red in her eyes, too.

She searched for a cup and poured herself a coffee before flopping down opposite William. The coffee was the instant kind; it was bitter and a little stale, but she drank it anyway, enjoying the warmth and alertness it brought with it.

"I see Dad planned ahead for you, too," he nodded at her new clothes and gestured at his matching set.

"Yeah, what about the others?"

"There are a few spare bits of kit lying around but I think they're going to pick up some things in town, Dad left quite a bit of local money for us."

"Do you think it's wise? Them going into town?"

"We've got to go some time, it's as safe now as it ever will be," he shrugged, but Kali noticed the tension in his shoulders.

"Have you explored much of the house yet?" she asked, hoping to distract him and herself from the idea of their friends alone out in the unknown.

"No, but I know Lenaria and Anissa have. I don't think Anissa had a great night."

"I feel bad for her. For Tannick," Kali stared into her mug, and a pang of regret lurched in her stomach.

William took a long drink of his coffee and set the mug down. "Don't. Tannick was a traitor, he made his own choice."

"You think that's fair? Me dropping the truth on him like that, how was he supposed to react?"

"Oh, I don't know, maybe not report you to Raikan literally immediately after? I don't see Amariel or the others handing you over to the Council, do you?"

Kali stayed silent, sipping on her coffee.

William sighed. "Do you want to explore the house before the others come back?"

"Yes, please."

She jumped up from the table and raced down the hall. William walked slowly, not trying to keep pace.

They found that the house had two levels; the top level was on the ground floor, where the front and back doors accessed the house. There were four bedrooms in total, a large living room with comfortable looking sofas and a large television, as well as the laundry room and the library that Kali found earlier. They also found a medical bay at the back of the house, equipped with two clinical looking beds and various pieces of machinery.

But it was downstairs that excited Kali. Situated beneath the house, was a huge training room and armoury, stocked with every kind of weapon Kali could hope for.

William let out a low, appreciative whistle as he ran a hand along the weapons at the near side of the room.

"Dad really out-did himself with this," he smiled.

"I can't wait to show Amariel, imagine what his face will be like!" Kali exclaimed, picking up a wooden pole and throwing it to her brother.

He caught it, grinning.

"Yeah, I think he'll be happy at seeing all this," he said warmly.

Kali rushed around the room trying to take everything in, scared to miss anything. There were stations for different weapons, for hand-to-hand combat, and agility training. Her father had thought of everything.

William laughed as he watched her scurry between the stations. "I should have known you wouldn't be able to sit still in here," he chuckled.

"Well, we could kill some time before the others get back," she suggested, gesturing at the pole in his hands and snatching up one of her own.

He laughed, taking up a defensive position after a moment's consideration. "Why not?"

The sparring session started amicably enough; they traded blows, laughing at each other when they broke through the other's defence, but it became rapidly apparent that they were each harbouring something unsaid. An unspoken resentment towards the other seemed to fester as the blows became harder and more ferocious, and it slowly evolved into something unexpectedly aggressive.

It was Kali who spoke first.

"So, do you think Liliana was after us yesterday or do you think us being there was just a coincidence?" she panted.

"Well, they were able to resist my power – that seemed pre-planned. Plus, *someone* needs to have told all those other demons not to attack you. I'd guess she was hoping we'd get caught up in it."

"Guess? I mean if you *knew* more than I did you would tell me, right?"

"Why would *I* know more about Liliana's plans?" William brought his arm down to disarm her, and she jumped back out of his reach.

"Oh, I don't know. You just seem to have a lot of information you choose not to share with me. You know that whole thing about our mother being a demon or the existence of this safehouse. You're full of secrets I know nothing about," she swung the pole at his head, and he brought his up to counter it.

"Maybe if you didn't seem to feel the need to volunteer the truth about yourself to anyone you spend five minutes with, I'd be more inclined to tell you things," he used the force of his counter to push her backwards, and Kali noticed he used more force than strictly necessary.

She regained her balance and stopped, staring at him in incredulity – the man who'd told his boyfriend about her behind her back was lecturing *her* about keeping secrets?

"What's that supposed to mean?" she challenged.

"You told Tannick about us and almost got us caught!" he answered, face flushed.

"Oh, so *you're* allowed to tell people, but not me?"

"That was different! That was Amariel—"

"I've known Tannick as long as you've known Amariel, Will, so that's bullshit!"

William ran a hand through his hair in frustration, his eyes moving briefly away from her before resting once more on the red flecks in her eyes, the only remaining evidence of yesterday's outburst.

"You exposed your powers to *everyone* yesterday, Kali! What *was* that? You looked like you were dying and Raikan saw you looking like a fucking demon!"

"I was trying to *save* us!" she retorted furiously. Now they were getting to his real source of frustration, she realised. Was he ashamed of her? *Scared* of her?

"Well, great work. If Raikan managed to get out alive then the Council probably know about you by now."

"Okay, next time I'll just let everyone die."

"Or just find a way that doesn't expose us all!"

"Well easy for you to say considering your powers were absolutely no help!"

They both fell silent, glaring at each other and breathing heavily.

He sighed.

"Fine, whatever. It's done now anyway."

Kali paused. "Do you think Liliana is still after us? That she can organise something like that?"

"We don't really know what she's capable of, or how she found us...last time."

They both looked away, trying not to think about the last time they'd come face-to-face with their mother.

"Do you think yesterday was about me?" Kali's voice came out smaller than she intended.

He deliberated for a moment.

"Not something on that scale, no. I think that was just a demon waging war because that's what they do. That's not to say she wasn't hoping to get to you, though."

"I wonder why she cares so much," Kali wondered aloud, questioning briefly if it was at all possible that their mother had retained any maternalism underneath her coldness and cruelty.

The wistfulness in her tone must have been apparent; William started to speak, stopped, and then sighed again.

"Kal...she doesn't care, not about anything. I know it's difficult for you because you never knew her before, but I need you to know that that woman is not our mother. Our mother died the day she turned. That *thing*...it doesn't care. There's nothing left of our mother in there, it just wears her skin."

Kali picked at a loose thread on the hem of her shirt, deliberately avoiding his eye. She didn't know where this sudden need to rationalise her mother's efforts was coming from. She'd always grown up without her mother – unlike her brothers, she'd never known any different. To her, her mother was never more than a phantom, conjured up in her imagination from the whispered memories of others, her view of her simple and unchanging. A kind warrior, a hero, a protector. She wasn't prepared for the fact that finding her again now would feel so much like losing her.

"But why is she trying so hard?" she refused to look at her brother, unwilling to see the pity in his face.

William looked at her hesitantly. "Kali, I don't know why she wants you so badly, but she doesn't love you. I need you to understand that. If she wants you then it's to have you as a weapon, maybe a sense of twisted ownership because she sees you as her property in some way, but if you're dreaming up scenarios where a little part of her is still your mother and she's doing this because somewhere in her demon brain she loves you, I need you to understand it isn't true. She does not love you. Demons aren't capable of it. They wage war because they crave chaos, and they'll follow anyone or anything that promises to give them it. That's all they know."

Nothing William said was a shock to her, she knew all of that was true, but for some reason hearing it hurt Kali more than she would ever be able to explain. Perhaps, on some level, she was guilty of romanticising her mother's pursuit of her. Pretending the demons were told to spare her because of motherly concern.

Maybe it made all the suffering they'd experienced a little easier, the idea that it came from some twisted form of love. The idea that somewhere, she still had a parent that loved her, cared for her. Because facing the truth meant facing how alone she was. Especially now the seraphs knew her secret.

Maybe she just needed to believe there was a glimmer of hope for her mother because it meant her own redemption was possible.

The noise of the others returning upstairs interrupted her thoughts, and she returned her pole to its original position, William following suit as they made their way back upstairs to their friends, a sad tension hanging between them.

They met in the kitchen, where Amariel, Anissa, and Lenaria were emptying bags full of food onto the table and the counters.

"Hey! Need any help?" Kali tried to sound cheerful, hoping to momentarily forget about demons and their mother, and to replace the thoughts with something normal instead.

"No, but you can come with me!" announced Lenaria at once. "I'll check you two afterwards," she gestured to William and Amariel, as William began helping Amariel put food away.

"I'll come too!" Anissa rushed to follow them as Lenaria shooed Kali from the room.

"William and Amariel are too perfect together and it makes me feel ridiculously third wheel-ish," Anissa explained as they stepped into the corridor. Kali suspected there was more to it after her exchange with William the day before, but she decided not to push it.

"Lenaria, you know I'm fine, right?" she said, slightly exasperated as Lenaria led them through the house to the medical bay. "I thought we were waiting until after breakfast?"

"Oh, please, she just wants an excuse to check out her new toys," Anissa grinned. Kali noticed that the smile didn't quite reach her eyes, which were dark and tired-looking, and felt a small stab of guilt about leaving Tannick behind. William was right though – he chose to betray her, and he chose to stay behind, and there was enough to be worrying about already.

They reached the medical bay and Lenaria hurried around the room, examining equipment Kali didn't know the name of and smiling to herself. Kali and Anissa exchanged amused looks as she made her way back over to them and instructed Kali to sit on the bed.

Lenaria strapped various devices to Kali, taking readings and muttering to herself as she worked. She examined Kali's cheek, the wound now mostly healed over, and her eyes with a mixture of worry and interest.

"Kali, I want to make sure you're okay after yesterday and your...well, you know. Are you feeling any after-effects at all? Your blood pressure is a little lower than I'd expect but your healing and everything else seems okay."

A strange look passed over Anissa's face so quickly that Kali wasn't sure if she'd imagined it.

"Honestly, I feel fine. No different than usual."

"Hmmm, okay. Well, you *seem* fine, but I'd like to run some tests on your blood just to make sure."

"Go wild," Kali held her arm out for Lenaria, allowing her to collect a couple of vials of her blood.

When she was done, Kali hopped off the bed.

"Send the boys through next, would you?" Lenaria called over her shoulder as she adorned the vials with labels and hurried over to the fridge to store them.

"Sure thing!"

She fell into step with Anissa as they left, and Kali thought about the night before. A curious look had crossed Anissa's face when Lenaria mentioned the use of Kali's powers, and she recognised it as the same look Anissa wore after Kali told them the truth about her, when she used her power to see if she was telling the truth.

"Ani, last night when you *felt* me, what did you feel?" she asked tentatively, unsure if she really wanted to know the answer.

"Oh, you know, just that you were telling the truth and stuff, nothing major or anything," Anissa did not meet her eye, and she was twisting a strand of hair around her finger with such force Kali thought it must hurt.

"*Ani*," Kali said firmly.

Anissa stopped short and bit her lip, looking worried. She faced Kali.

"I wasn't going to say anything, Kali. I trust you completely, okay? I believe you and I believe *in* you!"

"Ani, you're actually kind of freaking me out now. What did you feel? What...what am I?"

Anissa hesitated, as though trying to find the right words.

"I felt…I could feel that you're a good person at your core, Kali. I really did feel that," she wavered, looking away from her.

"But?"

"But…," she looked at Kali, and Kali almost felt like she was looking into her soul. "There is something… something underneath everything. Like an undercurrent, darkness that feels like it could swallow the world and under that again, there's just *nothing*. A kind of void I've never felt in anyone before, like there's no limit to it, it's just depthless. It feels like you might get lost in it and never find your way out again and I don't know how to save you," Anissa's voice was barely a whisper now, and tears shone in her eyes.

"Ah," Kali said, her heart sinking as she tried to quash the queasiness creeping up her gut.

She wasn't sure what she was expecting Anissa to say – she was prepared for the darkness, the unspoken part of her that resided within – but she was shaken by the revelation that the emptiness beneath it was something real, detectable. It confirmed her very worst fear – she was irreparably broken, and nobody could help.

"Well, that's not great," she laughed shakily, feeling like her lungs were made of paper, hollow in her chest.

Anissa looked at her sadly, seeming tired beyond her years, and walked towards the kitchen, leaving Kali in silence.

Chapter Sixteen

A few weeks passed by before the group finally agreed the demons hadn't tracked them to the safehouse, and that it was safe to stay. As they began to put down roots, it gradually began to feel like a haven to Kali, instead of somewhere she was banished to in exile. When it became clear they were in no imminent danger, she stopped planning escape routes and attack plans when her mind wandered and started sleeping through the night as undisturbed as she could hope to expect.

They were still cautious, and William decided that schedules should be drawn up for routine patrols around the house to make sure they weren't at risk of an ambush. Although they were particularly alert whenever they ventured into the town, they all found themselves becoming more relaxed, spending more time there with each visit and feeling less on-edge.

Still, Amariel warned them often about becoming complacent and insisted they each dedicate a few hours a day to training and learning new skills. Anissa and Lenaria were shocked to learn he meant them too, Anissa being a complete novice and struggling with even the most basic techniques in the beginning.

It was after one such training session that Lenaria approached Kali, red-faced and sweating, but looking rather pleased with herself. Moments prior she had managed to disarm Amariel, though Kali was still unsure if it was intentional or a fortunate accident on her part.

"Kali, I wanted to let you know the results of your blood tests, I've been studying them for weeks; the results were fascinating!"

Lenaria looked excited, but Kali felt a sense of dread. She wasn't sure she was ready to hear about yet another thing that marked her out as different, having spent days reeling from Anissa's admission weeks prior.

"Oh wow, that's great," she replied, hoping Lenaria would note her lack of enthusiasm and drop the subject. Lenaria however, seemed oblivious to Kali's discomfort and continued, undeterred.

"Your cell morphology is unlike anything I've ever seen before. It's like your cells are in a constant state of flux, caught somewhere between seraphic and not, always changing. You have proteins on your cells that I've never seen characterised before, they're entirely unique to you!"

"You can tell all of this from some blood?"

"Oh, why of course! The equipment out here is rather sophisticated too. Of course, it helps if you know what to look for," she explained with a hint of pride.

"Well, that's really interesting. Thanks, Lenaria," Kali turned to leave.

"Oh, I'm not even finished! Your potassium, calcium, and sodium levels are off the charts, but I can't see any ill effects from it that makes me think it's a disease state, I think your physiological range is just higher than an average seraph. Your levels of endocrine hormones are higher than I've ever seen in anyone, it's almost like your body is in a constant state of fight-or-flight!" she gushed enthusiastically.

Kali didn't really understand most of what Lenaria was talking about, and she might have been amused by her obvious excitement if she wasn't certain that all these things marked her out as some kind of abomination. It was just another confirmation to Kali of her "otherness," that she was an outsider right down to a cellular level.

"So, what does that mean?" she asked.

"Well, to be honest, I'm not sure! I just thought it was interesting. I could run more tests—"

"*No!* I mean, no thanks, Lenaria. I'm okay not knowing."

Lenaria looked disappointed.

"Oh, okay. I just thought I'd let you know."

"Thanks."

Lenaria smiled and began to walk away when Kali called her back.

"Lenaria, does that mean that if the Council were to ever run tests on me, they'd be able to tell that I'm—that I'm not...you know?"

Lenaria smiled sadly. "I'm afraid that's exactly what it means, Kali. It took virtually no digging to find these uh, abnormalities."

"Perfect," she muttered.

Armed with the knowledge that she was not only an aberration by way of her powers but also physically at a cellular level, too, Kali spent the next few days isolating herself from her friends. She spent time in the library or training, eating only when she needed to and talking as little as possible to anyone. She didn't know why she was punishing herself this way; she just knew she couldn't stand to be around them knowing what she knew. To spend time with them was to feel utterly alone despite being surrounded by friends. It was a powerful and strange sense of loneliness.

After several days of this, William approached her in the library one lunchtime. She looked up from her book when she sensed his presence, then continued reading.

"Mind if I join you?"

She shrugged.

"Listen, I don't know what's going on with you, but I know something's wrong. What's going on?"

"Nothing, it's fine."

"Kali."

"Look, it's fine. Lenaria just found some weird stuff in my blood – it isn't important."

"Weird how?"

"Weird as in not normal. As in not...seraphic."

"Ah," he said, understanding suddenly. "And this, does it shock you? I mean, when you think about it, are you surprised?"

"Well, not exactly but still..."

"But what?"

"Well, I'm some kind of mutant, it's official."

"Not being funny, Kal, but was that ever really in question?"

She glared at him.

"No, I'm not trying to be a dick," he said quickly, leaning back in his chair. "But I mean, look at your powers! Did you think that came from nowhere? Did you never think you might be physically different?"

"Well yeah but I never really thought about the physical side of it so much," she rubbed the back of her neck, realising how stiff it was. She must have been sitting in the library for longer than she realised.

"Okay well let me ask this: are you a different person now than you were before Lenaria ran those tests? Have the results actually changed anything about you?"

She paused for a moment. "Well…no."

"Then do they really matter? I don't want to take away from what you're feeling, I know it must be difficult; but if they don't change who you are or what you are then do they matter?"

"I guess not?" she replied, already feeling lighter.

"Okay, good. Because Lenaria's tests are great and all, but I can shoot fire from my hands and you can dematerialise at will; I don't see her blood tests explaining any of that."

Kali laughed and realised she was truly hungry for the first time in days.

"I haven't missed lunch, have I?"

"As a matter of fact, that's actually why I was sent to get you," he smiled.

"Thanks, Will."

"Any time."

* * * *

With the attack on Alarium getting farther behind them and the weight of worrying about what Lenaria's blood tests meant for her lifted, Kali became more and more at home in the safehouse and more relaxed with each passing day.

As the months passed, Amariel, Lenaria, and Anissa came to feel like family, and she saw William more comfortable than she'd seen him since before their father and Mattias died. Some days, if she tried hard enough, she could almost pretend they were family and friends living a normal life together, rather than fugitives.

They were still cautious, dutifully following William's patrol schedule around the area and looking for signs of demonic activity or signs that the Council had managed to track them, but they laughed a little easier every day. They did chores together, trained together, and at night they would settle down and watch the television – the others were fascinated when William and Kali explained DVDs and online streaming to them – switching between TV shows and movies, wondering aloud at the differences between human life and seraph life, and critiquing their attempts to accurately portray demons and angels.

"As if a human could wield such a weapon!" scoffed Amariel one night, although clearly enjoying himself as they watched a supernatural drama.

Kali watched William give him an amused look and move closer, the two of them sat together on the smaller sofa with the three women on the bigger one.

This, she reflected, was the single best thing about their move here. She'd watched Amariel and William's relationship go from cautious and guarded under the requirements and restrictions of the Guard to completely free, and it was truly the happiest she'd ever seen her brother. They brought out the best in each other, and Kali wondered if she'd ever love anyone the way they loved each other. On her darkest days, she wondered if being part demon made her incapable of it.

She watched the two of them, the way they seemed to gravitate towards each other when they moved, always in sync no matter if they were helping Anissa in the kitchen or training in the armoury in complete awe. The way they seemed to communicate in unseen and unspoken ways, how they made being together look effortless made her happy in a way she wasn't sure how to express.

It was perhaps the single one thing that Kali was grateful for from the past year or so, and it was the one thing she wouldn't change now. That love like that could exist in the world she knew to be a twisted and broken place gave her hope, and reassured her that if in the end, the darkness or the demons did claim her, that William would not be alone in the world. Amariel was her hope when she had none for herself, and she truly considered him a brother. She knew Mattias and her father would have loved him, and when she told William so one night, he pulled her into a hug without saying anything.

Each of them settled into a comfortable routine in the uneventful months that passed, which Kali considered a welcome break from the training, stress, and worry they knew before. It made Kali wish they'd come here sooner, although she reflected that if they did so, Amariel, Lenaria and Anissa would likely not be here with them.

She thought about Tannick from time to time, hoping that despite everything he was safe. She knew Anissa missed him terribly, but she seemed to be coping well. She volunteered often to cook and venture into town for supplies, clearly preferring to bake and read than to train or fight, although Kali thought she was improving in the latter.

The calm lasted until one afternoon, when Anissa and Lenaria returned from town in a state of agitation. Lenaria looked concerned, and Anissa was stressed and desperate-looking as she called everyone to the kitchen.

"Anissa, what's wrong?" asked Amariel.

Anissa clutched a piece of paper in her hand, looking pale.

"It's Tannick, he sent us a note!"

"He *what?*" roared William, jumping up from the kitchen table. "How did he find us? If our cover is blown, then we need to move!"

Kali didn't rejoice in the idea of moving yet again, but she couldn't help agreeing with her brother – if Tannick found them then others couldn't be far behind.

"No, I don't think so," Lenaria said. "I don't think we've been discovered; I think that Tannick might have used Nefuil mail."

"I thought that practice was stopped years ago?" asked Amariel.

"It doesn't mean it doesn't still work," shrugged Lenaria. "Look here"—she gestured to a small streak of blood on the bottom of the envelope, in which a small sigil was hastily scrawled in black ink— "if Tannick indeed sent this to Anissa, this would be all the blood that would be required. This sigil, it loosely translates into 'blood to blood'. It looks like Nefuil to me, though I've only ever seen it once."

Kali looked around the room at the others, hoping someone would provide some clarity, but Anissa was barely listening to the conversation happening around her and William looked as thoroughly nonplussed as she was.

"Um...can someone tell me what Nef— what you guys are talking about?"

Amariel turned to her, as Lenaria tried to coax the letter gently from a shaking Anissa's hands.

"Nefuil mail is an old practice. It fell out of fashion long ago due to its unfortunate similarities with blood magic. It was limited, too, because you could only communicate with other family members, but it meant you could get a message to a relative without needing to know their location."

Kali waited for more information and pressed Amariel when none followed.

"Yeah, but what *is* it? How does it work? How do we know Tannick used it and demons or the Guard aren't about to burst through that door?"

"Well, we don't know for sure he did, but Lenaria is correct that it looks like Nefuil was used here. The premise is simple: you write the name of the person the message is intended for, mark it with a sigil such as the one on this letter, and seal it with a small amount of blood. The message travels through the Inaustia seeking the recipient until it finds their location. The idea is that blood calls to blood. It's a very primitive method of communication."

"Can it be tracked?" William asked urgently.

"I doubt it, but anything is possible," replied Amariel.

Kali wondered what would make Tannick resort to such methods to find them, especially after months had passed.

"How did you find the letter, Ani?"

"It was lying on the ground, just out beyond the fence on the path!"

"Interference from the wards?" Amariel wondered aloud, talking to nobody in particular.

"I thought it might have been something we dropped the last time we were shopping but it's him, it's Tannick!" Anissa continued, brandishing the piece of paper wildly around her.

"What does it say?"

Anissa bit her lip and frowned.

"It says that he's in danger. The Council are accusing him of letting you escape and trying him with treason, but that he's tracked down information on Liliana that could let us prove we are innocent and let us go home! He says it might even help us get rid of her for good!"

"Information? Information like what? What does it say?" Kali leaned forward almost without realising, trying to read the letter.

"Nope. Not buying it." William cut sharply through Kali's questioning.

Anissa rounded on him. "What do you mean you're not *buying* it? I know my brother and I know this is from him!"

"How? How can you possibly know it's from him? It's a trap, Anissa. We should move on from here, we can't take the risk."

"Who died and made you the boss of all of us?" Anissa spat back at him. The words were scarcely out of her mouth before she clapped a hand over it, as though she could force them back in. She looked between Kali and William looking apologetic.

"Oh God, I'm so sorry! I didn't mean—"

"It's fine, Ani. Don't worry about it," Kali reassured her.

William poured himself a glass of water as Amariel placed a concerned hand on his shoulder, and Kali could feel the tension in the room rising like a tangible, living thing.

"Say this Nefuil thing works, you all realise that two of us technically share a bloodline with one of the people we're trying to stay away from? How do we know Liliana won't be the next thing we find at our door?" William demanded.

"I don't think that would be possible," said a worried-looking Lenaria, but she sounded uncertain.

"Lots of things aren't possible! Kali isn't possible. The demons passing through the wards at Alarium weren't possible. We have seen our fair share of things that shouldn't be possible recently!" William slammed his glass down on the counter, spilling water across its surface.

"If Liliana can use the Inaustia to track you or Kali, then we're as safe here as we are anywhere," sighed Amariel, giving William's shoulder a conciliatory squeeze and handing him a cloth.

The group looked around at each other, the insidious awareness they might be in danger momentarily silencing them. The possibility that their haven was more exposed than they realised or that they might one day come face-to-face with Liliana loomed over them, their monotonous patrols and training sessions seeming insufficient in its wake.

Anissa still stared at the letter as though it might come to life and tell her its origin, and William was muttering something under his breath. Kali knew further bickering would only raise the tension between them, and they needed to agree on what to do next; they might not have a lot of time to decide.

"Lenaria, you have a lot of equipment here, is there any way you can test the blood on the envelope against Anissa's and confirm if it is Tannick's blood?" she turned to Lenaria.

"Oh, I'm not sure. I could certainly try, I should have the materials I need here, we are very well stocked – there's an entire molecular medicine section I've barely touched!" Kali noticed she sounded a little too enthusiastic, given the circumstance.

"Ani, what else does the letter say?"

Anissa looked hesitantly at William before answering.

"Tannick wants to meet. On Friday night at this address," she showed Kali the address written in the letter, and Kali recognised Tannick's handwriting.

She gave Anissa a small smile. Behind her, William made a noise somewhere between frustration and incredulity.

"Okay: we find out if this is Tannick's blood on the envelope. If it is, we can be reasonably certain that he sent the letter, and we can *carefully* consider going to meet him."

Anissa beamed at her, but William shook his head.

"Kali, you can't actually be serious! This is far too risky! Even if it *is* Tannick, he already betrayed us once! What's to say this isn't him doing it again?"

"Will, I get it. But think about it; what's our game plan out here? Beyond surviving, beyond the next few months. Because I sure as Hell don't know what we're supposed to do next! This is the first potential lead we've got on trying to get back home or take down Liliana or *both!* If there's even a chance, then we need to take it. Otherwise, we're just hiding here until someone finally *does* find us, and we have more enemies than friends right now."

He considered for a moment.

"Fine. Whatever. But I'm not dying for Tannick, I don't care if he's got the secret to everlasting life. I won't put us in danger for him. If the Council really are out to get him after all of this, then I call that karma." He turned on his heel and stalked from the room, Amariel throwing them an apologetic look as he hurried after him.

Anissa looked disheartened.

"Hey, we're all a little taken aback by this, but he doesn't mean anything by it," Kali said gently, but Anissa wouldn't meet her eye.

Without William's objections, the kitchen grew quiet again. After a few minutes of silence, Kali left, her nerves peaked and seeking an outlet. She wasn't in the armoury for long when William arrived, followed soon by Amariel. They trained for hours, none of them voicing out loud their anxieties about the potential implications of the letter or how unprepared they felt at the thought of fighting should they be discovered. Dinner was strained that evening, what little conversation there was forced and stilted, and each of them went to bed earlier than usual. Sleep evaded Kali and she stared up at the ceiling, unable to close her mind to the chance they were in imminent danger. She wanted answers, no matter what it would reveal.

It took a further two days for Lenaria to confirm that the blood on the letter belonged to Tannick. William made it clear that it changed nothing for him, agreeing to go solely to help protect Amariel and Kali. Kali felt apprehensive too, but even after everything, Tannick was her friend and she owed it to him to try, betrayal or not. Emotions not-withstanding, if he did have information then it wasn't something they could ignore. Despite her misgivings, Kali was certain that for better or for worse, their actions over the coming days would change everything.

Chapter Seventeen

The night Tannick had requested a meeting for came around all too quickly, leaving little time to prepare. The coordinates provided by Tannick weren't particularly far from their safehouse, doing nothing to quell William's suspicions, which he vocalised frequently.

Kali privately agreed that it seemed too much of a coincidence that their meeting place should be only a few hours' drive away from their supposedly random location, but she still saw no alternative. This was still their best – and only – lead against Liliana and their only chance to return home. She repeated this to William until he was sick of discussing it, and Kali regarded this as a win all round.

They looked over the note one last time before saying goodbye to Lenaria, who was to remain at the safehouse. Gathered in the kitchen, they held hands as Kali focused on their intended location. They appeared in a filthy street strewn with litter and debris. The darkness around them was almost impenetrable, and a faint stench of rotting rubbish filled the air.

"Anissa, are you certain that this is where Tannick said he would meet with us?" Amariel wrinkled his nose in distaste.

"Amariel, *keep your voice down*. Yes, I'm certain, you read the same note I did!" Anissa hissed through the dark, looking around her as though fearful they were being watched.

Kali was on edge too, something was off about this place; the shadows were too still, the silence too unbroken. The air was heavy with tension, waiting for something to break it.

"I still don't know why we're giving this traitorous bastard the time of day," muttered William, earning a sharp look from Anissa.

"He made a *mistake!* Would you abandon Kali if you were in my position?"

He sighed but didn't answer.

"Thought so," huffed Anissa.

"If you are quite finished bickering, we should continue forward," Amariel said pointedly.

Kali felt as she always did right before battle, every muscle poised and ready to fight. The promise of violence seemed to hang around them.

"Something's not right...I think we should be careful. Stick together and watch your backs."

They nodded at her as they began to creep silently forward. Anissa had no real military training, save for that picked up at the safehouse, but she resolutely refused to stay behind with Lenaria when they asked her to. *"It's my brother!"* she'd spat, blocking their path until they finally relented and let her join them. But Kali worried about her now, out here in the open.

As they continued down the road, they saw a square up ahead; in its centre stood the figure of a man. Darkened paths and alleyways surrounded the square, and Kali stopped, throwing her hand out to stop the rest of the group.

Anissa looked surprised, looking between Kali and the figure. She opened her mouth to speak, but Kali shook her head, gesturing for her to be quiet. She looked to William and Amariel, who wore expressions that mirrored her suspicious apprehension.

"It's too open. If it's a trap then we would be surrounded," she whispered, as they nodded in agreement.

"A trap? Kali, I thought you were on my side; this is *Tannick!*" Anissa reasoned, but she kept her voice low.

"Is it?" Kali replied.

Anissa looked upset. "Kali, what are you saying? I *know* that message could only have come from Tannick! He talked about things only he could know about, and Lenaria tested the blood and it was a match! We need to help him and if he really does have information on Liliana then it could mean we all get to go home! *Please,* Kali, let's just go get him and take him back to the house. I know he hurt you and you don't need to forgive him but he's my *brother*," she pleaded.

Kali hesitated, guilty, but she still couldn't shake the overwhelming feeling that something was off. She looked again and realised, perturbed, that no living person could ever be as still as whatever stood in the square, least of all Tannick. There was no rising and falling of its chest, no nervous fidgeting the way Tannick would before a fight, checking his weapons over, no looking around to check its surroundings, and no matter what Anissa said, Kali was certain that whatever stood in the square now was not Tannick.

Shaking her head, she spoke mainly to William and Amariel.

"No, something…this is wrong, we have to go."

"*No!*" Anissa exclaimed. In the silence, her voice rang out like a gunshot.

Everyone froze. With the silence broken, the energy around them seemed to shift. The shadows seemed to crawl with movement as though things lurked within them just out of sight.

"Go. Go now!" Kali turned on her heel, dragging Anissa with her. If they could get somewhere less exposed, she could teleport them out safely, but Anissa was fighting against her, tears in her eyes as she twisted back to look at the figure in the square.

Kali turned to face her. "Anissa, I'm sorry, that isn't him, we need to go!"

But Anissa wasn't looking at her or the square now, and the terror in her expression as she stared beyond Kali, over her shoulder, turned Kali's blood cold. Time slowed as she looked in the direction of the source of Anissa's horror, and saw a monstrous dog-like creature emerging from the shadows behind them.

"*Hellhound!*" cried Amariel. She felt William's hands on her shoulder dragging her backwards, and she pulled Anissa with her. The hellhound slinked menacingly towards them, snarling between razor-sharp fangs, its eyes never leaving them.

"It's driving us back towards the square, we need to take it out before we get trapped there!" Kali cried.

Anissa let out a terrified sob. "It's a *hellhound!* Our powers don't hurt it like they hurt demons!"

"No, but these do," Amariel withdrew his weapons with an air of grim confidence.

"Can't we just teleport?" cried Anissa.

"Too exposed!" called William.
"Hellhounds are fast, if it strikes before we're gone it could rip us apart."

Kali shared a bleak look with William as they followed Amariel's lead and drew their weapons. The three of them started forward, flanking the beast as they closed the gap between them.

Behind them, Anissa screamed, and Kali turned in spite of herself, leaving her back exposed to the hellhound. She sensed a rush of movement from behind her at the same time she saw a demon grab Anissa and drag her back towards the square. Throwing herself to the side, she felt the hellhound miss her by inches as it lunged at her with startling speed.

"Kali, *go!*" rang her brother's voice as he and Amariel descended on the hellhound, hacking at its spine. Without looking back, she sprinted in the direction of Anissa, ignoring every instinct that told her not to follow.

She reached the demon dragging Anissa easily and drove her sword upwards into its skull. Dying, the demon released Anissa and she fell forward, stumbling. Kali reached out to steady her, taking care not to cut her with the sword, now slick with demon blood. Once again, Anissa struggled against Kali's grip to move towards the square, but this time, she stopped short.

The square was now completely empty, the figure gone; Anissa seemed to shrink beside her.

"Tannick?"

Kali tugged on her arm, desperate to get her away from the danger. She could hear Amariel and William calling to each other as they fought the baying hellhound – she wanted to help them and put as much distance between them and the square as possible.

But Anissa was rooted to the spot, looking desperately into the shadows for any sign of her brother. Without warning, something sailed through the darkness towards them, landing at their feet with a wet *thud*. Kali staggered back on weak legs as she recognised the face staring up at her. Tannick's head lay on the ground, discoloured and grey – it was clear to her that he had been dead for some time.

A terrible, wounded noise came from Anissa as she stared at her brother's head, her knees buckling from under her as she tried to back away. Kali caught her with her free hand, stooped and took Anissa's weight on her shoulder as she half-dragged her friend back towards William and Amariel, barely containing the urge to scream herself.

They met half-way, William and Amariel breathing heavily but miraculously unhurt.

Kali reached for them. "Take my hand, we are getting out of here, now!" she shouted over Anissa's sobs.

As her hand closed around William's, the darkness erupted around them. Demons spilled from every direction, boxing them in. She reached desperately for Amariel, but even as she did so, demons surrounded each of them.

"We can't take them back with us!" William pummelled the demon nearest him with his sword, his other hand still clutching hers tightly.

Claws raked down Kali's back, hands of demons eager to grab her as their prize. "I know that, hold on!" she grabbed hold of Amariel. "Anissa, keep hold of me!"

She concentrated, ignoring the increasing number of demons surrounding them, and took them back to the top of the road they started on, away from the horde. The demons that held onto them took a moment to adjust, and the group seized the opportunity to fall upon them, deftly beheading them and severing their spines.

Panting, Kali turned to face her friends, but the demons they had left behind were already gaining on them. Weapons – spears, daggers, arrows –began to sail through the air, an unwelcome déjà vu as Kali was reminded of the spear that killed Mattias what felt like a lifetime ago. She held out her hands, using her power to deflect the weapons, but she knew she couldn't keep her friends safe from the weapons and take them away from this place at the same time.

"You three need to run, now!" she called, straining with the effort of sustaining the barrier between them and the demons.

"*What?*" William stared at her, incredulous.

"I can't use two powers at the same time, and if I drop this barrier then we might all die! We don't have time for this, go!"

"No way, Kali, not happening!" William raised his sword and stood beside her.

The demons were almost on them, still firing weapons in their direction, trying to find a gap in Kali's concentration.

"William, *please!*" but she knew it was pointless; her brother would never turn and run from a battle if it meant leaving her to fight alone.

Amariel stood to her left side, weapons readied; William stood to her right, jaw set. Anissa stood just behind him, looking scared but determined. *This is it,* she thought, bracing herself.

The demons reached them and flew at them with ferocity; as the weapons stopped flying, Kali dropped her hands, snatching up her discarded sword. She knew their chance of victory was slim-to-none, but she threw herself into the battle as though it was assured. She sliced her way through the demons surrounding her, trying to keep eyes on her friends and brother. The fight had pushed them apart, and Anissa was already struggling. She saw a demon lunge from behind her friend, blade poised for a fatal blow.

"NO!" Kali cried, extending her hand desperately and driving back the demon with a burst of energy. Anissa began to thank her, then her eyes widened. "Look ou—!"

But Kali didn't hear the rest of her warning; taking advantage of her distraction, a demon threw itself at her, driving a mace down onto her leg with vicious force. Agony exploded in Kali's leg, and she was sure her knee was shattered as she fell to the ground with a cry of pain. She heard William shout her name as the demon grabbed her by the front of her shirt, forcing her face up to look at him.

"Long live the Queen!" he snarled tauntingly as he withdrew a syringe of venomous-green liquid and plunged it into her neck.

Kali wanted to fight back, to loosen his grip, but her vision was already fading at the edges, and her limbs felt heavy. She could hear her name being called as though from far in the distance, and the world was growing steadily darker. The demon lifted her effortlessly and threw her over his shoulder.

Her leg should hurt, she thought, but she had lost all feeling in her body. The demon whistled, barked something in a language Kali couldn't understand, and began walking away from the battle. Perplexed, Kali noticed that most of the other demons fell in line behind him to follow, turning their backs on the fight. Her last thought before she fell into unconsciousness was the realisation that they were only here for her.

* * * *

Kali awoke groggily in a dark room she didn't recognise, cold and – alarmingly –

wearing only her underwear. As her vision came into focus, she saw she was lying on a bed-like table in the centre of a windowless, brick room. She tried to move but found that she couldn't – her arms, legs, and head were bound to the table. Her breathing became quicker, each one sending little clouds out into the cold air as she shivered. Trying her best not to succumb to panic, she tried to summon the strength to teleport, to do something, but none of her powers worked. Her head was throbbing, and she felt weak as she struggled uselessly against the restraints. Her injured knee ached more with every effort to break free, the restraints holding her remaining unaffected.

Her movement limited, she tried to see as much of the room as possible, looking for possible weapons or escape routes. Feeling a sharp scratch in her right hand, she twisted her head up as far as she could in that direction. With a jolt, she saw a bag of bright and toxic-looking green liquid, similar to the kind the demon had injected her with before. It was set up like an IV, connected to a long tube that was attached to a cannula stuck in her hand, and Kali felt absurdly like a patient in a warped, terrifying hospital. She had never seen a poison like this or heard about demons being able to incapacitate seraphs with it and had no idea how to counteract it, even if she could figure out how to escape from the table.

She looked desperately to her left and saw nothing but empty room. Turning her eyes upwards and straining her head backwards against her bindings she could just make out a door which told her that the only way in or out of the room lay behind her. Heart now pounding, she tried again and again to activate any of her powers, to no avail.

She heard movement behind her, coming from beyond the room; voices coming closer and the sound of footsteps on stone. She heard them stop just beyond the doorway, voices hushed and excited, and a powerful sense of foreboding spread through her bones like lead.

A key turned in the lock and Kali heard the door creak open as several figures entered the room. As they approached the table, she watched three demons wheel a trolley loaded with an assortment of cruel-looking instruments past her line of vision, looking at her eagerly as they passed. She sensed someone behind her and was angry yet unsurprised to see her mother's face loom above her.

Unable to do anything else, Kali spat in her face.

Cold fury mixed with something unintelligible passed over Liliana's face as she wiped it with her sleeve, plastering on a wide smile.

"*Now child,* that is no greeting to give your mother *or* your Queen!"

"It's a good thing that you're neither then," Kali snarled.

Liliana stared down at her, and Kali held her gaze, hoping her eyes were full of defiance instead of the fear she could feel unfurling in her chest. It was like her mother was staring down into her core, taking her measure, and strapped down to the bed, powerless, it was unnerving to Kali.

"Well, how *disappointing,*" she smiled. "If that is how you feel then let's see if we can't *convince* you to pledge allegiance, hmmm?"

Kali struggled against her restraints again but couldn't break free. Her mother's eyes danced with dangerous anticipation as she leaned in close to Kali. Out of sight, she heard the demons chuckle excitedly.

"Let's not waste time with dramatic hyperbole or grand declarations of fealty," Liliana began, looking down at Kali impassively. "Let us speak plainly. I want you to join me. I know your soul, daughter. I know it calls to the darkness as my own does."

Kali remained silent, not trusting herself to speak. Icy terror burned through her veins as her mother spoke, and she didn't want her words to betray her fear, or the truth in Liliana's words.

Liliana gave a knowing smile, malice in her eyes.

"Heed my words, child. I am accustomed to getting what I want and destroying what I can't."

"Sounds like you need to hear the word 'no' more often, if you ask me," Kali muttered, finding defiance amongst her growing panic.

Liliana smirked.

"Your spirit is admirable, but your glibness will not serve you here. I promise that you will never know a moment of peace and your little friends will never know safety as long as you defy me. Tell me, are you prepared to gamble their lives for your soul?"

Kali dropped her gaze from Liliana and when she looked back, the smile on her mother's face was smug.

"You needn't put them in any danger. I have no quarrel with them. Join me now and they will be safe."

"To do what? Why don't you just kill me if you're so scared of the prophecy?"

Liliana laughed out loud. It was a chilling sound that held no humour.

"I don't put my faith into the ramblings of dead prophets. Prophecy or no prophecy, you have power, and I have other uses for you. I would prefer to have you with me than dead but make no mistake, I'd sooner see you dead than against me."

"So those are my choices? Join you or die? I think we've played this game before, *mother*. I chose death then and I'll choose it again. Sorry, better luck next time," jeered Kali, her heart thumping and the muscles in her jaw tight with the effort it took to stop her teeth from chattering together.

Her mother fixed her with a bitter smile.

"But darling, the rules have changed. We're playing my way now," she replied, her voice soft and filled with menace.

Kali tensed against her restraints, trying subtly to break free again. If she had to die to thwart her mother then she was prepared to, but not like this. Not trapped like an animal, defenceless and weakened. She doubted her death here would be swift and she didn't want to draw it out or suffer for some sense of twisted demonic satisfaction.

"Change whatever rules you want, my answer won't change," she hissed, finding no give in her ties, and feeling a sinking sensation in her stomach.

"We'll see," smirked Liliana, turning to confer with the demons Kali had almost forgotten about.

They spoke low and quickly in their demonic language, looking ravenously eager. Kali tried to break free one last time only to find that she couldn't: she was completely trapped.

Liliana returned moments later, arrogance and self-assurance dripping from her every word.

"Here is how we're going to play: I will ask if you are ready to join me, and you will answer simply 'yes' or 'no'," she began.

"Answer 'yes' and you will be royalty, you will want for nothing, and you will fight beside me to conquer the Earth piece by piece. Answer 'no', and my friends will reduce you to a whimpering slab of sinew and blood. Are we clear?" she smiled malevolently down at Kali.

Kali glared at her as the demons busied themselves with tools she couldn't see.

"Good. So, before we begin: are you ready to join me? Agree now and spare yourself the needless suffering."

Every sense in Kali's body was in overdrive, every nerve screaming at her to fight or flee but she could do neither. She lay rigid, trying to stop the uncontrollable trembling in her limbs as she realised there was no escape from this. She could only stare up into her mother's cold, empty eyes, as she felt the green poison trickle into her veins and heard the demons prepare different instruments with which to torture her. She wouldn't give them the satisfaction of letting them see her fear, she promised herself. She smiled up at her mother without breaking eye contact.

"You can burn in Hell, bitch".

Her mother stood straight and turned away from her.

"Do try and have some fun," she smiled indulgently at the demons now approaching the table, who smiled back.

"With *pleasure*, my Queen."

Liliana threw Kali one more contemptuous glance before exiting the room as the demons began moving hurriedly round the room. They spoke to each other in their harsh language as though coming to a decision; one approached her to check the IV, leering down at her as they ensured it was still flowing, whilst the remaining two began sticking something to her legs, arms, and stomach.

She squinted to see what they were doing, but the demon to her side roughly shoved a strap into her mouth, forcing her head back down. Almost immediately and without warning, Kali's body lit up with pain as electricity surged through her body. She felt her muscles contract involuntarily, so tight she was sure they were tearing under the strain. Her head felt like it was seconds from exploding, and she couldn't breathe. She told herself not to scream, but she wasn't sure that she even could if she wanted to. Everything was out of her control, her muscles screaming even if she wouldn't and her skin burning.

They turned the current off, and Kali gasped as much of the frigid air into her lungs as she could. She was vaguely aware of the demons talking and laughing amongst each other before the electricity burned through her again. Again and again, they turned the electricity on, upping the voltage and the duration until Kali was sure she would burst into flame. She refused to cry out, disappointing and angering the demons in equal parts. She thought of her father and Mattias and vowed to be strong for them. *"A demon feeds on fear and pain; give it any at all and it will only make it hungry for more,"* she remembered her father explaining to her one day in lessons. She resolved not to feed their cruelty.

Dissatisfied, the demons began tearing the electrodes from her, and Kali was sure her skin was tearing with it. After several rounds with the electricity, and with the poison still pumping round her body, Kali was barely aware of what was going on around her. She felt seconds away from unconsciousness. Slightly delirious, she considered that this seemed counterproductive for torture and that maybe she should be the one leading this session if this was the kind of amateur treatment she would be subjected to.

Her strange sense of amusement must have shown on her face because the demon nearest her suddenly hissed into her ear, *"I'll give you something to laugh about,"* before sticking a nasty-looking blade into her side.

Before the pain could even register, another demon seized her left arm with both hands and twisted, and she felt bone break. She bit back a groan of pain as one of them cut into her torso with a lethal-looking, hooked blade. Pain rolled through her and continued to grow as the demons sliced into her with fervour. She tried not to think of what else they had planned and thought instead about William coming to rescue her. He would, he had to. She just needed to hold out for him.

As time passed, Kali didn't know how long, she tried to block out the sickening sounds around her. The sound of her flesh being ripped apart, of the sharpening of blades, and of her blood hitting the stone floor and pooling beneath her as they carved her into something less seraphic. She was shivering, colder than she had ever been in her life, and all she knew was pain. A stinging-burning agony that blocked out everything else. Her vision swam, and she thought she was dreaming when her mother's face came into focus above her.

"Have you had enough? Are you ready to join me?"

The words didn't make sense, and Kali stared straight through Liliana and laughed. A laugh that sparked new agony through every part of her, that didn't make sense to her but that she couldn't stop. She was quite certain she had lost her mind, but quite certain that she didn't care.

A knife plunged into her, and her laugh changed to a strange gurgle as she tasted blood. As her mother left and the demons resumed their deconstruction of her, she wondered if they might kill her. The weapons they used didn't carry fatal runes, they were instruments of pain only, but the green liquid had weakened her, and she was barely hanging onto consciousness, holding on for a rescue she was growing less sure was coming.

They injured her with impunity, assuming they couldn't fatally wound her with these weapons, but Kali was sure she was dying.

They taunted her, feigning retreat then breaking bone, laughing. When they brought a blunt instrument down on her already injured knee, Kali bit her lip so hard she drew blood. As the hours passed, she thought of her mother's words *"...whimpering slab of sinew and blood." At least the whimpering part isn't true,* she thought.

She finally cried out in earnest when they pressed a burning metal instrument to her wrist, and the demons hissed with excitement in response. Emboldened by their success the demons entered a flurry of activity, setting down their weapons and equipping themselves with new toys to wield upon her instead.

The new pain was, she decided, the worst yet; it was a terrible and urgent kind of pain that demanded all of her attention, made worse by the fact she was *sure* she could smell her flesh burning. They took great pleasure in showing her as they prepared metal instruments, holding them in the flame until they glowed with heat, then pressed it to her skin. The metal welded itself to her, becoming one with her, joined in pain as it burned through layer and layer of her.

When she cried out, it seemed only to encourage them, and she cursed herself for showing weakness. Time passed – minutes, hours, or maybe days, Kali didn't know – and she was finding it increasingly hard to focus, impossible to stay awake. She was disoriented and confused; eventually, even the pain became dulled as she drifted into semi-consciousness.

A sharp slap to her face brought her back into reality, and her mother stood over her once again. She coughed, a metallic taste filling her mouth. Kali couldn't make sense of the words that Liliana spoke, but her gaze held such an intensity it seemed to burn into Kali's soul.

And, despite the defiance, the anger, the refusal to be like Liliana, there was a tantalising emptiness dancing just below the surface of her. That familiar darkness, growing stronger as she grew weaker, that promised to shut it all off. The darkness that promised to shut off not only the pain she felt right now, but all the pain she had ever felt – all the grief, the guilt, the struggle with her own identity – and to replace it instead with power.

Kali looked up at her mother, faltering. Is this how she wanted to live? Forever in pain, on the run, *weak?* What if she said 'yes' to the darkness and had the power instead? Would she lose herself entirely, or could she wield the power like the demons wielded their weapons on her, simply an extension of themselves?

Her mother seemed to sense her thoughts. Reading Kali's face, she drew back in shock and triumph. She drew close again until they were nearly face to face, Kali could feel her breath on her cheek.

"*Yes, child:* join me and the pain stops, join me and you will never know fear or loss again. I will guide you, my daughter, you will never be alone again."

Kali wanted to fight, but she had been fighting for such a long time. It was harder still to fight the darkness when it spoke to her in her own voice. It whispered to her the way it always had, but stronger now, telling her that she had it wrong. The darkness inside her wasn't the enemy, it was part of her, it *was* her. This wasn't giving up; it was grabbing the power to fight she had been denying herself for so long. This wasn't losing, this was having the courage to win. She was sure it was the right thing to do.

Her eyes met Liliana's, and she saw her own green eyes reflected in the cold black of her mother's. Triumph lit up Liliana's features as Kali prepared to let go. In the version of herself reflected in her mother's eyes, she thought she saw the whites of her eyes become threaded with black tendrils, as she imagined the darkness inside her uncoiling and rising like a snake prepared to attack.

Suddenly, an explosion in the distance ripped through the tense silence and rocked the room. Blood-curdling shrieks rang through the air, and her mother whirled on her heel, striding from the room.

"Guard her!" she commanded the demons as she slammed the door behind her.

Like a spell breaking, shame washed over Kali. How could she be so weak? How could she bend to Liliana's will so easily? She berated herself relentlessly, but she was just so tired; every ragged breath she took caught in her throat, every second that passed was another spent in terrible pain. It was getting harder to stay awake again.

Kali heard a commotion directly behind her, outside the room in what she imagined was a corridor. Shouting, the noise of fighting and weapons clashing, and muffled noises she couldn't make sense of rang through the air. She was so tired. The demons in the room flanked her, preparing to fight as pounding began on the door of the room. She thought that surely, with the demons distracted, it would be okay to close her eyes now, even just for a second. Her eyes began to close just as the door flew open and the fighting spilled into the room.

She was somewhere between conscious and not when she heard her brother's voice, his ill-disguised horror and fear as he moved closer, shouting her name. She supposed that she must look dead and tried to summon the energy to move a finger but found even that impossible. She recognised Anissa and Amariel's voices and heard the three of them clash with her torturers, slaying them where they stood, ill-equipped with their non-fatal weaponry.

Someone, she assumed William, stood over her, gently trying to rouse her.

"She's breathing," he sighed in relief, but his voice was frantic, "Kali, it's okay, we're here now. Kali, can you hear me?"

"We have to move, Will. We only stalled Liliana for a few minutes, she'll come straight here," Amariel's usually calm voice was urgent.

She was vaguely aware of her restraints being undone, and the cannula being removed carefully from her hand.

"Grab that bag, we should see if Lenaria can run tests on whatever that is."

Someone moved beside her to unhook the bag of poison, slipping slightly on the blood – her blood – on the floor, which sent a wave of revulsion through Kali. She felt hands underneath her, and then someone lifting her, causing pain to spasm through her. She groaned and opened her eyes.

It was William who was carrying her, dead demons littering the halls as they crept hurriedly along through a maze of corridors. He looked relieved when she opened her eyes, but he was pale, and his features were drawn.

"Hey, kid. We got you, don't worry, we're getting you out of here!"

She tried to say thank you, but every step was sending waves of pain pulsing through her, and she couldn't form the words. Instead, she rested her head on his shoulder, and let oblivion take her.

Chapter Eighteen

The next few days passed in a feverish blur for Kali. She was semi-conscious when they arrived back at the safehouse, met by Lenaria who had already prepared the medical room as a precaution. If she was shocked by the condition of Kali, she hid it well, calmly ordering the others to bring her supplies and setting to work, suturing and dressing wounds and setting fractures.

The fever that gripped Kali had no certain cause – seraphs usually weren't wounded long enough to develop serious infections (a very human affliction), but nobody could be certain what effects the strange, green poison had on her body. Then there was the poison itself, which could have caused unknown damage. Kali tossed and turned, dreaming and hallucinating all manner of disturbing and distorted visions until the fever finally broke.

When she woke, the room was dark, and she was unbearably thirsty. Remembering the last time she had awoken in a bed in a dark room, she felt her heart rate quicken and her breathing become harsh, setting machines she hadn't noticed beeping frantically. A figure in the corner of the room shifted, as William roused himself from an uncomfortable sleep in an armchair.

"Kali?"

Realising she wasn't in danger, Kali relaxed.

"I-I need water," she croaked.

He hurried to pour her a glass, and she took it gratefully, gulping it down greedily until it made her cough.

"Easy, easy!" William set the glass on the bedside table and handed her a tissue.

"Thanks," she choked.

William looked awful. He was pale, with dark shadows under his eyes and hair that stuck up at all angles.

"You look terrible, by the way."

He looked stunned for a moment and then burst into a fit of surprised laughter.

"Thanks. I'd hold off commenting on anyone else's appearance until you've looked in the mirror, kid." There was a sadness in his voice.

Kali tried to sit up from the bed and was met instantly with dizziness and pain.

Groaning, she leaned back on her pillows, willing the room to stop spinning.

"Kali, what are you doing? Just relax and stay put for now," William reached out to steady her, exasperated.

She wanted to argue, but threw her hands up in defeat instead, wincing at the fresh pain it brought. She looked at her brother, pushing the images of what might have happened if he hadn't arrived when he did from her mind.

"Will...thank you," her eyes burned and she looked away, blinking furiously, trying not to think of how close she was to giving in to the darkness, trying not to remember the pain or the fear she felt as she lay trapped on that table.

"Any time, Kal," he smiled, but he looked haunted too.

She took stock of her body. She was covered in bandages, sutures, and splints, but the pain was less now than before.

"How bad is it?" she asked quietly.

"You'll live," he tried to smile reassuringly.

"I want to see."

He hesitated. "Kal...I don't know if that's a good idea. Just focus on resting for now."

"For how long?"

"Lenaria doesn't know. You've been out for a few days now already. The green stuff, it seems to have slowed healing down, but we don't know much about it yet, or how it will affect you long term."

The green stuff. For a moment, she was back in the room with the demons; she imagined the cannula in her hand caringly placed by Lenaria was pumping her full of poison, and she scrambled to rip it out. William caught her hand, looking at her sympathetically.

"Kali, you are safe," he said firmly. She nodded, catching her breath, and he released her hand.

"I want to see," she repeated, feeling oddly detached from reality.

William sighed. "I'll go get Lenaria."

Lenaria wanted to perform all manner of tests and checks on Kali and admonished William for not fetching her the *instant* Kali woke up. Kali's eyes were heavy by the time she was finished, but she was determined to see what had been done to her body. She wanted to see it all, to document every injury and account for every agony, even if she didn't really understand *why* she did. She needed it to be real in a way she couldn't vocalise. She needed to see it.

Lenaria brought her a mirror, and William stepped outside. It took ten minutes of arguing for Lenaria to agree to let her stand, supported, and to remove most of the bandaging. She stood painfully on one leg (her bad knee unwilling to bear her weight), forcing down dizziness, and looked at her reflection. Lenaria seemed unable to look at her, but Kali couldn't look away.

This is the price of your refusal, a taunting voice in her head jeered. Looking at each wound, she could feel every knife edge, every burn, every bone break all over again. Her pulse quickened, earning a warning beep from one of the nameless machines, and Lenaria began to cover her back up. Still, Kali couldn't look away. The patches of skin that weren't ravaged by wounds and burns were mottled purple-blue. In some places, entire patches of skin were gone, her healing wounds raised in parts and sunken in others, her body an uneven tapestry of misery. Seeing it made it more real than the pain ever could. This was her proof. The proof that this had happened to her, and proof that she had survived. *Proof that you were weak,* taunted the voice.

By the time Lenaria helped her back into bed, the effort of merely standing had taken its toll on Kali and she was half-asleep. Lenaria did a few more checks before letting William back in and instructing Kali to rest and get some sleep.

"I've *been* sleeping," Kali protested, unconvincingly stifling a yawn.

William smiled at Lenaria as she lingered in the doorway. "I promise I'll make sure she rests."

With a small nod, Lenaria left, gently closing the door behind her.

"How did you find me?" Kali yawned, growing more tired by the second.

"A story for another day, Kal."

"Mother won't be happy," Kali said sleepily.

William froze. *"What did you just say?"*

"Hmm?" Kali closed her eyes.

William's voice drifted to her as she sunk into a deep sleep.

"Did you just call her '*Mother*'?"

* * * *

For the majority of the next three days, Kali slept, but by the time a week had passed since her rescue she was desperate to get out of bed. Her dreams, as always, were not peaceful. Every night she relived her torture. Worse, sometimes she was the demon, torturing William, Amariel, Anissa, and Lenaria, and sometimes she was torturing her father and Mattias. She thought if she could just leave the medical bay's unfamiliar bed and the IV behind, it would remind her less of that place and her nightmares would abate.

Nobody was enthusiastic about letting Kali get out of bed, but it was Amariel that eventually spoke on her behalf. He urged them to reach a compromise – if Kali passed Lenaria's tests then there would be no reason to stop her from moving around.

"I don't agree with this, you know," Lenaria told her as she hooked Kali up to different monitors and took readings that were meaningless to Kali.

"I know," Kali grinned.

"Hmm, well…your readings all seem fine. Not *great* mind you, but fine. Clothes off, I want to examine your injuries."

Kali feigned shock. "Why Lenaria, you haven't even bought me dinner yet!"

Lenaria looked at her blankly. "I've prepared your dinner plenty of times, but I fail to see the relevance here."

"Never mind," laughed Kali, as she peeled off the hospital-like gown they had put her in when she arrived. "Does this mean I can finally have a proper shower and change my clothes?"

Lenaria ignored her and began examining her injuries instead. She checked how wounds were healing and placed her hand on her, using her ability to assess how well the internal injuries were healing. After she was finished, she handed Kali her gown and was silent for a long time, taking meticulous notes.

Eventually, she sighed. "I strongly urge you to stay in bed a little longer, but I can see no immediate threat providing *you do not over-exert yourself.* That means no powers for the time being, no fighting, no strenuous activity of *any kind.*"

"Thank you, Lenaria!" Kali exclaimed delightedly, already moving awkwardly out of bed.

Lenaria rolled her eyes, exasperated, and moved to help her. When she reached Kali, she drew her into an unexpected, careful hug. "I'm glad you're okay, Kali."

Slightly taken-aback, Kali tensed in surprise before relaxing and leaning into Lenaria.

"Thank you for taking care of me," Kali was surprised to find her eyes were filling with tears, suddenly emotional.

She rested her head on Lenaria's shoulder and wrapped her arms around her. A few moments passed before Lenaria cleared her throat and withdrew from the hug, wiping her eyes.

"Come on, I'll help you to the kitchen, Anissa is making lunch."

"Thanks," Kali moved off the bed, standing carefully.

She found that her injured knee, although painful, reluctantly bore her weight and she was able to walk relatively unaided. Her left arm was now only moderately painful, and only the worst of the wounds still bothered her. Lenaria had her on a strictly regimented combination of pain relief and healing ointments and despite the poison's impact on healing, Kali's injuries were making steady progress.

Through conversations with the group, she learned that tests on the poison showed it was unlike the lethal kinds generally employed by the demons. None of them had ever encountered anything like it before or heard of any similar poison. Lenaria's tests revealed that it seemed to have a limited effect on regular seraph tissue; Amariel wondered out loud if it was tailored specifically for Kali, which seemed to concern him.

The testing also showed that the poison's primary purpose was immediate incapacitation rather than long-term damage, which was a welcome relief to everyone. Lenaria had quietly confided in Kali that she thought the poison may also contain some element intended to boost demonic power, and Kali rapidly changed the subject. She hadn't yet admitted to anyone how close she was to letting go and letting the darkness in, and she had no plans to.

As they entered the kitchen, she found everyone gathered together; they cheered when she entered and she smiled at them, taking a mock bow. Lenaria ushered her into a seat and William rushed over to help, Amariel watching him warmly.

Anissa fussed over her, pouring her coffee – which was instantly removed by Lenaria in favour of "healing tea" – and setting down a plate of pancakes with a flourish. Kali thanked her, but despite her initial hunger, after a few bites she felt nauseated. She pushed the food around her plate as Lenaria and Anissa left the kitchen, leaving only Amariel and William.

"What's wrong, Kali?" asked Amariel.

William was watching her intently. "Yeah, I've literally had to fight you for pancakes before. Nearly lost an eye."

Kali chuckled, but she still felt queasy. She opened her mouth to reply when a hand on her shoulder alerted her to someone standing behind her. Adrenaline coursed through her as she jumped up from the table, grabbing a knife as she stood, and spun round to face her attacker, ignoring the pain from her injuries as she pinned them to the wall.

She could hear Amariel and William shouting as she came face to face with a pale and wide-eyed Lenaria. Kali was breathing hard when she took a step back from her friend, her face becoming increasingly flushed. She dropped the knife at her feet, appalled and embarrassed.

"Lenaria, I'm so sorry! I don't—I thought…"

The threat and the panic in Kali's chest still felt real, and Amariel and William were moving around her in such a way she couldn't tell if it was concern or containment.

"I-I mean, it's okay, I shouldn't have, I…" Lenaria panted, startled.

"I have to go," Kali turned and limped from the kitchen, willing her injured leg to move faster. William caught up to her easily.

"Kali, wait. Where are you going?"

Kali ignored him as she made her way to the bathroom, William following but not touching her, for which she was grateful. As soon as she made it to the bathroom, she sank awkwardly to the floor and retched into the toilet. She could feel the strain on her semi-healed wounds each time she was sick and was relieved when she was finally finished. She leaned against the wall, breathing heavily, and noticed small spots of blood on the front of her gown.

"Well, I think this might count as over-exertion," she laughed shakily, not looking at her brother.

William closed the door and sat on the floor beside her. She expected him to speak but was glad when he didn't. A few moments of silence passed before Kali spoke.

"I thought she was a demon. I thought that she—I thought that I..."

"Was under attack?" William suggested quietly.

She nodded. "It was ridiculous. I feel completely ridiculous."

"It's not ridiculous at all. You've been through something ...something that had you on high-alert and in danger, you just haven't adjusted back to being in a non-threatening scenario yet."

She snorted. "You make it seem so logical."

"It is logical!"

"So, when will I adjust?"

"I'm not sure, Kal. In your own time, I guess?"

"What if that never happens? I mean we're constantly looking over our shoulder, we are *always* on high alert. Our whole life is one big threatening scenario! How and when am I supposed to feel normal again?"

William grimaced and offered no further advice, and Kali deflated.

"You've hurt yourself," William gestured to the blood staining the front of her clothes.

"It's nothing," mumbled Kali. "Will, I—" she hesitated and stared resolutely at the floor.

"What?"

When Kali spoke, it was barely above a whisper. "What if it isn't about adjusting? What if I'm just broken or evil or *wrong* in some way? When Liliana…right before you arrived, I was going to… let go. Will, there's a-a *darkness* inside of me that just keeps getting stronger and I know, *I know,* if I let it in then I'll be just like her, but I also know it will feel *good* to stop fighting it," the words she'd held back for so long were now spilling from her, unconstrained.

"Back in that room, I knew if I let it in, she would stop. I just wanted it to stop, I was so *tired* and I almost—" her throat burned, and tears streaked her face as she remembered how close to the edge she'd been.

She wiped them away furiously, white-hot shame in the pit of her stomach; she had led everyone on a life of danger, and she was a fraud.

Sadness painted the lines of William's face and Kali thought he had never looked older.

"Kal—"

"Don't say you understand because you *don't,* Will."

"I wasn't going to say that. You're right, I don't understand. But Kali, what they did to you…when I walked in, I thought they had killed you. Maybe you would have let go and maybe you wouldn't, we'll never know, but anyone that says they wouldn't have at least considered it is a liar."

"Mattias wouldn't. Mattias would rather have died than ever think about…that."

William frowned. "Yeah, maybe," he sighed, "but you are a *good* person, and yeah, I've watched you choke demons to death with their own blood without breaking a sweat, so I sort of figured about the whole darkness thing," he gave a weak laugh. "But that is not the same thing as you being evil or a bad person. We all have our own darkness, Kali, just not everyone's looks like yours. That doesn't make you evil."

"I just keep thinking about how disappointed Dad would be. I tried so hard to be strong for him, and Matt, but in the end, it wasn't enough. If he is watching me right now, I hate knowing I let him down. I let them both down." This time, she didn't bother to wipe the fresh tears away.

"If Dad is watching right now then I'd say he would be proud of both of us. We've stuck together like we promised we would, and we've looked out for each other. That's all he would have wanted for us."

"I'm pretty sure he wouldn't have wanted any of this for us to be honest, Will," she sniffed.

He considered her for a moment. "Yeah okay, fair point," he conceded, sighing.

"I find myself feeling almost glad he isn't here to see all this more and more recently," Kali rested her head back against the wall and looked up, wondering if it was possible her father was looking down on them from wherever he was now.

"I get what you mean," sighed William. "What those demons did was his worst fear, so in a way, I'm glad he isn't here to see it. But if he is watching, I want you to know that he would be more concerned with making sure you're okay than anything else. Matt too. And I'm sure they would be damn proud that in the end, you didn't let her win. Maybe there was a moment where she almost won, but hey, I came to your rescue because I'm the best, so no harm done, right?"

Kali smiled slightly. "You know I spat in her face; she was furious."

"See? Definitely a move for Dad to be proud of," he chuckled, shaking his head.

"I don't think Mattias would approve of spitting though."

"Hmm, maybe just in that one specific context he might have made an exception."

There was a pause, then they both sighed.

"Thanks, Will."

"Any time."

"So, any chance you could help me up? I don't want to survive this just to get stuck and die on the bathroom floor," Kali held her right hand out.

Standing, William grinned and helped her up.

"I hate to prove Lenaria right but I'm tired," she admitted. "But I *need* to shower and change into some clean clothes and I'm here now. Could you—?"

"I'll ask Anissa to bring you clean clothes, do you need Lenaria's help for anything?"

"Thanks. No, I'm fine."

William turned to leave, but Kali called after him. "Will...how is Anissa? After everything?"

He sighed and absentmindedly rubbed the back of his neck.

"She's pretty shaken up. I think she feels terrible that she never got to make up with Tannick, mostly. It's looking more and more likely that the demons had him this whole time, torturing information out of him and getting him to write that message. She's been having nightmares, but she thinks we haven't noticed. And on top of that, she blames herself for what happened to you."

"*What?*"

"Yeah. She says that if she hadn't pushed so hard to stay behind that night then none of it would have happened and that if you didn't need to protect her in the fight then that demon wouldn't have got the drop on you. I've tried to tell her that nobody thinks that, but I don't think she believes me. Especially since I was so against going from the start. Even the fact that she was the reason we found you hasn't seemed to help."

"What do you mean she was the reason you found me? You never actually told me how you found me."

William shifted uncomfortably, as though he would rather forget everything about it.

"Just focus on getting better just now, I'll tell you later."

"Will, come on. I want to know."

He made a face and rubbed his neck like it pained him to remember.

"Well, after the demons took you, we fought the ones that were left and by the time they were dead you were all gone. We knew the chances of them staying on the human plane were slim to none, so we found the Inaustia and sure enough, there were signs of demon activity – dead plants, footprints, blood, that sort of thing.

"I realised we didn't know how much ground we'd need to cover once we got through, so we went looking for a car. I managed to get it started and we went through the Inaustia, but then the trail went cold. There were tens if not hundreds of buildings – mostly abandoned ruins – to search and the road kept turning into this thick, dense forest and we'd get turned around.

"We'd been driving around for a while and I was starting to think we'd never find you when Anissa went pale. Really pale. She said she could *feel* you, and she started crying and said she knew how to find you—"

"Anissa *felt* her way to me," Kali looked at him, dubious.

A shadow passed across her brother's face.

"You were the only seraphic thing besides us for miles. She said what you were feeling was so intense that she was picking you up without trying to. That basically you were in so much pain it was activating her power, like she could feel you in her head," he explained, voice hollow.

"Oh."

"Yeah, *oh*. So anyway, she tells us to take a turn and then from there she's like a Kali GPS, the stronger she felt you, the closer we were to you. Eventually, we saw this castle-like fortress up ahead and we just knew that's where Liliana must be holed up. I created a little fire and explosion to get everyone as far away from where Anissa said you were as possible. But then Anissa said she couldn't feel you anymore and we thought..."

The memory of finding her seemed to subdue him, and he shuddered.

"So, she literally saved my life," Kali said in awe.

"Yeah, but she doesn't see it like that. You might want to talk to her if you get the chance later."

"I will," Kali nodded.

"Good. I'll go get her to bring you what you need."

He left the room and shut the door behind him, allowing her to peel off her bandages and step into the shower. The hot water stung at first, but she took comfort in the warm, clean water as it began to draw the furious itch out of her healing wounds. It was the first time she had felt clean in days.

She felt like she might stay there for hours, washing away the traces of the past week, until the heat made her dizzy and unsteady on her feet. Reluctantly she turned the water off and reached for a clean towel, cocooning herself securely in it as she wrapped it around her. The injuries she'd been so eager to see before were intrusive now and caught her attention unwelcomely as she did so. The red-purple of them, accentuated by the heat of the water, stood out against the rest of her skin, and the discoloured patches of fading bruises smeared the spaces between. Both were now a cruel reminder of all that had happened to her, inescapable proof that there was no washing it all away. She covered them as best she could, trying to calm the storm of emotion threatening to rise in her chest.

She opened the door an inch and peeked through, happy to find that Anissa had left clean clothes outside the door for her. She dried and changed into them, along with fresh dressings for her injuries, making a point not to linger on them for too long. She tied her wet hair up, and limped down the corridor, knee protesting angrily as she went. She found Amariel, Anissa, and William in the living room, and flopped down on an empty sofa.

"Perfect timing! We were about to choose a movie to watch!" Anissa beamed. Kali could tell she was trying very hard to be positive for her. She could also tell that she had recently been crying.

"What do you think, Kali?" Amariel sat down beside William on the sofa opposite her, holding up several DVDs.

"Don't mind me, pick anything!" she smiled back, far more interested in arranging the cushions into a more comfortable position. She hoped she could get Anissa alone for a chance to talk to her, to make sure she was okay, but she didn't want to make it obvious.

After some discussion between William and Amariel (*"we can't pick a horror movie, Amariel, think about what we've just been through!"*) they settled on some banal comedy that Kali didn't pay attention to. William and Amariel were tucked up together beneath a blanket, whilst Anissa settled into the space beside Kali. At that moment, they could have been anyone, just a group of friends spending time together instead of outcasts on the run together, recovering from tragedy.

"I love you guys," she mumbled sleepily.

She closed her eyes and felt Anissa take her hand tenderly.

"We love you too, Kali," she gave her hand a light squeeze.

Anissa's hand was warm and comforting in hers, and Kali smiled to herself as she drifted to sleep.

Chapter Nineteen

The events of the morning had exhausted Kali so much that for the first time in days her sleep was, mercifully, dreamless. When she woke up, she was still on the sofa, but her friends were gone. Someone had covered her with the blanket, which she moved aside as she sat up, carefully stretching out her stiff muscles. She could hear voices down the hall, likely coming from the kitchen, accompanied by the clinking of plates and the smell of food. Suddenly ravenous, Kali stood up slowly and made her way to the kitchen but stopped short of the doorway. Embarrassed, she remembered her outburst with Lenaria earlier in the day and wondered if she should go back to bed when she heard her name.

"Should we wake Kali or let her sleep?" rang Anissa's voice.

"She hasn't really eaten today; I'll go get her." William's voice was followed by the scraping of a chair.

"Please, allow me. Eat your dinner while it's still hot," Amariel's voice was full of a gentleness that was reserved only for her brother. Watching them together, it was almost easy to forget what a formidable warrior Amariel was.

She heard him move towards the door and with a start realised he was coming towards her. Before she could move, he was standing in front of her.

"Hello," he looked at her quizzically, "are you coming in or were you waiting for something?"

"I was just...yeah I'm coming in," she looked down at the floor and followed Amariel in, taking an empty seat next to Anissa. Lenaria watched her as she sat down but said nothing.

Everyone seemed in high spirits as the food was served, even Anissa, who despite her grief for Tannick seemed genuinely thrilled that Kali was back with them and out of bed, though she was considerably more reserved than usual. Kali let the conversation float by her without joining in; it was nice just to listen to her loved ones have conversations that were light and full of humour, to hear them laugh, and she felt a great rush of warmth towards all of them. As she watched them laugh freely, she wondered if she would ever experience joy so effortlessly again. For now, maybe experiencing their joy was enough.

As Kali began to eat, she found that once again her appetite disappeared after only a couple of mouthfuls. She moved her food around, hoping not to draw anyone's attention. When everyone else had finished, William collected the plates. He raised an eyebrow at the sight of her plate but caught Amariel's eye as he gave an almost imperceptible shake of his head and said nothing.

She smiled at Amariel, who winked back at her. Amariel was good for her brother, she reflected. William had been thrust into a world of uncertainty just as she had been, a burden of responsibility placed on his shoulders, and Amariel usually managed to counter whatever stress her brother was experiencing and stop an over-reaction before it erupted.

They stayed at the table for a while, chatting and laughing over the remainder of the bottle of wine, but as the night drew on, the conversation turned to patrols and next steps.

"We must assume we were followed, and prepare accordingly," Amariel spoke firmly but matter-of-factly.

"You keep saying that but clearly we weren't followed. It's been a week, what do you think they would be waiting for, a group invitation?" Anissa countered, sounding frustrated.

Kali met her brother's eye.

"Maybe they wanted to see what I'd do first," Kali remembered the triumph in her mother's eyes the last time they were face-to-face. The last Liliana saw Kali, she was preparing to give into the darkness; it was possible that she expected Kali to return to her.

The group looked at her in surprise, and William gave her a look that pleaded caution.

"Maybe they thought I would die or turn all demonic or something. Who knows what that poison was really meant to do? I just don't think we should get complacent. Not now, not after how they ambushed us last time."

A sombre chill fell over the group as they remembered the night of Tannick's – or rather the demons torturing Tannick's – trap. Kali saw Anissa tremble and knew she was picturing his head, bloated and discoloured, lying at her feet and felt a pang of sympathy for her friend, and one of grief for Tannick. She reflected, with some guilt, that she hadn't given as much thought to Tannick as she ought to, her grief for him lost somewhere in the trauma that followed.

"Kali is correct," continued Amariel, "we must ensure our safety has not been compromised."

"But surely we are safest *inside* the house?" Lenaria spoke up. "If you go back out there now then aren't you just giving them more opportunity to find us if they don't know where we are? Aren't we protected inside the building?"

"Fair point, but we'll need food and other supplies soon, so we need to leave eventually. I would rather know sooner rather than later if that's safe or not," William leaned back in his chair, his eyes flitting often to Kali and Amariel.

Kali thought back to her mother's threats with a twinge of alarm.

"She told me," she interrupted, her voice unintentionally quiet.

The group fell silent and looked inquiringly at her, but she struggled to find the words. The shame that she'd forgotten until now she was putting them all in danger was making her flushed.

"What did she tell you?" William pressed, leaning forward. Amariel rested a cautionary hand on his upper arm as Kali flinched back slightly in response.

"She um, she said that as long as I chose not to join her that none of you…" her breath hitched, and she faltered. "She said none of you would be safe."

She cast her eyes downward, guilt creeping through her. She expected them to demand answers as to why she was only mentioning this now, how she could have neglected to tell them about it. She expected them to be disgusted at her self-absorption and her ability to forget about the threat made against them.

"Yeah, no shit, Kali. Did you think we were hiding out here because of the scenic views?" William laughed, though not unkindly.

She looked up, surprised.

"I can't say a targeted threat from Liliana is a welcome prospect, but it's not any more than I expected," agreed Amariel.

"I believe we all knew the risks when we came here," nodded Lenaria.

"I would have died at Alarium without you anyway, Kali. We all would have," Anissa reached out and took her hand, gentle and reassuring.

Kali fidgeted with the edge of one of her dressings, finding it hard to look at them.

"Are you sure? I won't blame you if you want to leave. None of you signed up to be in Liliana's direct line of sight."

"Kali give us some credit. We know why we're here and what we're risking. But Anissa is right: Liliana came for all of us at Alarium and it was nothing to do with you. That's just demons being demons," William assured her.

"Kali, we're not leaving you now. We're not leaving you ever," Anissa gave her hand a small squeeze.

"I...thanks, guys," Kali smiled, choked with emotion.

Time and time again her friends proved her wrong. Whenever she thought she was bound to end up alone they rallied around her, and she didn't think they even knew how much it meant to her.

"So, is this the part where we have a big group hug and sing songs round a roaring fire?" quipped William, but he was smiling at her.

"I think we were discussing the necessity of patrols," Amariel shot a look at William and suppressed a smile.

The group began discussing tactics, patrols and potential battle strategies, and Kali quickly began to feel useless. She couldn't help them now in her injured state, and whenever she thought of facing the demons head-on, she experienced a near-debilitating stab of fear in her gut. Every time she thought of facing them, she thought of the green poison that could incapacitate her, and the suffering they were not only willing but *eager* to inflict – it made her feel incredibly exposed.

She silently berated herself for being weak when she was raised to be stronger than this. She was weak now for being scared of the demons, she was weak for nearly giving in to Liliana, and she was weak for not being able to get her friends out of the battle when they were ambushed...just like she couldn't help Mattias or her father all those months ago. She stood, looking at Anissa whose expression seemed to mirror Kali's frustration and sense of uselessness. She sensed her opportunity to get Anissa alone to talk to her.

"I'm really tired guys, I think I'm going to go to bed. Anissa, could you help me? My leg is still a little unsteady."

"Of course!" Anissa looked grateful for the excuse to leave.

Kali bade everyone goodnight, then followed Anissa to the door. Once out of the kitchen, she turned and hobbled in the direction of her bedroom.

"Uh, Kali? The medical bay is this way?"

"I want to sleep in my own bed tonight, Ani."

Anissa nodded and offered Kali her arm for support. Kali didn't really need it, but she accepted, hoping to maintain the pretence and encourage Anissa to open up to her. They moved slowly down the hall, and as Kali racked her brain for the best way to start the conversation, Anissa did it for her.

"I'm really glad you're okay, Kali," Anissa said quietly, "and I'm really sorry for everything."

"Ani, you have *nothing* to be sorry for."

Anissa wouldn't look at her, staring only at the ground as tears welled in her eyes.

Kali stopped and gently turned Anissa towards her.

"Anissa, listen to me. You have absolutely nothing to be sorry for, okay? William told me you feel like you're to blame but I want you to know that you're wrong. None of this was your fault. You *saved* me!"

Anissa looked up at her. "How can you say that? *I* insisted we went to find Tannick, *I* refused to listen when you said it wasn't safe and it was *me* who distracted you and let that demon capture you. The whole thing was my fault," she whispered tearfully.

"Anissa, we decided together that we were going to find Tannick, we all wanted to believe we could go home again. As for the rest, do you think that any of us would have reacted any differently if it were our family out there? Of course you didn't want to leave your brother behind," Kali gently wiped a tear away from Anissa's cheek as it fell.

"But in the fight—"

"Anissa, I don't for a second regret saving you or resent you for it. I'd make that same choice a hundred times in a row if I had to again. We were never getting out of there, that trap was designed to ensure of that. If that demon hadn't captured me when he did, you would all probably be dead, and I'd still be with Liliana. You need to stop blaming yourself, please. If it wasn't for you then who knows what would have happened, if they'd ever even have found me."

Anissa shook her head and squeezed her eyes shut.

"I abandoned Tannick. We never even made up and now he's gone," she finally said, her voice wavering.

"Anissa, he loved you and he knew you loved him. Nothing could have changed that," Kali tried to swallow the lump in her throat as she realised they'd never get the chance to reconcile either.

"But I never got to tell him that I forgive him, or say goodbye," Anissa's voice broke as she dissolved into tears.

Kali put her arms carefully around Anissa and she seemed to fold into her, crying on her shoulder with painful racking sobs that made Kali want to cry with her. Her heart ached for Anissa; she knew this kind of anguish and wished she could do something to take her pain away.

After several moments, Anissa stood upright, wiping at her eyes. She looked more tired than Kali had ever seen her.

"Ani, I'm so sorry. I'm sorry I didn't go back for him that day. I wish I did, I wish we'd just made him come with us. I'm so sorry," Kali sniffed, thinking about the boy who trained with her when they were children and the man who'd fought alongside her at Alarium. She suspected the death of her friend was yet to fully hit her.

"No, don't do that to yourself, Kali. William was right, going back would have been a death sentence and I know that now. I knew it back then; I just wasn't thinking clearly. You saved us, you did."

"But not him," she exhaled, trying to expel the heavy feeling in her chest.

"Not everyone is your responsibility to save," Anissa muttered, taking Kali's arm again and beginning to lead her to her bedroom.

Kali suddenly worried that she was imposing on Anissa's grief and that her own – both for Tannick and the resurfacing emotions of losing her own brother – was threatening to overwhelm her. She didn't want to take away from Anissa's sorrow by making it about her, but she couldn't stop thinking about all the days spent with Tannick at the lake. She could hear his laugh and feel his infectious energy, scarcely able to believe they'd been absent from the world all this time and she hadn't noticed.

"Ani, I can make it on my own from here. Thank you for your help, though," she stated, afraid if she cried about everything now that she may never stop.

"Are you sure?" Anissa sniffled.

"Yeah, will you be okay?"

Anissa nodded but seemed unconvinced, and Kali hugged her, wishing that something as simple as a hug could draw the pain out of her friend.

Kali started towards her bedroom, but she knew she held no desire to sleep. She didn't want to go to the place her nightmares took her, didn't want to relive the same awful scenes in her head. She didn't want to think about losing Tannick or her father or Mattias. She didn't want to think about being strapped to that table. She didn't want to feel weak anymore. She didn't want to feel any of it.

She shuffled down the hall and was only half surprised when she found herself at the top of the stairs leading down into the training room. Clambering awkwardly down the stairs, she ran her hands carefully over the weapons lining the walls when she reached the bottom, her hand coming to rest over a familiar-looking short sword. She recognised it as one of her old training swords, from when she was a child. Back then, it seemed so large to Kali; that seemed like another life now.

After a moment of hesitation, she withdrew it, taking up the balanced stance her father had taught her so many years ago, placing weight on her bad leg carefully. Gently at first, she worked through the different stances and techniques she knew, building up to parries and counters with imaginary enemies. It felt good to have a weapon in her hand again, to feel like a warrior instead of defenceless, to feel in control.

Against her will, she remembered how it felt to be trapped, remembered the fear and the pain. She remembered how it felt to watch her brother die, then her father, and she remembered how it felt to be betrayed by Tannick, to have to flee her home once more. She remembered Tannick's head landing at her feet, and Anissa's distraught screams as she dragged her away.

Her imaginary attacks grew fiercer as she sparred with her imagination, the blood rushing in her ears as adrenaline sung through her veins, numbed to any pain in her body. She teleported to the other side of the room, pushing down the dizziness it brought; tossing the sword aside, she began to pummel a combat training dummy with furious conviction, the memories of the past two years churning through her mind. Again and again, she struck the dummy, each blow punctuated by a different memory, creating a savage rhythm, her breath coming quicker and quicker until eventually, the dummy cracked in two.

Sweat poured down her face as she slowly sank to the ground. The pain she hadn't felt came rushing back now and her breaths came in sobs. She realised she'd been crying, her throat painful and raw. Too tired and sore to even entertain the idea of moving, she decided that she would rest here now, and sneak to her bed before anyone noticed. She lay her head down on the training mat and fell asleep instantly.

She awoke a few hours later to the sound of her name being called, rousing just in time to see William entering the training room, closely followed by Amariel. Her brother wore what was by now a familiar look of exasperated fury whilst Amariel seemed to be struggling to hold back his amusement and, if Kali wasn't mistaken, pride, as he eyed the broken mannequin.

She stared up at her brother, still half-asleep, and grinned at him, which apparently served only to make him angrier. He seemed to be literally lost for words as he looked around the room, taking in the dummy, the sword, and the fresh blood Kali just now realised was spotting her clothes. When he spoke, it was strained through gritted teeth.

"Report to Lenaria, *now.*"

Wincing, she stood up. His anger seemed to be contagious, infecting her and making *her* angry. She stood, staring him out and refusing to move, defiant.

"Kali, I'm not kidding. Move!"

Ignoring him, she picked up her discarded sword from the floor and, deliberately slowly, placed it back in its rightful place. She could feel his eyes on her.

"*Kali,*" he warned.

"I'm getting really sick of you always telling me what to do like I'm a child, Will."

"Stop acting like a child and I won't have to!"

They stared each other down, neither willing to concede, until Amariel cleared his throat emphatically.

"Kali, what I think your brother is trying to convey here is his concern for you. Lenaria has requested that you report to the medical bay so she may run some more tests," he reasoned, trying as ever to maintain his role as the peacekeeper.

"She's already run about a thousand tests!" Kali interrupted. "No, I'm done having her poke and prod me every other hour, I'm going to bed!"

Before her brother could argue, she teleported to her bedroom. *Good,* she thought, *that should piss him off.*

As with most of her arguments with her brother, Kali wasn't quite sure why she was angry, but she knew that she was too angry to back down. Stubborn, Mattias always called her – another way in which she and

William were alike. She expected to calm down as she always did, but in fact, Kali's sudden sense of anger didn't dissipate over the coming days, and as time went by, she began to feel increasingly separate from her friends and brother. She isolated herself more and more, spending time either in the library studying tactics of war and learning the demonic language, Daeathric, or in the training room, pushing herself back to fighting condition.

The latter resulted in one of the biggest arguments Kali had ever had with her brother, calming only once the rest of the group jumped in to mediate. As Kali pointed out, he couldn't stop her from training, although as a peace offering, she (reluctantly) agreed to allow Lenaria to do whatever checks she deemed necessary. Still, both Lenaria and William were unhappy about what they called "needless, strenuous activity", and Kali did whatever she could to avoid their company.

The truth was something had changed in Kali since her torture. The thing that scared her most now was not her own darkness, but rather how much she found herself longing to succumb to it. To be enveloped by it, taken over by it, revel in it. Though she knew it was self-destruction, the darkness whispered promises to her that were dangerously inviting.

Despite everything, she thought of how wonderful it would be not to have to fight anymore. To simply exist the way other people took for granted. To not have to pretend that she didn't harbour a bloodlust or have a desire to lose control. She had started to wonder again *why* she fought it; after all, the darkness was a part of her, it *was* her, maybe this was simply who she was meant to be.

Then she'd think of her family, and of her friends that put their lives on the line for her, and the pull to the darkness loosened its grip. Never enough to be free of it, but enough to fight it a little longer, at least.

As the days continued to slip by, Kali threw all of her energy into training – weapons, combat, cardio, weights on a loop – ignoring the combined protests of Lenaria, William, and her injuries until she could finally feel her strength coming back.

One day, Amariel joined her in the training room.

At first, he kept his distance from her, making a point of doing his own thing and not bothering her. When she didn't object to his presence, he approached her, watching her train intently. Thirty minutes went by without either of them speaking before Amariel cleared his throat. Kali turned towards him.

"I can continue to teach you if you like. Help you try to use multiple powers at once if you still want to pursue it."

She studied him carefully, unsure if this was some kind of test.

"William didn't send you, did he?"

"Surprising as it may be, Kali, I sometimes have my own opinions and do things of my own accord separate from your brother."

"Fair enough. So why do you want to help me?"

"Because we're friends. Because we're soldiers, and it's what we know," he replied simply.

"Okay," she nodded. "When do we start?"

Amariel gestured around them. "We're here, aren't we?"

She grinned at him and pushed her hair out of her face as he cleared a space for them.

Amariel was a good teacher, Kali knew that from their previous training sessions, but she was surprised about the intensity of his efforts this time around. She expected him to be over-protective on William's behalf, but he launched into her training without easing her into it.

"There's no point covering old ground," he said. "We know you can control your powers one at a time. We'll start with just using two simultaneously and then work up to using them in combination with physical combat."

Kali was determined, and she welcomed having something to work towards, to focus on. She thought that this was Amariel's intention – where her brother saw her as his little sister who needed to be protected, Amariel saw her as a soldier that needed to recover from a trauma in the only way she knew how. She realised with a rush of warmth how much she loved Amariel. As much as he was good for William, he was good for her too.

She followed Amariel's instruction, allowing her mind to access the power inside of her, trying to extend her concentration to two at the same time. On the surface of it, it sounded easy but after an hour, Kali was worn out.

"Why don't we take a break, get some lunch and try again afterwards?" Amariel said eventually. "There's no sense in depleting your energy for no reason," he continued when Kali opened her mouth to argue.

Begrudgingly, she nodded and followed him upstairs for lunch, desperate to feel anything other than the weakness that seemed to taunt her from within her very soul.

They worked at it for days, and the days became weeks until finally, Kali was able to use any two of her chosen powers at the same time. They were joined occasionally by William, who seemed less offended by Kali's training now her wounds were visibly healed.

Gradually, they began to settle into a familiar routine again, training together, eating together, and patrolling the grounds together. As the sudden interruption to their life got further behind them, the more things began to return to normal – or, their version of normal. Laughter crept back into their lives sincerely, muting and softening the tension that seemed to envelop them in the wake of Tannick's death and Kali's torture.

Once the strain between Kali, Lenaria, and William dissipated, they held a memorial service for Tannick, which Kali knew meant a great deal to Anissa. Back in Domeneum, he would likely be considered one of many who died in the onslaught at Alarium – an overlooked name on a long list of the fallen, the details of his death lost to his family and friends. Here, he felt properly mourned, more significant somehow and she hoped it helped Anissa find some peace.

Her mind wandered often to what those in Domeneum knew of their own fates; did Raikan survive and succeed in telling the Council about her true nature and her escape, or had he been captured or killed alongside Tannick? Was each of their names on a list of the dead? If so, what happened to their home now that the last of the Robereun family were thought to be gone? Were they considered tragic heroes, slain by demons, or did the Guard hunt her as they hunted all demons?

Kali could spend hours tormenting herself with these questions, never knowing which reality she'd prefer, but she tried to spend her time with Anissa instead, hoping she could help her friend through her grief and quash her own down in the process. Kali thought that although perhaps cliched, it was undeniable that the events of that night had brought them closer. Kali knew the grief Anissa was going through, and both were bonded by a shared sense of loss and trauma from that night; Anissa lost her brother, and often Kali found herself feeling like she'd lost not only her friend but a part of herself, too.

They grew accustomed to seeing their own tiredness mirrored in the dark circles around the other's eyes, both plagued by nightmares they spoke of only to each other, never daring to utter the horrors they visited each night within earshot of the others. Gradually, as they shared the burden, the weight lifted and their conversations turned more often to memories and laughter than to sorrow and tears. Kali began to hope that with each other to lean on, recovery was possible for all of them.

As they put distance between them and their recent trauma, the group found themselves eager to develop new skills and pass-times that didn't revolve around fighting. They split their time between training and patrolling, along with a various assortment of hobbies and interests they'd picked up. Anissa baked cakes that became increasingly more elaborate as time went by, and Lenaria began painting. Sometimes she'd paint calming, serene landscapes and at others, she'd paint violent scenes of death, the red paint mimicking blood too realistically for Kali to be able to look at for too long without disquiet setting in. Amariel developed impressive skills in woodwork, going so far as to handcraft a new dining table and matching chairs for the group, and William spent more and more time writing.

What he was writing Kali wasn't sure of, but they often spent hours together in silence in the library, him scribbling in a notebook he'd found at a shop in town whilst she read up on demonology and Daeathric. She wasn't sure if her brother approved of her new studies, but Kali thought given recent experiences it was important to arm herself with more knowledge about their enemies. To be able to understand them. To never be vulnerable in ignorance again.

She thought that studying demons would only fuel the nightmares that still haunted her but to her surprise, she found that the more she learned, the more they abated. With her physical strength returned and gaining more knowledge about the demons that threatened her, she felt more in control than she had previously, and far less defenceless.

Their routine was to shift ever-so-slightly when Anissa announced one day over breakfast that if she and Lenaria would be expected to train and patrol that Kali, William and Amariel should be expected to cook "properly" for the group as well. Dutifully they obliged, each taking turns cooking meals rather than simply helping prepare, Anissa eagerly perched over each of them spouting encouragement and hints or tips. Kali found this incredibly endearing.

Amariel was surprisingly adept at cooking much to William's delight, whereas both Kali and William were abysmal, having never cooked anything more elaborate than the most basic of meals.

"Dad did all the cooking whenever we actually ate at home or weren't camping in some forest, and then I ate Guard food for about a year straight!" William protested defensively one night after inexplicably managing to burn an entire packet of pasta to the bottom of a pot.

Kali fared only slightly better than William, too impatient to spend any time on a meal with a tendency to over- or under-cook most things.

"But if you need food then it should be quick food so you can eat and go back to training!" she complained to Anissa, who shot her a look of mock horror in response before laughing at her.

Despite her propensity for disaster in the kitchen, she enjoyed spending time with Anissa when she was in her element, which was unusual given the militant nature of their experiences thus far. Under Anissa's tutelage, Kali was not only making regular improvement in food preparation, but she was also beginning to have fun with it. One day she spent hours helping her bake a vast array of intricately designed cupcakes in a variety of flavours, and realised afterwards, tired and covered in flour, that it was the happiest she'd been in years.

Laughing with Anissa and concentrating on something that wasn't physically punishing or mentally exhausting, something that wasn't centred entirely around the idea of fighting demons or *being* part demon was such a wonderful escape. Anissa, she noticed, laughed more freely and was more relaxed than she had been since losing Tannick.

She cherished days like those. It was in these days that the darkness held the least pull, that she felt most in control of it. Sometimes she even forgot about it, however briefly, and that was the most bittersweet experience because as wonderful as forgetting was, eventually she would remember again. She wished she could live inside of those moments, sheltered from the evil in the world, and protected from the pain it caused.

It was on such an evening, however, that their newfound contentment came to an end. It was a quiet evening – William was in the library writing, and Kali sat at the kitchen table reading as Anissa hummed absent-mindedly preparing dinner. Lenaria and Amariel were out on a patrol, the former only recently re-instated on patrols beyond the wards after numerous uneventful sessions.

When Kali heard the door slam shut she glanced up in mild irritation at the interruption to her concentration but thought little of it, until she heard Lenaria's wail of distress coming from the hallway.

She stood at once, moving in the direction of the noise without hesitation. Behind her, Anissa dropped the plate she was holding, where it shattered loudly on impact with the floor.

She met William in the hall as he sped towards Lenaria, wide-eyed and concerned looking. They approached her and saw she was bleeding from a gash on her forehead, looking anguished.

"Lenaria! What happened, are you okay?" Kali rushed towards her.

"Where's Amariel?" added William.

Tears streamed down Lenaria's face as she staggered towards them, dazed. Anissa arrived silently behind them.

"D-demons," she sobbed. Kali's heart sank, and William looked ashen.

"What about them? Where is Amariel?" William repeated urgently, fear burning in his eyes.

"They t-took him. They at-attacked us and Amariel s-saved me," she wailed. "He t-told me to run and I *s-swear* I thought he was behind me," she looked desperately at William as she spoke, "but when I looked back, he was g-gone!"

"Lenaria, how many demons are there? Where are they now?" Kali placed her hands on her shoulders as she sank to her knees, forcing Lenaria to look at her.

"About six or s-seven? I d-don't know where they went. They couldn't get through our wards."

William turned to her urgently. "They might still be out there."

She looked at him, desperately wanting that to be true. "Let's go."

"*Go?*" cried Anissa. "You can't go, what if it's a trap?"

"It probably is, but we're not leaving Amariel out there," said Kali firmly. "Take Lenaria to the medical bay. Look after her. We'll be back soon."

"Kali, you've already been taken by them once," Anissa pleaded.

"We're ready for them this time."

"Let's *go!*" William was already moving towards the door, and Kali hurried after him.

She always stayed armed now, ever since she was captured, and she knew William did too. She'd never been more grateful for that than in that moment as they made their way out into the darkness.

They sprinted out the front door calling Amariel's name, giving up on discretion knowing their location was already compromised. They searched for ten minutes, becoming increasingly desperate until William tripped over something, gleaming softly in the darkness. He picked it up and Kali felt sick as recognition, then despair, passed over William's face as they both realised the item was Amariel's sword, splattered with blood.

Studying the area around them, it became apparent there had been a struggle, with scuffs in the dirt and drops of blood staining the ground. The trees surrounding them were scarified with roughly drawn demonic symbols, and they were smeared with more blood. Kali recognised the markings well enough from her studies to conclude that they related to portal or transportation-related magic. Her chest felt heavy.

William sank to his knees and stared at the sword as though it might come to life at any moment and share the secret of Amariel's fate with them.

"Will, we can keep looking."

He looked up at her, glassy and unfocused. "No, he's not here. They've taken him, I know it. We would have heard them or seen something by now, plus..." he looked desolately at the sword in his hands and gestured at the crudely drawn markings on the trees around them.

Kali knew, as was the constant truth, that this was her mother's doing. She had waited until their guard was down and fulfilled her promise that her friends would suffer for her refusal. Had she been watching them for all these months? Had she chosen to strike when Lenaria was on patrol sensing she was more vulnerable? Had she managed to track them through some other, nefarious means?

Kali wasn't sure what to believe, but she knew there was only one thing she could do. She'd stolen the last few months of freedom, but that was never her life, and could never be her future. This cycle of violence didn't end unless she ended it, and she only knew of one way to do that.

She rested a hand on William's shoulder and looked him in the eye. "I am going to find him, and I am going to get him back to you. I promise you."

William blinked and stood up. "I'm coming too!"

"No, Will. You can't come with me this time," she turned and walked back to the house before he had the chance to argue.

She knew that it was time to face the inevitability she'd buried since she first learned the truth about herself. She knew that it was time for her to end this once and for all.

Chapter Twenty

William caught up to her in the kitchen. "Kali, it's *Amariel*. I can't lose him, I can't!"

"I know that Will. I know! But this trap is for *me*. She knows my biggest weakness is you – my friends, my family. They know I'm vulnerable if I'm worrying about protecting you. I can get him out of there, I promise you I can. But I need to be alone. *Please,* Will, let me do this."

Kali had never seen her brother look so tortured. He looked at her like a man on fire, crazed with pain and fear. She knew he was imagining, as she was, the cruelty they'd inflicted on Kali being inflicted on Amariel. It was an unbearable thought that she couldn't seem to shake from her mind.

"Kali, you can't go in there alone, they will kill you and then they'll kill him. Let me at least sneak in behind you, once I free Amariel we can help you fight your way out," he pleaded, desperately.

Kali fought down the panic rising in her throat. Every second they spent arguing was another that Amariel was left to the mercy of the demons. She knew she wasn't coming back from this, and she knew on some level that William did too.

"What difference will two of us make against an army, Will? What will both of us dying achieve? Don't you see? This is never going to stop. This isn't something we can just wait out; Liliana will never stop coming for us if I stay. This never ends, not unless I stop it here and now, one way or the other. But either way, I will get Amariel back to you, I promise."

"Kali, if you go there alone then you know how this ends. I'm not letting you die, not after everything we've been through!"

"If I go there with you then I'll spend the time I could be fighting worried about you, and I risk losing you *and* Amariel."

"Do you honestly think you can fight your way out alone?"

She looked him in the eye. "No, I don't."

He opened his mouth to argue, looking wretched, but she cut him off before he could speak. It was time she was strong for her brother after a lifetime of him protecting her.

"Will, my life has been on borrowed time since Dad hid me as a baby. There was never a normal life out there for me, but you can have it with Amariel. This life has already taken so much from you, from us. Please let me do this one thing. Let me know it hasn't all been for nothing. Let me do this now, on my terms, helping the people I love," she beseeched him.

He stared at her, looking broken, knowing she was asking his permission to die. He cried out, and in one swoop, overturned the dining table, smashing the glasses and empty plates that still lay prepared expectantly for dinner. The place where his hands rested on the surface of the kitchen counter were scorched, and Kali couldn't remember a time where he'd lost control like this before. It broke her heart, and she knew that she had to get Amariel back to him, that she could not leave him alone in this world.

"It can't end like this," he whispered through tears, with his hands on his head.

Like a dam breaking, she felt everything they had been through and knew her brother felt it too. She knew at that moment that his tears were not exclusively for her; they were for the mother he lost, the childhood burdened with the truth, their father, their brother, the future they'd never have, and for Amariel, who might already be dead.

Stepping closer to her brother, she looked him in the eye, trying to convey the conviction of what she felt now. The assurance that this was the right thing to do, that it was something she *needed* to do.

"Will, I cannot live my life running like this, hiding behind other people and wondering who will be next to die. I would rather it ended like this than with one of you dead. We've lost too many people, and I can't lose any more. Let me do this. Let me get him back for you. Let me go out on my own terms doing something worthwhile. *Please,* Will. Please let me do this alone."

He stared at her as though not truly seeing her, then nodded silently.

The only thing she heard as she turned and exited the room, feeling hollow yet determined, was the sound of her brother's broken sobs.

* * * *

Kali spent the next fifteen minutes preparing weapons and trying to form a strategy, alone in the training room. She couldn't stand to see anyone, not yet – she was scared her resolve would break if she spent too much time with her friends. She knew that this mission was one-way for her, that the two paths facing her once inside would be to turn like her mother wanted her to or die. She was prepared to die, she just hoped she'd find Amariel first. She tried not to think about the former, about whatever her mother had in store for her. *At least I don't need to form an escape plan for myself,* she thought drily.

Satisfied with her preparations and unwilling to waste any more time, she set the books she was studying aside, clipped her weapons into place and made her way to the kitchen. William, Lenaria, and Anissa were together, pale and silent. They looked up when she entered, and Anissa immediately burst into tears.

Kali was at a loss for words. What to say to people who had risked everything for you as you left on a suicide mission? There were no words that encapsulated her love for them, that articulated what each one of them meant to her, or how grateful she was to have known them. There were no words, and so she said none. She walked to the middle of the room and drew them all into a hug. When she withdrew, her eyes were the only ones that were dry.

"Thank you, for everything. I love you," she said, turning to each of them.

She looked to her brother last, holding his gaze. Tears stung at the back of her eyes as she smiled at him before she closed her eyes and prepared to teleport into the bowels of Liliana's stronghold.

Just as she felt that familiar shift somewhere in her gut, she felt a hand shoot out and grasp her upper arm. Too late now to stop the power she'd set in motion, she opened her eyes in alarm to find William's determined face looking back at her as they fell momentarily into nothing.

They materialised into the only place Kali really knew in her mother's fortress – the room in which she was tortured months before. It was empty now, and she saw her brother's stance relax as he stopped scanning the room and turned back to her.

"What are you *doing?*" she hissed at him in a low voice, checking reflexively over her shoulder to make sure they were alone.

He fixed her with a stare, looking remarkably calm for the situation.

"Kali, don't ask me to sit this one out. Not when it's him. Not when it's you," he looked down at her, eyes blazing and determined.

Kali opened her mouth to argue, then simply nodded. His mind was made up, and to argue would only waste time. A knot of fear pierced her heart, momentarily robbing her of breath as she considered the possibility of something awful happening to him. She'd inadvertently brought him here, to this terrible place that cultivated only suffering. This now-empty room felt dense with the memories of her own, and beyond the door lay the promise for more. She shook herself impatiently, thinking instead of Amariel. Having William here made it that much harder to do what she needed to do, but she took comfort in the fact that Amariel would not be left to escape here alone.

They moved cautiously towards the door, listening for movement on the other side. It was silent. Exchanging wordless nods, weapons readied, they gently pushed open the door. They flinched as the hinges creaked, amplified in the stillness around them, but were glad to find it unlocked. They crept out into the hallway, turning in the opposite direction that William had taken her when they escaped previously. Following the dimly lit corridor as silently as they could, Kali prayed that they were going the right way.

At the end of the corridor lay an antechamber; two guards were stationed outside of a large, wooden door.

Two guards wouldn't be difficult to kill, but they didn't know what lay beyond that door and that left them at a disadvantage. Kali couldn't afford to be captured before they found Amariel, and she couldn't bear the thought of William falling into their mother's grasp too.

She gestured to William to stop and motioned for him to stand behind her, both of them with their backs against the wall. Hiding in the shadows behind a pillar, she raised her hand and carefully knocked a burning torch from its sconce. It hit the ground with a loud clatter, and the guards' heads snapped in their direction. Unable to see them, they shifted restlessly. One called out in Daeathric and Kali stayed silent, willing them to leave their post and investigate. Behind her, William began to tense, shifting his weight in anticipation. She heard the demons confer briefly in low tones before one of them slowly made its way towards their hiding place.

She watched it come closer, weapons raised, and she focused all her energy on it – all of her rage, and hatred, and grief – and she saw it drop its weapon, clutching desperately at its throat. It gurgled as black blood poured from its mouth, followed soon by its eyes and nose. Black veins spidered across its face as it choked, falling heavily to the ground and eventually, lay still. Behind her, William shifted uncomfortably.

The second demon called out to its partner, struggling to see through the darkness. Imitating the way she had heard them speak before, and thinking back to the books she studied, she called to it in a deep, gravelly voice using the Daeathric word for *"help"*. At once, the other demon charged forward, barrelling into the corridor brandishing its weapon and freezing on the spot at the sight of its friend's bloodied corpse.

Kali sprang forward, using her power to pin the demon to the wall. She noticed with some satisfaction that her powers seemed stronger here, and more in her control. Helpless, the demon looked at her with contempt.

"*Where is the prisoner?*" she spoke in its language, but it only sneered at her.

She imagined every vessel in the demon's body bursting, every nerve screaming, and directed all her energy at him. His muscles stiffened and his back arched against the wall, still unable to move.

Two powers at once – thank you Amariel, she thought as the demon writhed in pain. Blood burst from its eyes and mouth as it gasped for breath. William stopped midway towards them, a breath catching in his throat. Kali stopped and spoke to it again in Daeathric.

"*Your death can be swift, or it can last for days, beast. Where is the prisoner?*"

"*With...the...Queen,*" it panted.

"*Where is that?*"

"*Through...door. Upstairs. Room on the left.*" Unexpectedly, it laughed, spilling more blood down its chin. "*She is...expecting you...will die...here,*" it mocked.

"Yeah, that's what I'm counting on," she muttered as she drove her sword through its neck, beheading it. She let its body fall as its head hit the ground, coming to rest near his fallen partner.

She turned to William, who seemed to shrink back from her as he looked at the gore lying at her feet.

"What did it say?" he tore his gaze from the slaughtered demons to look at her. Kali thought he looked pale, a muscle twitching in his jaw as he waited for her answer.

"They're upstairs, through that door."

He nodded, a strange distance in his eyes. "Anything else?"

"She's waiting for us."

"Then let's not keep her," he replied darkly, already moving towards the door.

"Will, maybe you should wait here," Kali suggested, her chest tight at the idea of bringing him further into the fortress.

He stopped, his shoulders squared in determination and his sword clutched tightly by his side.

"I'm not going through this with you again, Kali. This is Liliana's playing field and her game, we'll never out-strategise her here. If saving the man I love means walking into a trap then that's what I'll do. Without you, if

I need to," he replied over his shoulder without looking at her.

"Fine," she shook her head. "But you leave Liliana to me. You get Amariel and you get out of here, no discussions."

He turned back towards the door without answering, and she hurried after him, fear and anticipation coursing through her as they reached it.

This is it, she thought, adrenaline pounding through her with every frantic beat of her heart. *Through the door, upstairs, left...you can do this.*

Braced for combat, they shared a tense nod and threw open the door, hoping to catch whoever or whatever lay waiting on the other side of it unprepared.

But the demons were expecting them; they stood in perfect lines facing the door, armed and waiting, so still that Kali momentarily mistook them for grotesque statues. Their appearance broke the stillness; the demons lunged at them immediately and with terrifying speed, putting them instantly on the defensive. The sheer number of them made it impossible to do anything but parry their blows. Kali threw out a couple of bursts of energy in quick succession to try and put some space between them and the demons – anything to get a moment to regroup – and William followed them up with jets of fire, but the demons persisted on. Some immune to the flames like those at Alarium, some determined to push on though their skin charred and flaked.

"Don't let them get behind us!" William cried.

Even as he spoke, Kali heard the clanging of metal armour and the thundering of footsteps from the corridor behind them, alerting her to the arrival of yet more of her mother's demons.

"We're surrounded!" she panted as she swooped low to cut a demon in half at the waist with her sword and spun to catch another across the throat. She impaled a third, kicking him off of her blade and using the momentum to carry her back towards William. The demons were endless, impossible numbers of them coming from all directions. It was like Alarium all over again.

As she looked at the grim expression on her brother's face, a memory tugged at her. Not the memory of the battle at Alarium itself, but rather the ghost of a feeling. A delicious feeling, a solution to the onslaught of demons they faced.

Last time, when she called upon it out of desperation, the power burned through her. This time it was almost effortless. She felt the power building before she'd consciously decided to do so, an automatic reaction to the thought forming in her mind and the power rousing in her core. A barrier of energy had cocooned them, separating them from the demons until she was ready.

And this time when she willed the demons dead, it wasn't a fury or a hatred that carried the wish, it was a cold and calm resolution. There was no dizziness here, no slow trickle of blood betraying the toll of the power – she was solid, rooted. For a fleeting moment, she felt like she was home.

William turned wildly in all directions as the demons fell with grunts and cries of agony. He reached out to her, offering a hand to steady her but faltered when he saw her, upright and composed.

She took in the carnage and, once she was sure no demons remained alive, began to pick her way through their corpses to reach the stairs at the other side of the room, her mind back on Amariel. The sudden calm was eerie and incongruous, and Kali felt a familiar knot of tension in her stomach once more.

William remained silent as he followed her, slipping occasionally in the blood pooling in the spaces between the slain demons. They reached the stairs and started to climb them, on guard and senses trained on any movement or noise up ahead of them. Kali could almost feel how close they were to Amariel, following not only the demon's directions but also some innate instinct within her.

She couldn't explain it, but her senses felt heightened here and she felt *different*. It was as though her energy was operating on a new frequency, expanding rather than diminishing with every use of her power. The slaughter she'd inflicted on the demons had not tired her, but instead awoken a new energy in her, glowing like an ember somewhere deep inside. She began to hope in earnest that she could get Amariel and William out of this unharmed.

Their footsteps left a bloody trail behind them, leaving them open to being tracked – although, Kali considered, the scene they'd left behind them was far from subtle. They tried briefly to wipe the residual blood from their shoes, their success limited as the gore began to thicken and congeal into dark sludge.

"Every time we fight these things, I find new ways to be disgusted," Kali sighed as they gave up and pressed on.

William continued forward wordlessly, every muscle tight, his expression strained, as they listened for the sounds they hoped not to hear. The sounds of more demons, their mother's voice, Amariel's screams.

The stairs brought them to another corridor, a long passage that got darker the further they moved along it until they were straining to see as their eyes adjusted. In the near-darkness, Kali imagined threats in every shadow. Anxiety simmered inside her, acidic and hot. She almost wished demons would attack again, just to break the tension and give her nerves an outlet.

Finally, she saw a door on the left up ahead of them. She placed a hand on William's arm, making him jump.

"*What?*" he hissed.

"There. They're in there."

"How do you know?"

"The demon said upstairs to the left and I…I can feel it."

A troubled look flitted briefly over William's face, replaced quickly by hope. He rushed forward and Kali scrambled to keep pace with him. He ignored her whispered pleas for him to be careful, striding towards the door with sole focus.

He was yards from the door when a handful of demons melted out of the shadows, the first to reach him taking advantage of his surprise and sinking a dagger into his side. He groaned and staggered back as he swung his sword round to meet it. Kali watched as it fell to the ground, where the remaining demons trampled its remains in their eagerness to reach her brother.

She teleported between them, bringing her sword up in defence. They didn't strike at her like they did William – Kali guessed they were ordered not to by her mother – but seemed unsure of what to do instead. Demons were creatures of torment, not restraint. Holding back was not in their nature, and it made them easy prey. She lit a flame in her hand, enjoying the warm sensation it brought with it, the potential for destruction, and directed it towards the demons. They hissed at her as they caught alight and she cut them down with slashes from her sword.

She heard her brother cough and turned back to him, panic lancing through her. He lifted the front of his shirt carefully, the dagger still embedded in him, to assess the wound. Kali hurried over to him, fear choking her as she tried to push it down and stay calm.

"Easy, let me do it," she told him. He nodded and leaned back against the wall, sweat on his forehead.

Kali looked at the wound, recalling their basic field training and hoping it would be enough. It didn't look too deep, but her heart sank as she saw the wound turning sickened and green at the edges. A toxic border where blade met skin.

She closed her eyes as though she could unsee it. As though not seeing it would somehow make it not real. *How can this be happening again?* How could she be living in this same nightmare over and over again? Was this how life was to be forevermore – the same formulaic disaster on repeat again and again until nothing remained?

"Listen," she looked up at him, voice shaking. "I need to take this out bec—in case it's poisoned, okay?"

She raised a trembling hand as he nodded.

"Okay, on three. One—" she pulled the dagger out as gently but firmly as she could, hoping the blood would carry away the last vestiges of the poison and trying to think of anything, *anything,* other than Mattias lying dead on the grass.

William gave a grunt of pain low in his throat as it came free, then stood away from the wall, his hand resting over his wound. He lumbered towards the door, clutching his side.

"Will, you have to rest!" Kali tried to stop him, but he swatted her away.

"Just…get me to him."

"Will, I need to get you to Lenaria. I can come back for Amariel. I swear I'll come back for him."

"Kali. Please." There was sadness in his eyes as he met hers.

She hesitated, torn on what to do next. If she didn't take William home now, he might die. If she did, Amariel might die.

Unwilling to wait for her approval, William pushed past her towards the door with surprising agility considering his injured state.

"*Will!*" she hurried after him again, reaching him just as his bloodied hand reached the handle of the door.

"I need to find him, Kali," he paused only for a moment, talking over his shoulder to her.

Then he pushed the handle down and opened the door to the room where Liliana lay in wait.

Chapter Twenty-One

They spilled into a room that contained only Amariel and their mother. She was seated and facing away from them, but turned as she heard them enter, fixing Kali with a terrible smile.

"Welcome, darling. Returning home at last, I see. How *wonderful.*"

Kali looked at Amariel. He was standing, tied to a post looking bruised but relatively unharmed. Relief rushed through her, but in his eyes, she saw only fear and despair.

"*William,*" he exhaled, taking in the blood staining the front of her brother's shirt and the way he now leaned on Kali. "You shouldn't be here! Please, go!" he called to them, looking desolate.

Kali turned away from him, and spoke directly to her mother, trying to sound brave.

"This fight is between you and me. Let him go, and we can settle this."

Her mother let out a hollow, high-pitched laugh, laced with spite.

"Let him *go?* Why he is here as your guest! The witness to your ascension! Your *gift* to enjoy afterwards," she gestured to knives and wicked-looking instruments that lay to the side of her, some hauntingly familiar to Kali. "I see you've brought another along for the fun, too!" she added, her first acknowledgement that her son stood bleeding in front of her.

Kali felt repulsed as she understood.

"You brought Amariel here so *I* could torture him? Are you out of your mind? I would *never* hurt him! Let him go!"

"Now why on Earth would I do that?" taunted Liliana.

"Let him go and I'll stay."

"Kali, no!" Amariel cried out, tugging on his restraints. William stood protectively, though unsteadily, in front of her.

Her mother looked past him, looking only at Kali, smiling dangerously.

"Well of course you're staying, child. That was never in doubt. You amuse me with your presumption of choice. It's what you do once you're here that matters to me. You've displayed a flair for martyrdom in the past, but I doubt you could really hurt me, and I would prefer to have a weapon like you on my side."

Kali stayed silent, knowing they'd been through this discussion before.

"I'm sure you've already felt the pull, the effect that being here has had on you. Your powers, are they stronger here?"

Reluctantly, Kali nodded, avoiding Amariel's gaze. William looked at the floor.

Liliana's eyes glittered. "The darkness sings to you as it sings to all creatures borne of it."

"Enough of this! *Let him go!*" Kali demanded, moving out from behind William and raising her sword.

Her mother stared at her appraisingly for a moment before speaking.

"Very well, my offer to you is this: yield your weapons and swear your allegiance to me, and I will trade your friend's freedom for your own."

"Done!"

"*Kali!*" Amariel looked distraught.

Her mother's expression was victorious. "*Wonderful!* Well, I rather think this calls for a celebration!" she turned, striding towards a large wooden partition, and carefully plucked something out from behind it.

Kali tensed, expecting a weapon of some kind, and was confused to see that it was a beautifully intricate black dress.

She held the dress up for Kali to see. "Your subjects will be thrilled to meet their new second-in-command! Your ascension rites will begin shortly, and I expect my heir to be presentable!"

Kali stared at her, nonplussed. She would have been more prepared to battle a thousand demons than this.

William gave a snarl and brandished his sword at Liliana. "She's not going anywhere with you!"

Liliana looked at him coldly. "Kali, darling. You're aware this one is dying, aren't you? My, my, you do burn through brothers rather quickly, don't you?"

A potent mix of rage, hatred, and despair scorched through her. Without conscious thought, she felt concentrated hatred surge out of her and watched as long, deep gashes opened in her mother's face, arms, and chest.

Liliana blinked, surprised. It was the first time Kali had ever seen her seem perturbed by anything. The expression was gone as swiftly as it came, replaced by her usual infuriatingly cool composure. She smirked at Kali as the wounds knitted together as they watched.

Kali was breathing heavily, her lip curled in loathing. William fell to his knees beside her with a groan and Amariel began struggling against his restraints as Kali stared down her mother.

"If you had any thoughts about reneging on our deal and teleporting out of here, or foolishly attempting to harm me again, know that the poison currently killing your brother is one of my own creation to which only I have the antidote. Slow-acting, *agonising,* fatal. To leave would mean certain death for poor William," she chuckled cruelly as she strode towards Kali, still holding the dress.

"What do you *want* from me?" she asked through gritted teeth. "I've already agreed to stay, let them go!"

"They will be released once you have completed the rite of ascension," she pressed the dress into Kali's hand, then placed her own under Kali's chin, forcing her head up so they were face to face. "You see child, *I always get what I want.*"

Kali wrenched herself out of her mother's grasp, hate pulsing through her, like a corruption threading itself through every fibre of her. She turned her attention to William as her mother left the room, locking the door behind her and giving no indication of when she would return.

Kali threw the dress and her sword to the floor and dropped to her knees beside William. He looked feverish and pale, his face contorted with pain.

"Amariel," he whispered.

"I'll get him," Kali assured him.

She ran to where Amariel was restrained, feeling like she was living in one of her nightmares. As she reached him, she saw the same look painted on Amariel's face.

"Amariel, are you okay? Did she hurt you?" she untied his hands, her own shaking slightly. As she loosened his restraints, she noticed a sigil engraved into them which she recognised from her studies as the Daeathric rune for "suppression." She realised with a start that her mother was well-equipped with restraints and weapons to counteract seraphic powers. The thought chilled her.

Once free, Amariel moved past her immediately, his eyes on William. He staggered to his side and sat beside him, cradling his head in his lap, and holding his hand.

"You shouldn't have come here," Amariel breathed, looking down at her brother as he stroked the hair away from his forehead.

"You know me, I'm a sucker for a heroic rescue," William grinned before wincing in pain.

Kali joined them on the floor. "William, I need to check on your wound. Lie still," she instructed.

She pulled back his shirt and with a pang of despair saw that the discolouration had begun to spread. She bit her lip and looked at Amariel.

"It's moving too fast; I don't know what to do."

"We need to get him to Lenaria."

"But Liliana said she has the only antidote," Kali balked.

"And you believe her?"

"You *don't?* After everything she's done so far?"

William coughed and they turned again to him, feeling helpless as his breathing became harsher and the poison continued to spread.

"It doesn't matter. You're not staying here with her, Kali," he grimaced.

"Do you have a plan?" Amariel asked her.

"I *had* a plan. To get you out of here and tear this place down as much as I could, but then…" she gestured sadly at William.

Comprehension dawned on Amariel's face, followed by sadness. "You never intended to leave here with us." It wasn't a question.

"She wants me here; she doesn't really care about either of you. Maybe…I'll counter-offer that you leave before this ascension thing and then I'll take as many of them out as I can. You can try and find a car or something like you did last time once you're through the Inaustia."

"She won't agree to that, not when you can just teleport out of here when we're gone," Amariel countered.

William gave a weak, humourless laugh.

"I'm her only real leverage. We need to go now Kali, I'm sure Lenaria can find a cure for whatever Liliana has given me."

Kali looked down at her brother, at the pain on his face that was becoming harder to conceal, and all she could think was that he couldn't die like this. Not because of her. Not like Mattias and her father. She wasn't doing this anymore; she couldn't watch anyone else suffer.

"No. We are doing this my way. We don't know anything about the poison she gave you and I don't think we can beat her in a fight. Please just trust me."

William fell silent, and Amariel repositioned himself to make sure he was comfortable, as Kali stood. Amariel looked up at her, looking as helpless as she felt.

She eyed the dress with distaste, picking it up from the floor.

"I suppose if I'm going to convince her, I may as well look the part," she sighed. She turned her back to them, heading towards the wooden partition, feeling distinctly ridiculous as she donned the extravagant dress. She wondered how she'd ever be able to fight wearing it and considered that may be exactly the point.

* * * *

When Liliana returned, she looked smug at the sight of Kali in the dress. Kali suppressed the overwhelming urge to attack her, thinking instead of William, who was becoming visibly sicker.

"I have a counteroffer for you," she stated.

"Oh?" her mother raised her eyebrows, amused.

"You give William the antidote now, and you let him and Amariel go. Then I'll do your absurd ascension thing. But they go free right now."

"Child, how naïve do you think I am? What would stop you from disappearing out of here the instant I cure him?"

"I'll take the poison – the green one, like before. I can't use my powers with it. It will assure you I can't leave."

Amariel looked up at her sharply and William sat upright in protest, but both women looked only at each other, sizing the other up.

"We have a deal," smirked Liliana, placing a hand into her pocket and producing a syringe of green liquid.

A thrill of fear ran through Kali at the sight of it, and she realised that Liliana had the poison with her all along, ready and expecting to incapacitate her. She steadied herself and offered up her arm, ignoring William's pleas to stop and the voice in her head that told her things were going the way her mother planned all along. This wasn't part of her original plan, but she couldn't see any other way to ensure William survived. Amariel looked on forlornly but made no move to stop her, both of them unified in the hopeless realisation that it was the only way to cure William.

Her mother took her arm, and far more gently than she was expecting, slid the needle into her skin and lowered the plunger. The effect was almost immediate, and Kali felt her power drain from her, leaving her dizzy and unsteady. She knew she wouldn't be able to kill Liliana like this, but she found comfort that at least William and Amariel would be free.

Her legs gave way, and she sank to her knees as she watched her mother turn on her heel and walk towards them. When she reached them, she thrust a syringe of clear liquid into William's chest. His response was almost as immediate as Kali's; the clamminess and pallor dissipated, and he seemed to regain some composure.

"See, child. I am true to my word. Your friends are safe, and now they are free to go. Consider it my show of goodwill."

Kali merely nodded. There was a hope in her now for her brother and friends, hope that they would be safe, but the reality of her own impending end was looming over her. It was huge and all-encompassing, the knowledge that all her suffering, all that she fought for and loved, none of it meant anything. Everything still brought her here, to this moment. The residual call of the darkness she was growing too tired to fight whispered to her again. She began to feel very far away from everything.

A commotion brought her abruptly back to reality.

"We're not leaving her here with you, you murderous, demonic scum," William snarled, heaving his sword into Liliana's chest as Amariel rushed to Kali.

"Kali, we need to go," Amariel commanded urgently as he reached her.

But Kali couldn't move, only look on in dread as Liliana laughed, removed the sword with the air of someone swatting a fly, and turned to her brother menacingly.

"Amariel!" cried Kali as Liliana lunged at William, "help him!"

William, still injured, couldn't get out of the way in time. Even as Amariel sprinted towards them, Liliana's hand closed around his throat, and she lifted him into the air. Kali watched in despair as Amariel reached them, only to be thrown back with a flourish of Liliana's free hand; he hit the wall opposite with great force, fell to the ground, and lay still.

Her mother turned to her, fixing her with a cold smile. "I gave you a chance, but I am finished playing games, girl. Turn. Give in to your true nature. Right now. I want this over with. They may leave afterwards if you still wish it."

William's legs kicked out at Liliana to no avail as he choked and clawed at her hand. He lit a flame and watched defeatedly as it danced around the skin of her hand, harmless. In response, Liliana used her free hand to push into his still-open wound and he gave a strangled cry of pain.

"*Stop!*" Kali cried, pushing herself to her feet with some difficulty.

"He's dying Kali. Like they all have. But you can save this one, this time. Just turn and it will all be over," Liliana urged.

"How do I know you won't just kill them anyway?" she looked at her brother's purpling face, feeling like she too was slowly suffocating.

"I care little for them. I have no reason to kill them. But if you refuse me, they die anyway. It is your gamble to take, and right now you are too weak to stand and fight."

Kali's mind was on fire. *He's dying! He's dying! Do something!* It screamed at her over and over. Flashbacks of Mattias and her father dying tore at the edges of her, the image of Tannick's dead face, how he looked at her when she told him the truth about her. *People you lost, people you killed,* taunted the voice in her head. *Are you ready to add two more to that list?*

"They'll never be safe, child. If you defy me then they will die. I will never stop hunting them. It's time to let go, now," her mother echoed the voice's sentiments.

She knew her mother was right. She'd brought pain and misery on everything and everyone she touched, but this was her chance to save them, to end it. Maybe if done willingly, it would be something she could control. It was part of her, after all, perhaps it didn't need to consume her.

"Kali don't...do...it," William choked, and she opened her eyes to look at him, a dull weight in her stomach. She couldn't stand to lose anyone else. She couldn't. Not William. Not any of them.

"Please, Kal," William gasped, pleading with her once more.

But she had already made up her mind.

Ignoring him, she turned to her mother. "You'll let them go?"

"You have my word," she smiled, coldly.

Kali's lungs felt empty as she stared at her, defeated. This was so much worse than dying, but it was the only way she knew to save them. She clenched her fists and her nails dug into her palms, the sensation of it the only thing tying her to reality.

She didn't know how she knew what to do, but ever since her arrival here, ever since her torture, the darkness felt closer to the surface than ever. All she needed to do was call on it, to give herself over to it. She drowned out her friends, her brother, and instead thought of every painful memory, summoning the darkness like an old friend.

She closed her eyes and called upon every ounce of pain and grief within her, every weakness, every time she ever wished she was more powerful, and she stopped fighting the darkness inside her. She let the evil she knew resided in her surge forward. Her only wish was that William and Amariel weren't there to witness it.

White-hot pain raced through her veins and she cried out, doubled over in pain. It burned like it was ripping through her, tearing up everything in its path. Someone called out to her as she fell to the floor, but it was her mother's voice that she listened to.

"If you resist, it will take longer," came Liliana's mocking tone, "embrace it, revel in it. You might even find you enjoy it."

Kali gasped and opened her eyes as her muscles seized and watched in transfixed horror as black veins began to creep up her arms and chest. She looked around, panicked and hoping William and Amariel were alright. William was standing with

Amariel, both looking unsteady on their feet.

"Kali!" William cried out in anguish.

Amariel leaned against him, blood trickling from a small laceration on his head. Each of them seemed to be supporting the other. William looked at her desperately as Amariel tried to pull him away, looking heartbroken.

"Get...out...of here," she gasped.

Amariel looked hesitantly at Liliana, but she was watching Kali, wholly uninterested in the others.

With relief, Kali realised that her mother really was going to let them leave, and she felt herself relax. This wouldn't be for nothing. They would be safe. Their involvement in this nightmare would end here.

She felt the cold stone of the floor against her cheek as the world swam in and out of focus, but Kali thought that it was peaceful, calming. She closed her eyes once more and found herself enjoying the sensation of fire searing through her. The sensation of the darkness snuffing out the weakest parts of her piece by piece, leaving only the strong.

It was like being re-born, and, in that moment, she loved it. It was the fighting, she realised, that caused her pain. The fighting to stay ahead of the darkness that lived within her, the fighting to resist the urges she pretended she didn't feel, fighting against the desire to fall into the chaos, the pain, and the blood. Fighting was pain. This was the peace she wished for all along.

In place of fear, grief, and anguish, she now felt nothing. It burned everything out of her, hollowing her out and leaving nothing but a feeling of absolute power, and with it, a simmering, dangerous potential.

She felt her mother approach her and opened her eyes. Slowly, she sat up. Amariel was in the doorway, and William stood in the centre of the room staring at her now in horror, his sword half-raised.

She grinned at him, noticing that her teeth felt sharper as she did so. She cocked her head at him.

"Hey, guys. Did you want to stay for the fun after all?"

Tears streamed down his face as he stared at her, unable to speak. He stood for a second longer, then turned and ran from the room, dragging Amariel with him.

Her mother laughed.

"Shall we give chase, daughter?"

Kali pondered for a moment.

"Their cause is over, they are outcasts, and my brother has just lost the last family he had left. I rather think that torment far exceeds any superficial pain we could inflict here," she smirked, and Liliana smiled back.

"Very well. Shall I introduce you to your new home?" her mother asked, as they moved towards the door.

As they walked, Kali came across her fallen sword. She picked it up, lingering momentarily on the site of her own black eyes reflected in it, before handing it to her mother.

"Lead the way," she smiled.

Printed in Great Britain
by Amazon